Some Doubt About It

Some Doubt About It

a novel

MARION MCNABB

LAKE UNION
PUBLISHING

This is a work of fiction. Names, characters, organizations, places, events, and incidents are either products of the author's imagination or are used fictitiously. Otherwise, any resemblance to actual persons, living or dead, is purely coincidental.

Published by Lake Union, Seattle

www.apub.com

ISBN-13: 9781662517129 (paperback)
ISBN-13: 9781662517112 (digital)

Cover design by Shasti O'Leary Soudant
Cover image: © Val_Iva / Getty; © JOJOSTUDIO / Shutterstock

Printed in the United States of America

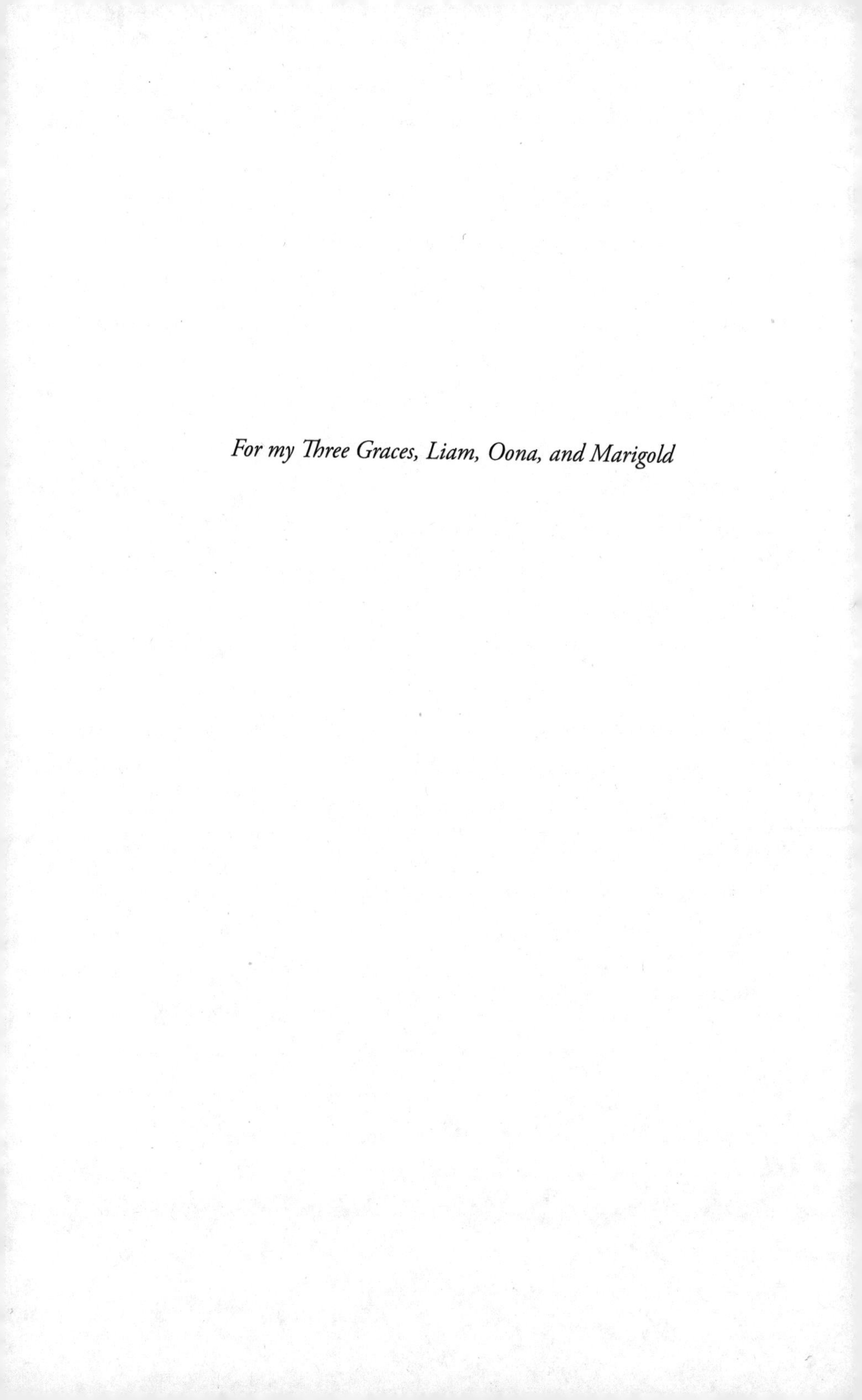

For my Three Graces, Liam, Oona, and Marigold

CHAPTER ONE

CAROLINE

The stage lights burned hot above Caroline Beckett's head as she sat center stage, the rapt studio audience hanging on her every word. Diana Sweeney, the talk show superstar, sat across from Caroline with a thoughtful, probing look.

"I mean, how have you done it, Caroline? And so quickly?" Diana said. Caroline was known by the moniker "Success at Life": a bestselling writer, an oft-quoted guru to the stars, a self-help maven extraordinaire—someone down to earth and relatable while simultaneously aglow with an otherworldly sparkle. "How do you stay 'in the zone'? How are you happy all the time? Don't you have bad days? I mean, help us out here!"

The audience giggled. Caroline relaxed into her seat. She was prepared for this question. She always got it. She paused, contemplative.

"Well, Diana, really . . . honestly and truly . . . it's a choice."

"A choice?"

"Yes, it's a choice. Choosing to be happy. Like I said in my book, *Kiss My Abundance*, I wake up every day and I choose happy. I don't think about the past or any of the struggles on the difficult road I experienced getting here. I think about now. The present moment. I *remember* to be here, right now. Just like in the book, I say the mantra 'I think, therefore I am' . . . and then I fill it in with whatever it is that I want. I think, therefore I am happy! And that just sets the tone for my whole day, and it all just takes off from there. And by doing this I really know that I'm a magnet for all the things I want to obtain in this world. I make the choice between good or bad. I focus on good!"

"A magnet? Meaning you attract what you're putting out there into the world? The law of attraction?"

"Exactly."

"Come on. It's a *choice*? Puh-lease! It's not that easy!"

"I know, I know. But look, this isn't new information. Really! It's just like I outlined in the book. As you know, it's a step-by-step guide to living your best life, influenced by the writings of Descartes and Saint Teresa of Avila."

"Oh, okay, okay—Descartes? He's the 'I think, therefore I am' guy. Right?"

"Yes! Exactly."

"And Saint Teresa of Avila? Somewhat lesser known. Why her?"

"Well, because Descartes ripped her off, of course!"

The audience reacted with conflicting moans and laughter.

"The drama! Okay, Caroline, well, break it down for us, woman. We all want to be happy. Right, everybody? What do we need to do?"

Over the applause Caroline said, "Well, first you have to buy the book." This was met with more applause and approval from the audience, and then she continued. "Look, in all seriousness, it was Descartes who said, way back in the seventeenth century, 'It is not enough to have a good mind. The main thing is to use it well.' And when I read that, well, it just really resonated with me. I make it a point to be very mindful of my thoughts and to use my mind to make things happen for me the way I'd like them to. I repeat his principle, the mantra—'*I think, therefore I am*' . . . and then I add 'what' to the end of that. What do I *think* I am? *What* do I want? That's what I ask myself. I say, '*Caroline, what are you feeling you need? What do you want?*' And then I release every doubt I have about manifesting it, and I focus my whole mind on that thought, and it appears."

"Well, that is impressive. If that's all it takes." Diana put her finger to her temple, closed her eyes, and said, "I have decided to receive a yacht and a billion dollars!"

Hoots and hollers from the audience.

"Hey, if that's what does it for you, then yes! Whatever speaks to you, it can be yours. I'm living proof. I wanted more happiness in my life, so I decided I was not going to stop until I found the way to be happy. So, I did the research. I literally studied purpose and meaning and happiness in life. I studied philosophers, and I worked up a how-to guide. And it's all right there in the book. Anybody can do this. By putting into practice the steps I outlined in *Kiss My Abundance,* anyone can manifest whatever they want in life!" Caroline looked out at the excited audience. "Do it! It feels so good!"

After the applause died down, Diana continued. "Now, I am just amazed by all this—tell us, how did you come up with the idea to link all of this modern thinking with an old philosopher and a nun?"

Caroline felt a little tingle at the back of her neck. She sat up a little taller in her seat and smiled. "It just sort of came to me. I read a lot. It just seems so obvious."

"Well, bravo! Thank you for sharing all of this with us. And now you've got something new coming out, right? Can you tell us a little bit about it?"

"Oh, well, yes, I do! I've been working on this idea for a long time . . ."

"What is it? Come on! We'd looooooove to know . . ."

"Well, okay, and that's just it. Whereas *Kiss My Abundance* was a guide to really becoming your best you, this next book will tack onto that and be a step-by-step guide to building on that foundation and finding love, finding the right partner, based on Plato and the Greeks! I mean, we all think about it and talk about it, want it, but when it comes right down to it, what the hell is love? How do we define it? How do we give and receive it? Do we know it when we see it? Do you know what I mean?"

Just then an audience member shouted, "I love *you,* Caroline!"

The audience laughed.

"So sweet! I love you too!"

A smile spread wide across Diana's face. "I mean, who doesn't love you? Who could *not* love you?"

Applause and laughter from the audience as Caroline humbly clasped her hands, one on top of the other, on her chest.

"Well, I'll tell you, Diana. It's all got to start right here," Caroline said, pressing her palms against the left side of her chest. "I had to do the research. And I had to do the work on myself to get to the place I am in my life, in my work, in my marriage. You just have to decide to take control of your life and to open yourself up to love. That's the first step. Decide! And it's a constant journey. But oh, wow, is it worth it! And this new book will be an easy-peasy guide to finding an enduring and everlasting love!"

"Can't wait to read it. And you know I could talk to you about this all day, but I know you've got to run—have fun at the Emmys, woman!" Diana said as she clapped, and the audience once again roared its approval. "And good luck!"

"Oh, thank you! I don't believe in luck, but I'll take all the good vibes I can get!" Caroline beamed. "Thank you, Diana. Thank you, everybody." She turned and faced the adoring studio audience, waving and smiling until the producer gave the cut sign and the cameras stopped rolling.

Diana detached the microphone from her crewneck sweater. "Good interview. I wasn't sure what to expect, but you were very convincing. Seems like you actually believe this crap."

Caroline was caught off guard. She felt her face begin to redden.

"Either way, good luck, kid," Diana continued. "Ride the wave while you can."

"Oh, um." Caroline steeled herself, steadied her gaze directly at those light-blue eyes. "Like I said, Diana. I don't believe in luck."

~

"Are you ready, Ms. Beckett?" The limousine driver turned to face Caroline.

"I am," she said, finishing applying her lipstick and shoving it into her tiny Gucci purse, which was *still* buzzing. "I'm as ready as I'll ever be." Her phone had been going off since she'd left the hotel, but Caroline had no time to talk. She needed a minute to focus, to meditate, to sit in stillness and center herself before hitting the red carpet. So much attention and excitement swirled around her, and she was beginning to feel disconnected. She needed to pull back and focus and get her footing again. Nothing good ever came from her feeling disjointed. And so she inhaled deeply and repeated her mantra: *"Everything always works out for me."* Ready for the burst of energy just outside, she knocked on the window, and the driver pulled the door open. She slipped a long leg out of the limo and planted one Louboutin, then the other, onto the red carpet. She smoothed her dress down over her Spanx, pulled her shoulders back, pushed her chest out, thrust her chin forward, and plastered a smile on her face. She dangled there on the precipice of the lavish entryway to television's greatest awards show—the Emmys—and smiled, taking it all in. She basked in the energy, opulence, and self-importance surrounding her on the carpet and then followed a young man with a clipboard and headset as he directed her to file in with the throng of somebodies lining up at the steps.

Limos pulled up, and as the occupants spilled out, their names were announced over the sound system as they made their way past the press and into the theater doors at the opposite end of the carpet. Electricity charged the air as formally dressed publicists, reporters, photographers, actors, writers, directors, and more—counting into the hundreds—milled about in one hot, congested tented area.

Caroline stood at almost six feet in her four-inch heels. She smiled and made brief small talk with a fellow celebrity, who laughed when she said she felt like a salmon swimming upstream. Caroline felt the energy pulsing around her, but she ignored the strong vibration coming from the still-buzzing phone in her Gucci. And so she was caught completely unaware when a young, bespectacled reporter thrust a microphone into her face and said, "That video was pretty damning. I assume that's why no Grant this afternoon?"

What video? "Grant is working and isn't able to be here." Caroline was cool, direct, but she couldn't help thinking the wind had shifted like a candle had just been blown out. The Spanx tightened around her like a python. But Caroline was a pro. She had been doing this for years now. The "live from the red carpet" period always involved questions about what dress she was wearing tucked in around the personal leading questions about her relationship with her husband, handsome celebrity photographer Grant Beckett. There was always an artificiality to the scene. The promenading, the outfits, the questions—all manufactured and formulaic. The good news was, if you knew the formula, you were set. The bad news was, the components always changed.

"I'm really happy to be here and to be included in television's greatest awards show," Caroline said. "Especially since *Kiss My Abundance* has been so well received, and I can turn my attention to my own show. We're finalizing some of the details to get it on the air as soon as possible. I'm really proud and incredibly grateful for all of it."

"Yes, *Kiss My Abundance* has been a big success. But, Caroline, come on, give us the scoop. Are things really okay?" the scrappy reporter asked. "The video is . . . well, it's pretty *in your face*. Forgive the pun."

And it was in that moment when that little flicker, the twitch in Caroline's otherwise unflinching face, betrayed her, and that was all the reporter needed. She pounced.

"Wait . . . you haven't seen the video?"

Caroline felt hot. Sweat beaded up around her hairline, and one salty drip had started at her shoulder blades and was sliding all the way down her nearly bare back. She was wet and somehow felt itchy. She wanted to rip off her dress and scratch at her damp skin.

Instead, smile still spread across her face, she looked down at the smug reporter, and, guessing, said, "Thank you, I don't delve into the salacious hearsay of social media and such."

Caroline looked beyond the gossipmonger, spying the doorway in the distance. Her pulse was quickening, but she held her own, choosing not to focus on the sweat filling up her shoes. She abruptly noticed a more than average interest from the photographers and reporters looking at her, photographing her, shouting her name, and filming her every move. There was more than enough eye candy on the carpet to keep the overzealous media enraptured, but suddenly they were interested in her—more interested than ever—and Caroline felt the heat of that attention. It made her dizzy. And in the nanosecond it took her to scan the crowd and become aware of it all, the reporter pulled out her phone and shoved it into Caroline's sight line.

Caroline tried graciously to look beyond the little rat's outstretched hand, but there was nowhere to go. Caroline inched her foot to the right, a feeble attempt at an escape, and bumped up against a wall of humanity. The publicity line was completely backed up. A sea of people lay before her, and no one was moving anywhere. And worse, it felt like every one of them had turned their focus directly onto her.

Away in the distance, the open door to the venue—the way out of the carnage—looked like it was inching farther and farther away. Where the hell was Thérèse? If she couldn't count on her manager in times like these, why the hell was she paying her so damn much?

Caroline swallowed and mentally prepared a standard "Oh, yes, of course I've seen that video" type of response, but what she actually saw in the video was beyond what she was capable of brushing under the rug with a shrug and her megawatt smile.

The screen lit up. The pale backside of a pasty man with a golfer's tan and a tattoo of the words *carpe diem* over a drunk sombrero-wearing Chihuahua pulsed up and down. The camera panned out to reveal two chunky Fila sneakers flapping on either side of the grunting man.

Caroline felt a muscle begin to twitch in her right cheek, but her smile remained fixed in place. She knew that back. She knew that stupid tattoo. She knew those ridiculous sneakers. And she knew what that sex tape was . . . evidence of her brokenness and imperfection.

She was at once faint and furious, as though she could chew the tacky acrylic fingernails off the little weasel's outstretched hand. Why was this happening? How could this be? If she was to be publicly humiliated, why couldn't she have just tripped and fallen in front of everyone and landed spread eagle on the carpet? Or even just had one of your garden-variety wardrobe malfunctions, a flash of a slightly droopy boob or a good old-fashioned crotch shot? Unshaven even. Why did her embarrassment have to be the public documentation of the ripping, tearing, gouging out of her heart from her chest, leaving her open, bloodied, empty, raw, and on display for millions to witness? And then to rewind and play again and again?

Caroline didn't know what to do. She felt oddly aware of the pulsing of her phone, but she knew she had to look elsewhere. Her brain screamed, *Wake up!* She didn't know where to center her gaze. She only knew she could no longer keep looking at the reporter's phone rolling the video of a naked man in his fifties—her husband—with a young, nearly naked woman in her early twenties, now straddling him and pushing her breasts into Grant's smiling face.

"I'm so sorry, Caroline . . . but that *is* your husband, isn't it? And isn't that your assistant, Oaklyn Reinhold?" the reporter asked, thrusting the microphone into Caroline's face like Oaklyn's boobs into Grant's.

"Caroline?" A woman's voice cut through the whoosh of blood-pumping, pushing, pulsing chaos in Caroline's brain. *Thérèse. Finally.* "Sorry," Thérèse said to the reporter. "Ms. Beckett is needed inside immediately. Thank you so much. Caroline, would you mind please coming with me?"

Thérèse turned to go, a protective arm around her client, but Caroline couldn't move. She was stuck. She couldn't put one expensive shoe in front of the other. She looked down at her feet and thought, *Move*. But nothing happened.

The reporter jumped. "Caroline? Are you okay, Caroline?"

"She's fine," Thérèse said. "Thank you so much. Come on, Caroline."

But it was as though Caroline could see herself through the lenses of the cameras that were focused squarely on her. She looked straight into the *How to Hollywood* camera. She traveled into the lens and out the other side, becoming the cameraman with his point of view and benign perspective of the whole situation. Zoom in. Hold it steady. Pull out. It felt comforting to be so distant from herself, to be outside her body. And then she heard a voice: *Everything is okay. This is not who you are. You are more than this. You are more than what you think about this.*

She blinked and immediately was back inside her own skin. Back in her body. Back in the spotlight.

"Caroline?" Thérèse said again. "You're needed inside."

Caroline looked at the reporter. The reporter shoved her microphone ever closer.

"Caroline? Your thoughts?" the reporter said.

"Thoughts?" Caroline said. She blinked.

"What?" the reporter said, a look of confusion on her face.

"Thoughts," Caroline said. "I think . . . I think, therefore I am . . ."

"What? What are you, Caroline?"

"I am—I am . . . I . . ."

But before Caroline could answer, Thérèse was finally able to put enough weight on Caroline's lower back to pivot her away from the microphone.

"Wait! She didn't answer!" The reporter was desperate. "Caroline—what is it? Who do you think you are? America wants to know!"

"So sorry, dear, she's needed inside!" Thérèse called over her shoulder while gently pushing Caroline on down the carpet, past the screaming reporters, photographers, and lookie-loos, out of view, safe for the moment. As she shuffled along the carpet, Caroline couldn't help but wonder about the voice she'd heard earlier, the one in her head. Who was that? And if she wasn't this person, or who she thought herself to be, well then, just who the hell was she?

CHAPTER TWO

DEVORAH

Devorah van Buren dipped a french fry in clam chowder and fed it to Mary Magdalene, her sixteen-year-old Chihuahua, who rested next to her on the barstool. The waterfront bar here in Hyannis, Massachusetts, was her favorite spot. In between sips of her Maker's Mark manhattan, Devorah alternated french fries—one for herself, one for Mary.

Devorah adjusted her body on her barstool. She found it increasingly difficult to feel comfortable these days, the elastic waistband of her cotton lounge pants like a noose around her fleshy stomach. The backless barstool was no match for her ample bottom, and parts of her spilled over the sides like beer in a pint glass. Her seven decades of life experience made this joint achy and that joint swollen. But the bourbon would soon heal her aches, and this way she didn't have to clean the dishes.

The only other people in the bar were an on-their-way-to-getting-buzzed-in-the-middle-of-the-day husband and wife in their early sixties and the mousy Irish bartender, Siobhan. Siobhan wore her curly dark hair piled on top of her head in a scrunchie and wiped down the bar like she was spit shining a Cadillac.

Now that it was September, most of the summer crowds had gone. Locals rejoiced. They got their island back. But the truth was, the locals, the visitors, whatever—it made no difference, as they were all basically strangers to Devorah. Over the years, her circle had shrunk to nonexistent. Would that make her circle just a straight line, then? Or would there be no mark at all? Would there be just nothingness? Or worse, a black hole sucking in all that surrounded it? Folding in on itself and growing into a larger empty chasm?

Mary licked her chops, working to get at some ketchup caught in her whiskers.

The woman across the bar cackled, pulling her attention over to them. The couple wore identical lemon yellow T-shirts with *Fort Lauderdale* stretched across their matching potbellies. Devorah rolled her eyes in disapproval.

"Tourists," Devorah said, leaning sideways and whispering to Mary, now eating clam chowder straight from the spoon in Devorah's outstretched hand. "Thank God for you, Mary," Devorah cooed. "Locals are bad enough, but tourists are worse."

The woman tourist rambled on about the weather—so hot—and how cool it had been yesterday—freezing—and how rainy it might be tomorrow.

Siobhan washed glasses and looked up at the television braced above the far corner of the bar. "You interested in the Emmys, Mrs. Van Buren?" she said with a brogue.

"Nope," Devorah said, but looked back at the screen anyway. "Just another Hollywood awards show with all those celebrities patting each other on the back for God knows what. You'd think they'd all cured cancer or something." Devorah would have preferred watching mind-numbing baseball to this crap. Wasn't there a game on? And then another squeal from the biddy down the bar ricocheted off the bar walls.

"Oh, look, that's Caroline Beckett," the woman said. "She's from this area, you know, honey."

"That right?" her husband said, sipping his beer.

Devorah looked up at the screen and saw Caroline Beckett staring blankly into the camera like a deer caught in headlights. Devorah's breath caught in her throat. It had been years since she'd seen her. Caroline looked the same. Or if there was any possible way for her to look younger than she did almost twenty-five years earlier, when she was Devorah's assistant, she did. And, well, it was Hollywood—so yes, it was possible. There was always a way to shave off a few extraneous years and come out looking thinner and more refined. Looking at Caroline, so far away, but her face larger than life and her voice filling up the room, made Devorah feel something in her chest she hadn't felt in a long time. It was like a beesting.

". . . I think, therefore I am . . . I am—I am . . . I . . ." Caroline's voice rang out from the television.

"What?" Devorah said to Mary Magdalene and laughed. "What did she just say? I think, therefore I am . . . ? Oh, jeez Louise, what do you know about that, Mary?"

"Oh, Jesus. 'I think, therefore I am . . . I am!' Well, she's gone full Hollywood batshit crazy," the tipsy bar woman said, once again pulling Devorah's attention. The woman pointed and laughed. "Look at her. Off her rocker! I swear there must be something in the purified water out there, right?"

"Maybe," the husband said.

Devorah paid the woman no mind. She sipped her bourbon and looked at the screen. The camera was tight on Caroline, and it became obvious that something was wrong. Caroline wasn't moving or speaking. Devorah squinted, as best she could, zoning in on Caroline's eyes. What the hell was wrong with her? Caroline was frozen. Her mouth hung slightly open, her eyes glassy. Was she on drugs, for Chrissake? Maybe all the Botox was seeping into her brain? Devorah laughed to herself but felt a crinkle of worry deepen on her forehead. A sensation of dread, like a heavy stone, dropped into her gut.

"What the hell is wrong with her?" the bar woman said. "Look at her! Wow, what a mess! Guess another one bites the dust, huh, honey?"

"Ah, yup," her husband said, looking only at his nearly empty beer mug.

Devorah was irritated but kept her focus on the television, on Caroline. Devorah willed her to move, to speak, to blink at least. Something was very wrong, and frankly, no matter their history, it was unsettling to watch. Why the hell wasn't Caroline moving? It was like watching a kid wet her pants in the front of the class. Just a shame, an absolute shame.

"Yup. She grew up right around here," Siobhan said to the frowning couple as she stacked glasses. "Over on Scudder Lane. Humble beginnings and all that."

"She come back here often?" the woman asked.

"I've never seen her," Siobhan said, pausing to check for water spots on a glass.

Nope, Devorah thought. *She does not. Doesn't call either.*

Devorah thought she might have heard from Caroline when her husband, David, died four years ago. It was a small town; people still talked. But nothing. That was a terrible, somber affair. David was the great love of Devorah's life, seven years younger than she and a Martin Sheen look-alike. He was lean and fit, which made his sudden death that much more unexpected, that much more devastating. Of her three husbands, he was far and away the one she loved the most. He was the lid to her pot. But he was gone. And gone with David went the full, happy life they'd shared together and the promise of tomorrow, of forever, of sailing off into the sunset together. The dinners out at this very bar, the laughter, the conversations, the hand-holding, the double dates, the friends, the travel, all vanished.

And now, except for Mary Magdalene, Devorah was all alone.

The bar patron continued to chatter to her uninterested husband, who looked like he'd been ignoring her observances for the better part of thirty years. "Hmm, just like the rest of 'em, forgets where she came from. And I don't like the dress. And her hair's awful. And you know, all that fancy-pants Hollywood stuff . . . it's all recent. Just a few years ago, she was nobody like the rest of us, and then she writes a blog, then a book about living your best life or loving yourself or something, and bam. Oprah's giving her a TV show. I mean, I could do that. Ha. Right, Gary? And all that woo-woo crap? Please. She doesn't have anything figured out, except how to make all kinds of money off unsuspecting losers who buy her book. Gimme a break."

At this point, Devorah had reached the bottom of her drink, which always meant that she had not only no more alcohol in her glass but also no more control.

"Pffi," Devorah said. The couple looked over.

The woman arched her eyebrows. "Yes?"

"You don't know her."

Siobhan closed the dishwasher and stepped in front of Devorah. "Mrs. Van Buren, more cocktail peanuts? Dessert?"

"What was that?" the tourist said.

Devorah leaned to the left and looked around Siobhan, who was tiny and not much of an obstacle. "I said—you don't know her."

"I didn't say I did know her. Did I, Gary?" The woman looked at her husband. "Did I say I know her?"

"What?" Gary clearly didn't want to be involved. Poor Gary.

"Well, if you don't know her, why don't you just shut the hell up?"

"Mrs. Van Buren," Siobhan said. "More chowder?"

"How dare you tell me to shut up? I wasn't saying anything. I was just saying—"

Devorah sat up taller, gave her the stare. Mary Magdalene began a low growl.

Siobhan tried again. "Mrs. Van Buren, maybe you'd like a coffee?"

Devorah tilted her head toward the couple and said, "Maybe I'd like this one to hit the bricks?"

The woman had had enough. "And you know what else?" she said. "Your ugly little dog stinks. I can smell that little rat all the way over here."

That was the last straw as far as Devorah was concerned.

~

Later, after the police had questioned both women, Devorah's head began to ache, and she sat down on the hood of her old black Mercedes.

"Mrs. Van Buren, you can't keep starting these arguments with other patrons," Officer Sorrenti said. "This has got to stop. You're in danger of not being allowed back, and I know you've already been asked not to return to Sonny's."

"First of all, Sorrenti, Sonny's is a dump. I wouldn't step foot in there if it was the last place on earth. And secondly, I wasn't arguing with anyone," Devorah said. "There was no back-and-forth whatsoever. That woman was openly bitching and negative, so I calmly told her to shut her big, fat mouth."

"You threw hot soup at her, Mrs. Van Buren."

"It was tepid at best. The soup here's never hot enough."

"Mrs. Van Buren."

"Okay, fine. But listen to me, Sorrenti, she's nothing but a complainer. Okay? She's insane."

"Mrs. Van Buren, one of these times someone is going to get hurt, and you're going to find yourself in a whole heap of trouble."

"For what?"

"You're lucky those people aren't pressing charges."

"They're not people, they're tourists," she said. When Devorah said the word *tourists*, it always sounded more like *terrorists*. "Look at them. They're losers. Good riddance."

Officer Sorrenti looked over to see the couple piling into the back seat of a blue sedan with an Uber sticker in the front window.

"If they weren't so drunk, this could have gone a different way, Mrs. Van Buren. And then my hands would have been tied. Regardless, you have got to control yourself. You have to watch your temper. Is everything okay? My mom said you don't show up for book club anymore."

"My eyes are bad. I can't read."

"You could get an audiobook."

"You finished or what, Sorrenti?" Devorah asked.

"You have to stop being so angry all the time."

"Why?"

"Because it doesn't seem like it's really working out for you."

"Anyway, I'm not angry." She lowered herself and Mary Magdalene into the car. "I'm just fed up."

CHAPTER THREE

CAROLINE

The bougainvillea wound its way around the porticos of the Becketts' Pacific Palisades mansion, drawing observers' focus, distracting with its vibrant fuchsia, and concealing the razor-sharp thorny wood underneath. It wasn't unintentional. Caroline had requested it.

Now, she looked down from her bedroom window and scowled. The foliage needed trimming.

The only unattractive thing on the entire smooth facade of the big house was Caroline's grimace and her swollen, puffy eyes that grew wide as Grant's black Range Rover sped up the long, dramatic driveway, like a lead bullet piercing the perfection Caroline had worked so hard to achieve. She liked everything just so. Pretty. Ordered and sharp. All obediently in its place and controlled.

She turned away from the window, but the gentle Pacific breeze blew at her back, bringing with it something a little more ominous than salty sea air. The winds of change rolled soft and gentle, biding their time before dropping their full weight.

The front door slammed. Caroline ran to the bathroom and splashed water onto her face. She would be damned if she would let him see her this way. As she felt the cold water tingling on her skin, she pictured him racing up the winding stairwell, past the Marc Chagall painting and the Lucian Freud etching of a fish head, down the hall past one empty bedroom after another until stopping outside the door of the last room at the end of the hall. The massive oak door—to the room they'd shared for nearly a decade—like a barricade protecting her.

Keep him there. Don't let him in.

Her buzzing phone illuminated the dark room, revealing a text from Thérèse: We need to talk.

Caroline closed her eyes. It had been fourteen hours since the debacle at the Emmys. She'd skipped out after the awards show, which seemed to go on for eons, and returned home before the vulturous paparazzi could hound her. She'd spent the rest of her night alternating between throwing crap at the wall and self-indulgent crying fits on the bedroom floor. She reached over to her nightstand and picked up the photo of her and Grant on a balcony with Monte Carlo in the background. Taken ten years ago, the photo showed them much younger, tanned and glowing, as they looked at each other and laughed. Caroline had always loved this picture. It seemed like the perfect reflection of who they were and what they meant to one another. Love, laughter, and friendship.

The picture, in its Waterford crystal frame, sailed through the air, smiles spinning round and round until they made contact with that big dark door and shattered into a thousand pieces.

And then, in contrast, a gentle knock.

Caroline braced herself as the door swung open and Grant entered, the wind pushing at his back like he was Venus on a scallop shell. He wore dark-rimmed Clubmaster Ray-Ban eyeglasses that made him look sophisticated and wealthy and intensified the deep brown of his snake eyes.

"Caroline," he said, stepping over the debris that littered the carpet.

She said nothing.

Grant looked around the room at the carnage. His shoulders dropped. God, he was always so dramatic, and so handsome. Aging suited him well. Of course it would, the bastard. He was tall, over six feet, but standing there, framed in the giant doorway in his golf shirt and plaid pants, he looked almost human.

"Caroline."

She applied cream to the soft space under her swollen eyes.

"Darling, Caroline, please."

"Don't you dare." She turned around to face him. "Don't you dare call me *darling*."

"I just wanted to . . . I just . . . I have to say . . ."

What? What was he going to say? What could he possibly say?

"I told you not to come here."

"I got on the first flight back, oh my darl—" Grant started to say and then caught himself. "I'm just a wreck about this. I'm so—"

"Don't. I don't care what you have to say."

"Caroline, please. It wasn't what it looked like."

"It wasn't you screwing my assistant?"

"Come on. It's not about her. I have to be better. I just . . . I'm a mess . . ."

Caroline looked at the items on the vanity in front of her. Expensive creams and perfumes, all designed to make her look and smell attractive. *To whom?* How much time and money and energy did she invest in that?

Grant took one step closer to her.

If you say "Sorry," I swear to God I'm going to throw this stupid, ridiculous Tiffany crystal perfume dispenser at your head.

"I'm sorry," Grant said.

And through the air the stupid crystal perfume dispenser went before missing Grant's head, hitting the wall to the right of the doorframe with a big thud, and falling to the floor.

"Hey," Grant called out. "What the hell?"

"Get the hell out of my house." Caroline turned around and applied a little eyeliner to her eyes, as though she were going to leave the house or had showered or didn't have matted hair or a fear volcano bubbling in her chest. Grant stared at the back of her. She ignored his reflection in the mirror as long as she could; then, finding his eyes in the mirror, she said, "Please leave."

"I'm sorry this happened."

"Oh, Jesus."

"Really, Caroline, I'm sorry things spiraled this way. And I am so very sorry."

"I don't care."

"Yes, you do."

"I. Don't. Care. Now. Leave."

"I don't believe you don't care," Grant said. "You do. You care about us. We have to work this out. Please. Hear me out. Have compassion. Isn't that what you're always saying, what you're preaching to your adoring fans—compassion?"

"Love. That's what I talk about. I preach love. You're just too stupid to understand that," she said, and paused for a minute. Her heart was racing. Heat rose at the back of her neck, and sweat started to build. She willed her body not to betray her, not to lay bare the depths of her brokenness.

She stood and walked over to the closet and pulled out a floral sundress, the one she knew Grant liked. The one he always told her was his favorite. She turned back around to him and, mustering an inner strength she was unaware she possessed, looked him in the eye.

"She's a total moron, you know. She is literally dumber than that lamp over there," Caroline said, pointing to the gorgeous French table lamp she'd imported from Paris. "But she looks good in a corner. Just like that lamp. Pretty and stuffed in a corner. Contained and ready to turn on when you need it."

"It was all just a dumb mistake. I never meant for any of this to happen. Things have not been great with us for some time, and I just—"

Caroline paused, twisting the dress in her hands like a murderer armed with rope in a 1950s noir film. "Oh, I see, so it's my fault you screwed my assistant?"

"Stop. Stop it. No. I never, ever meant for this to happen."

"Yes, you did. Of course you did. You're looking for attention, like you always do. Especially when I've got the spotlight. And I do. You're not as in demand as you used to be, but I got the option and the show and the press. And now you're the golf-playing, wife's-assistant-banging asshole who wants to stay forever young and thinks that screwing a twenty-five-year-old nitwit is going to do the trick. Well, I've got news for you, pal. It ain't. You're going to die like the rest of us. And, God willing, before I do, so I can spit on your pine coffin and dance on your unmarked grave."

Grant paused a moment, letting Caroline's words hang in the air. "Wow. Well, that doesn't sound very loving, very on brand."

"I guess it's kind of like your love for me and how it went straight out the window when you started banging that skank. *In my house.*"

"Our house."

Caroline looked around for something else to throw at him.

"Wait, wait. Look, I know how difficult this must be for you." He took a step toward her. "The press is ruthless. I'm being followed everywhere. There's an army of paparazzi at the gate to the neighborhood."

"Oh, that must be so horrible for you."

"I'm not . . . I'm not saying that for me. I don't care. I deserve it. I get it. I understand—I am an imperfect man. I broke my vow. I hurt you. And for that, I am disgusted, but I'm here because I'm concerned for you, about you. You have an image to project."

"Wait, are you concerned for *me* or my image?"

He stared at her.

"You think I only care about my image, you heartless shit?"

"No, that's not what I mean. That's not it. But look, you have built an entire wellness empire based on the fact that you have 'figured life out.' There is, literally, a billboard on Sunset Boulevard calling you the life expert. Come on. We've been married for ten years. I care about you. I love you. I messed up."

Caroline pulled her pajama top over her head, exposing her bare spray-tanned chest and taut belly.

"I think *you* actually care about my image because I made a lot of money on my image, and you enjoy having and spending that money."

"It's not the money."

"And isn't it just a wild coincidence that you're pulling this crap a month after our ten-year anniversary. Covering your bases, huh? California law, alimony for life after ten years—well done, you."

Grant looked shocked. Appalled. "I was never in it for the money."

Caroline pulled the sundress over her head. "Uh-huh."

"No. No way. Not *uh-huh*. No, no." Grant wiped at the lock of pretty white hair that fell across his brow. "I love you. I love you so much. I messed up. I'm sorry. But I'm here now."

He paused, and they both stood staring at each other. From somewhere in the neighborhood, the sound of a gardener blowing someone's dirty leaves into another neighbor's yard filtered in.

"Please, please tell me what to do," Grant said, his eyes cast downward at the mess around him on the floor.

There it is. But no, not enough; it was never enough. Words were not enough.

Grant dropped to his knees. "Forgive me. I'll do anything. Look—I know there are details. We'll have to get Thérèse and the publicist involved and—"

"I will handle Thérèse. Don't you worry. I'll take care of my image. It's your own that you should focus on."

"Caroline, darling. I will take whatever scorn I deserve in all of this. Of course I will. This was never about you. But please don't give up on me—don't give up on us. You changed my life. You have inspired millions of people. I just . . . I just didn't know where I fit into all of it."

"Good God, you're a narcissist. I mean, what a load of bull."

"Caroline, look at me. Caroline. Caroline."

"Grant. Grant. *Grant.*"

"She meant nothing to me. It's you. It's always been you. Please, please forgive me. I love you."

As Caroline stood before him, partially clothed, she suddenly felt overcome with exhaustion, like all of her resolve had disappeared. Her anger rose up and out of her body, hovering over her like a cloud, and her eyelids felt heavy. She noticed it was taking effort just to breathe. She felt like she was watching some terrible highlight reel from the movie on the demise of her relationship. She reached out into the air to hit pause.

"Are you okay?" Grant asked.

"Stop," Caroline said, fighting to maintain her composure. "Please."

Grant took a step toward her, extending his arms toward her.

"No," Caroline said, but there was no conviction in it. She was so weak, yet she was terrified of how alone she knew she was. Grant's arms felt warm, almost as hot as the tears that were spilling from her tired eyes.

"Shh," Grant said and kissed the top of her head. "My girl. You're my girl."

Caroline let herself be held. She leaned into it. How had they gotten here? How could this be it? She tried to push the thoughts away. Maybe she was too involved in her work? Maybe she needed to make more time for her relationship, for her marriage.

"I'm sorry I hurt you. I love you so much."

Her voice came out soft, raspy, as she said, "I'll speak to Thérèse. She'll spin it, and hopefully it won't hurt the sales of the book."

She could feel Grant nodding as she focused on her breath. She *did* need him. She hated herself for it, but she needed him. She needed someone. And here they were, back in each other's arms again.

This feels better. I have to do the things—I have to think *the things—that make me feel better. I can find my way through this. Hell, I might even be grateful for it.*

CHAPTER FOUR

DEVORAH

Devorah hung up the phone. She didn't leave voicemails. She'd been trying for the better part of three days to get in touch with Caroline Beckett. Why was she not picking up? Who the hell did Caroline think she was, anyway?

There was a knock at the door; then, a few seconds later, a deep voice called out, "Mrs. Van Buren? Your friendly fireman slash handyman slash devastatingly handsome tenant here to take a look at that wonky drawer."

"In here," Devorah said, and sat at the wide round table. It was set just off the kitchen, in a circular bay window that overlooked Nantucket Sound. Devorah loved this window. She could look out and see something different every single hour of every single day. The beach, the ocean, always changing, never the same. Rhythmic and hypnotic, chaotic, frenetic: no matter what the energy of the water, it always made Devorah feel like she was tethered to something. Something permanent in its impermanence. There were days, lately, where she lost herself for hours looking out at that dark water, and then Mary Magdalene would move, and she'd come back to reality and realize how much time had passed. *Where did I go? What happened?*

"Morning, Mrs. Van Buren," Diaz said. He was tall and lean, with dark-brown eyes that matched his slightly feathered hair. He had wide, full lips that sloped slightly down on the left when he spoke.

"Diaz," Devorah said, bristling as she always did when he called her "Mrs." It was so formal, she hated it.

"I've got some time to do the drawer before I head down to the station. That work?"

"You really need to find yourself a girlfriend," she said, then added, "You really don't need to do all these repairs and stuff."

"I like helping out."

Devorah looked down at the book in her hand, *Kiss My Abundance*. She ran her fingers over the cover.

"Doing some reading?" Diaz said as he dropped his toolbox on the kitchen counter and flipped open the lid.

"Sort of. More like investigating," she said.

Diaz struggled to align the drawer back on the side runners. "Saw Sorrenti at the ball field last night," he said.

"Oh, Jesus, I don't care what that dipshit had to say."

"Well, what he said was you got into some trouble at the Shanty."

"So?"

"So, what happened?"

"Well, what did Sorrenti and his big fat mouth tell you happened?"

He laughed. "He said you got into it with a terrorist."

"Look, I don't have time for gossip, Diaz. Okay? Great minds discuss ideas, average minds discuss events, small minds discuss people."

Diaz continued to smile as he pulled a bandanna from the back pocket of his Levi's and sprayed some WD-40 on the drawer hinge. "Right. I think he was just concerned for you."

"Why? I handled the situation fine."

"I'm sure you did."

"Think you're going to be able to fix that damn thing? Or should I just junk the whole drawer and get new cabinets?"

"It's just a screw that needed some tightening. I'm on it, Mrs. Van Buren. You don't have to get a new kitchen."

"Oh, Jesus, will you just cut the crap with the 'Mrs. Van Buren' stuff? What am I, a hundred years old? And if you say 'No, ma'am,' I swear I'll throw this saltshaker at you."

"As you wish, Devorah." Diaz laughed again and squirted some more WD-40 onto the drawer's runners.

"You comfortable out there?" Devorah looked out past Diaz, beyond the large side window in the kitchen to a small mother-in-law apartment over the two-car garage to the right of the main house. Both structures were shingled with redwood, now grayish white from time and the salty sea air.

"Yes. Thank you."

"You're not burning any candles out there or anything, are you?"

"No, ma'am," he said.

Devorah squinted. "Fires can get started that way."

"Well, I am a fireman, so I do know something about that—"

"So, what? Firemen can't fall asleep with a candle burning and burn the damn house down?"

"I suppose it happens, Devorah. But I'm not a candle guy, so rest assured, no candles burning out there."

"Well, what if you have a girl over?"

"And look at that," Diaz said, pulling the drawer out. "Like butter."

"Huh." Devorah rose from her chair and approached Diaz and the counter. Mary Magdalene looked up but decided against following her. Devorah pulled on the drawer. "Yeah, okay, it works. That's great. Thank you, Diaz. Guess you're not just a pretty face." Devorah looked around the kitchen. "Kinda wanted new cabinets, though."

"Well, we can do that, too, if you want, but these are only a couple of years old. I don't think you need it. Save your money."

"Why? What the hell am I saving it for?" Devorah shrugged and turned back to the window and her dog. "I've got no one but Mary Magdalene over there, and she doesn't give a damn about these stupid cabinets. My crazy sister went and died. She's got a couple of screwed-up kids I can't stand, so they're not getting any of it. Can't take it with me. So, I'm telling you, if it wasn't such a goddamn mess to rip out a kitchen and replace all of it, I'd do it. I'd do it in a heartbeat."

"Yeah, I get that," Diaz said.

Devorah walked back to her seat at the table, her knees and hips creaky and knocking her side to side like a boat on an angry sea.

Diaz pulled the kitschy bird clock down from the wall and pulled the battery case open and said, "So, I'm just going to change some of these batteries here. And then I'm going to replace this faucet for the one you wanted with the fancy spout in here, and then I'll recaulk the sides too. I'm just waiting for Larry to call me and tell me the part's come in."

Devorah nodded. "She's an idiot, you know," she said, and turned to Diaz, who met her eyes for one brief second. "Michelle. She really is."

He turned back to the sink. "Mind if I grab a cup of coffee?"

"Course not, but you'll have to make it yourself. Just grab one of those cups and press the button. And you should just take it. It's all yours. I can't drink the stuff anymore. My stomach is not what it used to be. Don't get old, Diaz. It ain't for wimps."

"You calling me a wimp?"

Devorah laughed and turned to check on Mary Magdalene, who stirred a bit in the nest of soft towels she'd made in her dog bed, then blinked and rested her head back down.

"It is better than the alternative," he said and dropped his tools back in his toolbox.

"What is?"

"Getting older. You know . . . it's better than *not* getting older, if you know what I mean."

"Actually . . ." Devorah paused, then looked back out the window. "I'm not sure I do."

~

Devorah had three remote controls, and one of them was always missing. She looked around on the table and ran her hand in between the couch cushions and suddenly paused, remembering. She used to get so mad at David and blame him for losing the remotes, but maybe it had been *her* misplacing them all along? She thought about his face, with its ruddy complexion, and his laughing eyes and what he looked like when she was mad at him, how his shoulders slumped, and the deep wrinkles that folded in on each other between his eyes. *David, you sweet man.* It was at these times, the seemingly insignificant moments, when his absence felt almost unbearable. Captured somewhere within the everyday minutiae, the depths of her heart were laid bare, exposed and unwilling to be shoved out of view one moment longer. These were the times when the loss of sharing the smallness of life, and the gaping hole left by David's death, took her breath away. Was that love? What kind of love? Platonic love, or what Plato defined as lasting nonsexual love, as their relationship had grown to be. Over the years their connection had expanded from the carnal attraction toward individual bodies to the attraction toward souls. They grew to ever greater levels of closeness, to wisdom and true beauty.

"David?" she said out loud to the room and then waited a minute. "Where did you go?"

Her hand, still stuffed between the cushions, hit something hard. She pulled the missing remote out and turned it over in her palm. Her fingers tightened around it, and she thought about throwing it against the wall but instead pressed the power button, turning the television on, grateful for the sound that sliced through the deafening silence of her empty home.

David van Buren had been a beautiful companion. They'd traveled extensively through Europe and Asia for two years after Devorah retired, or, more accurately, when she'd finally waved that white flag of surrender, allowing herself to be forced into retirement by the university.

They were restructuring, they'd said, and they offered her full benefits and an early retirement. She knew the supposed "restructuring" pertained more to the fact that she struggled with the university's new online learning system and asynchronous approach to the curriculum. There was also their push toward sensitivity training and her confusion surrounding correct pronoun usage in the classroom. Academia was becoming even more of a circus than ever, and now, when she could finally enjoy the spoils of her triumph over the sexist tradition she'd slogged through, she was cut off at the knees by pedagogical ideologies and technology that only seemed to separate student and teacher. It felt like a vitriolic concoction of protocol with a cancel culture chaser, and it made her feel dizzy. And disconnected. And pissed off. She didn't know what the hell everyone was so damn sensitive about anyway. Bunch of pansies! Everybody was so precious these days.

She'd loved her independence and teaching philosophy. She felt a desire to express herself and to connect with others. She loved being a professor. She loved the classroom; she loved the discussions and debate. But when she found herself relegated to the diminutive tasks of committee work and meeting note-taking, she saw the writing on the wall.

David, himself retired from a prestigious career as a corporate attorney, encouraged her to take the department's offer, sell their condominium in the South End, and live out the rest of their lives comfortably untethered with Cape Cod as their home base. He was a bit selfish in this way. The only thing Devorah ever really faulted him for was that maybe he didn't value her work quite as much as she deserved. They'd fought about it, and to compromise, he suggested she finish the book she'd been writing for years, and they could travel and live out of a suitcase. They could have the best of both worlds. Before meeting David, Devorah never could have imagined agreeing to leave her professorship for anyone, especially not either of her other husbands. Never in a million years.

They didn't need the money. Devorah earned a good living and had made some good investments two decades back, and David himself had been left very comfortable after his retirement from his firm. He wanted to go places, see things, with her. He wanted to shop on Orchard Road in Singapore, hold her hand as they strolled the beaches of Vietnam, light a candle with her in the Santiago de Compostela in Spain.

And so she relented, and they did it all. They traveled for months out of the year and never fought when they vacationed. The shared experience of exploring exotic places brought them even closer. She was grateful they'd taken the time to do that together. She appreciated having those experiences with him even though his almost obsessive desire to have all her attention pulled her away from the writing of her book. After she'd experienced so much heartbreak and abuse at the hands of unworthy men over so many years, David had truly ignited a love and trust in Devorah that she had never known. He was not perfect. But he had loved her and been endlessly devoted to her. Until he was gone.

And she had never finished the book either.

Sweet David, my heart, where did you go?

Will I ever see you again?

She had to stop. That was all over now. So what now? Devorah looked down at the book *Kiss My Abundance*, staring up at her, almost taunting her from the coffee table. She picked it up and flipped to the back cover. Caroline Beckett's super glammed-up face stared up at her. Devorah rolled her eyes. She read the back cover out loud: "Beckett's groundbreaking step-by-step guide to thinking your way to living an inspired life is based on her years studying philosophy, which have culminated in this truly masterful and modern work as yet unseen in the world of self-help." As Devorah read, she drew her eyebrows together, and a fiery feeling slithered up her spine.

"No, she didn't. You've got to be kidding me," she said, her eyes wide as she opened the book and read page after page. "That snake!"

When she finished the book, Devorah raced out of the living room and into her study down the hall. She flicked the light on and opened the closet door. She pulled out a Bankers Box, tore the lid off, and lifted out a stack of papers. She laid the pages down on her desk, licked her finger, and scanned through them until she found what she was looking for.

"Well, I'll be damned," she said and sunk into the ergonomically correct office chair. Then she picked up her phone and dialed.

After a moment, she said, "Hey, it's Devorah. I think you'd better give me a call. I bought your book."

CHAPTER FIVE

CAROLINE

Hands in prayer pose over her heart center, legs crossed, Caroline sat on a yoga mat in her home studio. The room was mostly bare, except for one side of the wall, which was lined with oversize, ornately decorated Indian pillows, a dark wood table, two large pedestals with statues of a meditating female Buddha, and a trickling fountain. Candles burned on the intricately carved wood table, and next to them, a cone of incense sent a thin plume of white smoke skyward.

Sunlight cut through the dark wooden blinds and onto the floor in front of Caroline, whose eyes were closed. The sound of water slapping against river stones and the gentle whir of the overhead fan blended with the easy rhythm of prerecorded wind chimes and Caroline's gentle inhalations and exhalations. Despite her surroundings and her correct posture, every now and then, Caroline felt the furrow of her brow, and her inhalation would grow deeper and more intense, followed by an equally loud exhale.

Stay the course. Caroline cleared her mind, focusing only on her breath. *Go away. Let me be, please, please. I don't want to think anymore.*

She pushed all the negativity out and away from her. She was in control of her thoughts. She tried to think of all the bad things as clouds and watched them drifting past her. She wasn't going to think about

Grant and her humiliation on national television and what that could do to her brand.

Oh no. Breathe, just breathe. Clouds. Clouds.

She leaned into her meditation practice, concentrating on her breath, working hard to clear her mind.

As Caroline settled in closely to just this side of nirvana, the door swung open, as did Caroline's eyes.

A female voice rang out. "Oh, shish kebab. Sorry. Are you meditating?"

"Um, yes, I was," Caroline said, squinting as Susan came into focus. Everything about Susan was round, from her face to her glasses to the too-tight polka-dot sweater wrapped around her short, round frame.

"Oh, Caroline, I do this all the time. I'm so, so sorry," Susan said, brushing her fried frizzy hair into a clip at the back of her head.

Susan was right. She did do it all the time. Susan was Caroline's new assistant. Her predecessor, Oaklyn, had abruptly quit a couple of months before the sex tape was released, and now Caroline understood why. Her sudden defection had left Caroline desperate for help, and she'd hired Susan, a temporary replacement sent over from an agency.

Caroline had been so caught up in the mess of her life, she hadn't found anyone more permanent. Or appropriate.

Caroline sighed as she stared at her assistant. Susan Noonan-Bunin was nearly forty years old and single. She'd told Caroline numerous times that she had been married briefly more than a decade ago. She loved to repeat the story of her wedding—that, on a drunken night in Las Vegas, she met an offshore crewman, Hugh Bunin from Lünen, who strangely smelled like cumin, and he sent her swoonin'. And the next thing she remembered, she was spoonin' Bunin. She was hungover and had no recollection of the actual wedding ceremony (or the tattoo, but that was a different story, which she also liked to tell). Quite soon, Hugh Bunin got moving and had the marriage annulled. Susan hyphenated her name, thinking it gave her a certain gravitas.

Caroline inhaled slowly and deeply. The smile on her face grew wider, though the panic in her chest remained. Meditation wasn't working. Her anxiety was at full throttle, but she covered it up. "It's okay. I was just finishing up. Did you need me for something?"

"Oh, yes. I do. Are you sure?" Susan said. "I don't want to bother you."

"Susan, be direct. Assert yourself." Caroline was proud of her ability to diagnose everyone else's problems. And Susan's was that she didn't have enough confidence.

Susan pulled her feet closer together. She stuck out her chest and her chin and pushed her shoulders back. She inhaled and nodded.

"That's it, yes," Caroline said, encouraging and patient with Susan. Having her around to transform definitely took Caroline's focus off herself for a few brief moments.

"They didn't have any of the caffeine-free organic Oregon Chai tea at Whole Foods, but they did have the caffeinated one, but then they also had the Tazo-brand decaffeinated chai tea, and so I stood there and I wasn't sure what to do, and I was going to call, but I know how you said I should be assertive and do what I want to do and make a decision based on the information I had and just to plunge in and do it and make a decision. So I did. I got both."

"Okay," Caroline said, rising from her seated position and bending over to touch her toes, which seemed to get farther and farther away from her fingers with each passing year. Her hands, her toes, her body felt different to her. Nothing felt in line.

"Was that okay? Was that what you wanted?" Susan asked. "Was that the right thing?"

"It's fine, Susan. Thank you. Did you get the salmon?"

"Yes."

"Wild?"

"Yes, wild, of course! Cut into six equal pieces of one pound each, skin on, sliced vertically."

"Okay, great. Thank you."

Susan began to cough. And then hack. “Sorry, my asthma. It’s just the incense.”

“Right.”

“I never remember to bring my inhaler.”

“Was there anything else, Susan?”

“Oh, yes,” Susan said, tucking her hair behind her ears and smiling at Caroline.

Caroline dabbed at the water in the fountain and touched the back of each ear. She clasped her hands in front of her heart and bowed her head. “Namaste,” she said to Buddha. *Help!* was what she wanted to scream, but now wasn’t the time. Caroline turned to Susan. “Did you want to share that with me?”

“Oh, yes, sorry. You’re just so patient. Oh my gosh, ha ha. Anyway—yes, first off, and I’m sorry to be the one to tell you this, but the neighborhood association is having some issue with the paparazzi at the gate, and there have been a lot of complaints.”

“Still out there, huh?”

“Slow news cycle. It’ll pass.”

“Right, thank you. Do you know where Grant is?”

“Yes!”

There was a pause; then Caroline said, “Would you share that information with me, Susan?”

“Ha! Yes! Of course, I will!” Susan said and paused. “He’s on the phone—or texting, anyway. Just passed him on my way to you.”

“Oh, okay,” Caroline said and, taking note of the uncomfortable silence, asked, “Is that all, Susan?”

“Oh, sorry! No. It isn’t. Jeff, your attorney, is here.”

“He’s here?” Caroline asked, frowning. “At the house?”

“Yes.”

“Hmm. Okay, well, wonderful. Thank you, Susan. Will you have him meet me on the veranda?”

“He’s there waiting for you right now. I know how you like to have him meet you on the veranda, so I told him to go there. Well, actually, he just went there on his own. Because he said he knows how you like him to meet you on the veranda. So, yeah. Yay! He's on the veranda. I just love it when things work out. Like that, how that just worked out. So cool. Veranda."

Sometimes Caroline interrupted Susan, and sometimes she just let her carry on—somewhat interested in the woman's frequent misunderstanding of social cues.

After all, Caroline was the mental/emotional/social authority on living one's best life. All day. Every day. It was an all-encompassing, time-obliterating occupation. Caroline wanted—but had no time for—friends or relationships that scraped beneath the epidermis. She surrounded herself with people all the time. She had an exciting life. She was a much-sought-after dinner party guest.

But for years, so much of those dinner conversations had skewed toward her social companions' children, and as Caroline was childless, she had very little to offer and wasn't really interested in anyone else's. She *had* wanted to be a mother. She had tried, and she had failed, and Caroline didn't like failure. She was terrified of failure.

"Oh, and one more thing," Susan said.

"Yes?"

"You got a phone call," Susan said.

"O-kay . . . ," Caroline said, waiting for more to be revealed.

"Or, I should say, phone calls. Plural. From someone called Deborah van Buren. From Cape Cod. She said you'd know her."

"Devorah? Devorah van Buren? Huh. She took his name. That's funny." Caroline felt a pinprick at the back of her neck. She adjusted her shoulders, and the pain went away.

"Oh, I'm sorry. Did I do something wrong?"

"No, no, of course not. So she called me? When?"

"Earlier. Right. Sorry. So sorry. Anyway, I told you. But I didn't, you know, answer your phone or anything. I never answer your personal phone. Not anymore. I know now I'm not supposed to do that since that last time when I answered and your doctor was talking about your—*vagina.*"

"Susan, what did she say? Did she leave a message?"

"She wanted you to call her. And I don't mind telling you she was just this side of ornery."

"She was?" Caroline said. "Wait—are you listening to my messages?"

"Um," Susan said. "That's a funny story, actually. I tripped, and when I landed—"

"No, stop." Caroline's eyes rolled toward the ceiling. "What do you mean? What did she say?"

"She just asked you to call her. And sorry about the vagina—the vaginal stuff. Such a funny word. *Vaginal.* Did you know that, in botany, or botanical terms, a vagina is a sheath formed around the base of a leaf? Comes from Latin, for *scabbard* or *sheath*. That's so weird. Do you ever think about words and where they come from?"

"Susan."

"Sorry, Caroline."

"It's okay," she said and then pursed her lips. She had a bad feeling. "Shoot."

"Something wrong, Caroline?"

Caroline felt a little sweaty, like someone had turned the heat up. She felt the pinprick in her neck again.

"Can you take care of all of this?" Caroline said, indicating the candles and incense.

Then she walked quickly out of the room toward the veranda.

CHAPTER SIX

DEVORAH

"Everything is temporary," Devorah said, adjusting the black plastic cape around her shoulder. "Right?" She repositioned herself in the salon chair. Her back was bothering her. Why did they make these chairs so uncomfortable?

"Isn't that just the truth?" Kayleigh said, snapping her gum and tightening the plastic bag around Devorah's hair. "So what made you decide to kick your color up a notch? Got somewhere special to go?"

"I have a feeling I might be . . . getting some attention soon," Devorah said. "I want to look my best."

"Good for you, Devorah! That's the spirit!" Kayleigh said.

Devorah was slightly annoyed at her hairstylist's chipper vote of confidence. What did she mean by "that's the spirit"? Did she really look that bad? Sure, she had let herself go a little bit, but that was before. Now was different. She had made a decision. She wasn't done yet.

"And maybe redheads have more fun?" Devorah asked, smiling sweetly at Kayleigh. "I guess I'll find out." The sun beamed through the front salon window, making her hot. "You want to turn the AC up a bit?"

"Are you uncomfortable?"

"It's warm in here. Are you not warm?"

"Sure, let me go check the setting."

Devorah fanned herself and felt the prickling of the hair dye as it did its work. She looked around the salon. There were three other women, all her age, all with the same damn haircut. At least Devorah was mixing it up a little. Devorah pulled out her cell phone to check—still no phone calls. Well, Caroline could try and ignore her, but Devorah wasn't going to take it lying down.

Devorah had an agenda, and a style refresh was just one item on it. Earlier that morning, Devorah had subscribed to a food delivery service. She would have three meals a day delivered, which was guaranteed to help drop those extra twenty pounds she'd been carrying. Okay, thirty. And she had a dentist appointment scheduled for the following morning. After she went in for her annual physical last week—which was frankly a biennial because she'd put it off for two years—her doctor gave her a good chewing out. She needed to lose weight and stop drinking. She needed to get herself moving every day and eat balanced meals. And while all of that was good motivation, it wasn't the main reason she wanted to get herself back into fighting form again. No, the reason she was getting herself back on track was much simpler. If she was going to stir up the hornet's nest, sue the traitorous Caroline Beckett, and subsequently publish her own book like she had always meant to do, she would no doubt be photographed, and dammit, she was going to look her best while doing it.

She knew how the world worked, and she was going to present herself in the best manner possible. In the court of public opinion, appearances meant everything. She was not going to sit back and be lauded as the spiteful last rose of summer. She was going to look every bit the professional when she exposed Caroline for the fraud that she was, and she would use the publicity to sell her own book in the process. This was going to be Devorah's swan song. And she was going to nail it.

The timing was right, too, of course. It always was. Devorah had been looking for a way out of her melancholy, a way to use her brain. And here was her chance. All the signs were pointing to Devorah's triumphant return, her rebirth. Just yesterday, while picking out soaps at Bath & Body

Works, Devorah had run into a former colleague from her professorial days. Veronica Miller was several decades Devorah's junior and had served as an adjunct professor of moral philosophy and civil polity in the department for a few years before Devorah was pushed out.

"Devorah? Is that you?" Veronica had said, searching Devorah's face. "Wow, I hardly recognized you. It's been ages."

It had only been seven years, not quite ages, but Devorah was disappointed to note that Veronica looked exactly the same as she had then, and knew that she, indeed, did not. Actually, Devorah was reluctant to admit, she did at least look like it had been ages and ages.

"Oh, hello, Veronica," she said. "Just on the Cape for a visit?"

"Yes, I'm summering with my family in Dennis."

"Summering, huh? Great." Devorah hated it when people made up pretentious verbs out of innocuous little nouns. She forced herself not to roll her eyes. Veronica had always been snooty, but it was a philosophy department. There were quite a few pretentious eggheads.

"You've been well, then?" Veronica asked, with some concern.

Devorah laughed a little. "Yes, don't I look well?"

"Yes, yes, of course you do. You look absolutely great. You do. You look fine. You do. Retirement suits you," Veronica said.

And it was the "retirement" bit that had really pushed Devorah over the edge. Devorah wasn't stupid. She knew that Veronica knew Devorah hadn't wanted to leave her position. *So what are we talking about here?* Devorah knew there was the slightest bit of ageist crap in Veronica's assessment of her physically. But it was a Tuesday afternoon in September—nobody was going to the Emmys. Just a simple outing to pick up some hand soap and maybe a candle. Was Devorah supposed to put on a ball gown and a fancy updo? Did she have to shower? Brush her teeth? Run a brush through her hair? It was as though Veronica felt the need to go way out of her way to convince Devorah that she did indeed look well. *Just wait until you're my age.*

"Well," Devorah had said, and held up a three-wick candle. "Guess I'd better get back to my *candle-ing.*" Devorah turned back to the stack in front of her and continued sniffing loudly. She turned back to see Veronica had raised her eyebrows, likely surprised at Devorah's rudeness. Before leaving, Veronica said, "Always a pleasure, Devorah. Bye-bye."

Devorah had waited a few seconds before she allowed herself to watch Veronica's form disappearing down the long mall corridor. Later, as Devorah walked through Macy's to get to the exit, she caught sight of herself in a store mirror. *Wow. Who the hell is that old woman?*

"I really do look like hell." She laughed and then looked over at a young boy about ten years old, who appeared to be frightened by her.

"You said a bad word," he said and ran away.

Jesus. She'd been talking to herself out loud and didn't realize it. She'd noticed here and there that she was doing that more often, the consequence of being alone too much, she thought. She continued to her car. Once inside, she called and made the hair appointment for the next day. The voice on the other end of the line had told her she hadn't been to the salon in more than two years. Could it really have been that long?

Yep, she was taking back the reins. To hell with Veronica, and to hell with Caroline Beckett, perhaps the biggest betrayal of them all. They'd underestimated her. They'd all written her off. She raised an imaginary fist in the air and deepened her frown lines.

As Devorah sat with her head under the hair dryer, she looked up at the television, following along by reading the subtitles. The movie was *Miss Congeniality*. Par for the course for a salon to play a rom-com about an ugly duckling who gets a makeover. Despite her own intention to get herself made over, she felt irritated by the whole idea of it: "I'm pretty, now you can love me." Appearances—was that really what it was all about? Beauty. Youth. Love. *Love me.*

Devorah closed her eyes to quiet her mind. She liked the darkness. It didn't feel scary or isolating. All the screeching of tires and tirades of words and thoughts and things slipped away. The noise from the hair dryer enveloped her, providing a backdrop of white noise in which Devorah quickly became lost. She waffled back and forth between acknowledging the breath traveling in and out of her body and the thoughts and ideas that popped into her head and distracted her. She knew the people in the salon probably thought she'd fallen asleep, but she had not. She was enveloped in the stillness, the quiet of her mind. *Shhhh,* the voice said. The part of her that was both her and other. The part of her that was always present and quiet and observing. It was only a couple of seconds that she was tuned in and one with the voice, the observer. Devorah felt a nudge, an inkling, a voice telling her to wake up. And then she came crashing back into the reality of the busy salon.

She blinked and looked up at the television. The rom-com was over, and after a commercial break, *Hollywood Minute* came on, once again splashing Caroline Beckett's image across the screen. *Well, she should know by now,* Devorah thought. Devorah wasn't going to take it sitting down. She was suing Caroline's ass. A flicker of a feeling, an inkling of doubt about what she was doing, crossed her mind, but she swatted it away.

A clicking sound as the hair dryer turned off. Devorah looked to her right and saw a woman gesticulating at her. She pushed the hair dryer up off her head and said, "What?"

The woman was very excited. "That's Caroline Beckett. I'm reading her book." The woman held the book up as proof. "It's so good! You should read it! She's from around here, you know."

"Yeah, I do," Devorah said and leaned back into the uncomfortable salon chair.

~

After the salon, Devorah stopped in at the grocery store to pick up some food for Mary Magdalene and some maraschino cherries for her manhattan. She had a spring in her step—she felt twenty years younger with her new fiery red hair. She loved how it felt as she walked—light and bouncy.

"Well, well, well, looking real fine, Devorah," a voice called out from the frozen food aisle.

Devorah laughed and turned to see Diaz and several other firemen with a large shopping cart full of food.

"Don't be such a flirt," she said and smiled.

The guys laughed and slapped Diaz on the back. They continued down the next aisle, but Diaz hung back.

"I would've shopped for you, Devorah. If you'd wanted me to. If you'd let me."

"Well, obviously I didn't want you to. I don't need you to. I'm perfectly capable of doing my own shopping," she said, then, softening, added, "But thanks."

"You're welcome, *Red*. I'll see you at home," he said and rejoined the other firemen.

Devorah laughed and shook her head, loving the way her hair smelled. She picked out her items. She finished up and was on her way to the cash register when something in the stationery aisle caught her eye. There, on the endcap, was a selection of mass-market bestsellers. And there, smiling out from a small poster next to the display, was Caroline Beckett, again. Devorah pursed her lips and paused for a moment.

Another customer, a woman, seeing Devorah with the book, leaned in and said, "Oh, I absolutely loved that book. That's Caroline Beckett, did you know that she's—"

Devorah pivoted on her achy feet and said, "Yeah, yeah, yeah, I know. She's from around here."

Devorah returned the book to the shelf and turned around, but she hadn't pushed it in far enough, and it fell to the floor. Devorah spun back around and looked at the book on the ground, then up at the other shopper, who raised her eyebrows in judgment, with an "Are you going to pick it up?" look on her face. Devorah never broke eye contact with the woman as she extended her leg, flexed her foot, and kicked the book into the middle of the aisle.

The woman looked on in horror as Devorah sauntered on her way to the checkout line.

CHAPTER SEVEN

CAROLINE

Caroline couldn't help feeling like something big was afoot when she walked onto the veranda to find Jeff Truman with his back to her. He rested his arms on the railing, looking out over the hilly expanse of the Palisades. He had a tall, athletic build, which he complemented well with expensive stylish clothing from Gucci and Prada. His was a calculated look—Caroline assumed he'd honed it over the years by careful examination of the most successful, most influential men on the planet. Jeff needn't have worked so hard. He was handsome and could've passed muster in H&M or Gap clothing, but she knew Jeff had standards. Jeff had ambition. That was why she'd hired him. You were nothing in this town if you didn't have a good attorney—and Caroline was not available to be thought of as nothing.

"Jeff, darling, you're looking well," Caroline said. Jeff was not only her attorney but also a friend.

"Caroline, as lovely as ever," Jeff said and kissed Caroline's left cheek, then her right.

Caroline smiled and reminded herself that she was the life expert. She had everything figured out. And she and Jeff were friends, and it was perfectly normal that he should stop by her home.

So, then, why were butterflies flittering around in her stomach? Was she nervous?

"Tell me some good news, Jeff," she said.

"Wish I could. But, darling, you're being sued."

Caroline attempted to hide the chill that trickled from a pinprick at the base of her neck all the way down her spine. She took a deep inhale and remembered that people were always suing successful people. It was a given. You couldn't call yourself truly successful until you'd been sued by the best of them, and at least a half dozen times. This—whatever frivolous claim it was—would not derail her. She was tough. She'd built herself up—a no one from nowhere. Nobody was going to take it away from her.

"Interesting," she said. "Who and why?"

"Well, it's about the book," Jeff said, fixing his dark-brown eyes on Caroline.

Caroline felt a change of electricity in the air. She knew the other shoe was about to drop.

She tried not to show her nervousness. "The *book*? My book?" she asked. "*Kiss My Abundance?* It's been out for a couple years now. What about it?"

"This person is coming in just a couple weeks shy of three years, love. The statute of limitations on copyright infringement is three years exactly."

"Copyright infringement? Someone's saying I stole their work?"

"Devorah van Buren is saying you stole her work."

Caroline tried to remain steady. "Are you serious? Devorah?"

"I am serious. Ten-million-dollar suit in Los Angeles County Court."

"Well, that is hilarious. And ridiculous. And—there's got to be a mistake. Devorah and I are old . . . friends."

Jeff straightened his posture. "Caroline, this is big. What a lawsuit like this could mean to someone with your notoriety will make ten million dollars look like Monopoly money. This—on top of the raised eyebrows from the video—is bad news for the brand. You. Your whole identity. What you stand for is in jeopardy. Look, I've been dodging calls all day, and that's just about the Grant stuff. You've got the sympathy vote for the time being, but it's just a second until the wind changes direction and you're painted with a less flattering brush as a cold fish who's hard to get along with, or whatever they decide to put on you."

Caroline visibly shivered; the pinprick in her neck twinged again.

"Sorry, love, I'm not trying to be harsh, but I'm here to tell you we need to take this seriously, and we need to make it go away. Fast. If this gets out—plagiarism—we're talking loss of endorsements, investors backing out, the TV show, everything. So, who the hell is she, babe? And, more importantly, what do I need to know?"

"She called me. She's been calling me, I guess," Caroline said, grabbing the railing. She felt a bit dizzy.

"Well, what did she say?"

"I don't know. I didn't talk to her. I was meditating. I was busy." Caroline sat down. "Why would she do this? What would cause her to do something like this?"

"I don't know, Caroline. But, as your attorney, I gotta ask you, whose book is this?"

"It's mine!"

"Sure. Fine. Okay. Then, who is she? And can you shut her up?"

"She was my employer—my mentor of sorts. Wretched woman. I haven't spoken to her in years. She's a pretentious old windbag. And, of course, yes, I'll call her. I will get this sorted."

"If we can keep this out of court, that would be best. You don't need any more bad publicity."

"Tell me something I don't know."

"Look, I'm your attorney, so be honest with me. Is there any basis for this?"

"How can you even ask me that?"

"Well, that's not a *no*. Anyway, this reminds me of that Edna St. Vincent Millay quote. Do you know it? 'A person who publishes a book willfully appears before the populace with his pants down.'"

"Right, well, thanks for that." Caroline, raising her arms into the air, shouted, "What next?"

And then came a strange rumble. First, the ground began to buckle and shake, the windows rattled in their frames, and an expensive glass vase on the side table fell to the ground, shattering into a million pieces. But the rumbling roar of the earthquake was so overpowering, it drowned out the shattering glass and took off on its own.

"Oh my God, Jeff," Caroline said, "what in the—"

Jeff heroically grabbed Caroline around the waist and pulled her into the frame of the veranda doorway. Jeff's water glass on the table teetered and then fell off the edge and crashed on the ground.

"What are you doing? Oh my God!"

"That's what you're supposed to do, right?"

"No!" Caroline shouted. "You stop and drop or something!"

Birds sped through the air, escaping their shaky nests. The water from the swimming pool swayed from side to side and splashed over onto the tiles.

"Stop, drop, and roll is fire," he said as the walls threatened to pull apart at the seams. "Oh, wait, I think you're right. You're supposed to drop and cover up your vital organs or something like that."

"And get under something."

"We are under something."

"We are in something, not under something."

"We are under a doorframe."

"We are in a room."

They continued to argue while the walls rattled and the earth released one final massive tremble. It sounded like an enormous dump truck was driving, literally, over, into, around, and on top of the house.

And then, just as suddenly as it started, it stopped.

"Was that . . . is that . . . is that it?" Jeff said.

"I guess so. Yeah," Caroline said. "Jeez."

There was a brief pause before Jeff jumped up and said, "Wow. Well, that was fun! What a whopper. Where's my phone? Oh, in my hand. Ha ha ha." He shouted at his phone, "Siri—earthquake. Los Angeles. Today."

Caroline felt shaken as she called out, "Grant! Grant, we're out here!"

There was no response as Jeff whirled around like a dervish, and Caroline realized she felt stuck. Frozen with fear despite the adrenaline pumping through her veins. She surveyed the area around her. *It's over. No big deal.* Minimal damage—just the vase, the water glass, and a few picture frames. The shattered glass spread out, and Caroline was barefoot. She pressed her hand against her chest to stave off the anxiety and nausea that were piling up, building inside her. Caroline slid her back down the wall and sat on the floor, kicking her legs and bare feet out in front of her.

She heard movement behind her, from the hallway.

"Grant?" she called out. "Grant! I'm okay! Grant?" And she immediately felt stupid. Ridiculous. Why? She didn't know, but her arms felt shaky. Jeff was yelling and laughing delightedly into his phone as he paced in front of her.

The panic rose, and Caroline fought for her breath. She remembered this feeling—panic. She knew she needed to reframe her thoughts and focus on something other than the bile building up in her stomach. She willed her mind to think of her favorite place in the entire world and immediately transported herself to the long stretch of beach she used to frequent as a child on Cape Cod. She envisioned herself sitting on the sand, staring out at Nantucket Sound. And she was there. *Now.* She could feel each grain of sand and smell the salty air. She felt the warm breeze from the vineyard and Nantucket roll in and spread through her hair.

She immediately felt calmer, more relaxed. She would not come undone. She didn't do that anymore, she told herself, remembering. *I don't come undone. I am a success at life.*

And then fervent, clamorous footsteps coming from the interior of the house and heading toward the veranda grew louder, almost as loud as the earthquake itself. Susan's panicked voice screamed, "Caroline? Caroline! Oh my God. Caroline, there was an earthquake!"

"Yeah, I know that," Caroline said, feeling her grip on Cape Cod slip away.

"Oh my God, are you hurt? Are you okay? Caroline!"

"I'm fine" was all she could muster. She felt like she wasn't entirely inside her own body, as though she were watching the scene from afar, like it wasn't all real. Ever since the Emmys, she'd felt disconnected and disoriented, more and more outside herself. She heard herself say, "Where's Grant?"

"He's upstairs. He's on the phone. I passed him on my way to find you." Susan turned around, truly taking in Jeff and the mess on the veranda for the first time. "Thank God you were here."

Jeff laughed. "Thank God, listen—I was trying to stop, drop, and roll!"

"Ha, that's for fire. It's drop, cover, hold on," Susan said, acting out dropping, covering, and holding on.

Caroline was trying to catch her breath.

"Right. Cover the vital organs! That's it," Jeff said.

It was just an earthquake, Caroline reminded herself. As a resident of Southern California for well over a decade now, she'd experienced plenty, but this one rattled her. *Why?*

"I just felt it and came running to find Caroline," Susan said.

"Where is Grant?" Caroline said, interrupting.

"What's that, Caroline?" Susan said.

"Did you say Grant was on the phone?"

Susan said, "Yeah, he was . . . on the phone."

"With who?"

Susan shrugged. "Not sure."

There was a beat. A moment of silence, until Susan broke it saying, "By the way, did you know you're trending on Twitter?"

"Oh, boy," Jeff said.

~

The veranda was now cleared of all broken glass, but Caroline was still stepping carefully on her way inside to check on Grant when Thérèse called on FaceTime in all her managerial glory.

"That was a rough one!" Caroline said.

"Tell me about it, I was getting a wax. It's like a crime scene down there. Anyway, have you been able to speak to this Devorah person?"

"No. I don't know why she's doing this," Caroline said.

"Well, and bear with me here, sweetheart, because I have to ask: Is it because you stole her work?"

"You know I can still fire your ass, Thérèse. Just because we've been working together for years doesn't give you the right to—"

"So that's a no? Good, stick with that."

"Every single word I wrote in *Kiss My Abundance* was the truth. The truth, and that's the truth." Caroline was inside now and made her way down the hallway toward the upstairs room that was Grant's study.

"Truth is great, and I don't even care whose truth, darlin', but you pay me to tell you this stuff. You've got a potential PR disaster on your hands. So just who the hell is this lady?"

"She's . . . a philosophy professor. A wealthy woman. She lived in town. I was her assistant a million years ago. She knew my mother. My mother cleaned her house."

"O-kay."

"It was a complicated relationship, I guess. She was a bit salty but very smart, a very clever lady. And it was a difficult time for me, personally. Our life at home, mine and my mother's, was challenging, so we spent a lot of time at Devorah's. Both of us working with and for Devorah. She was harsh, but I think she could relate to what we were experiencing at home, my father's drinking. His temper. Anyway, it was an escape, and I was a very good assistant. She was working on a book herself at the time. I guess it contained similar ideology to what I created. It had some of the same players, Saint Teresa and Descartes, and I think she was talking about how the action of changing their thoughts impacted the trajectory of their lives. I remember saying back then that everything I was reading seemed like a road map to happiness. But she never said anything about it being a guide, and I don't think she ever even did anything with her work. She just plain quit. But, I mean, hey, I'm pretty sure the teachings of seventeenth-century philosophers are in the public domain. Right? I mean, come on, it was my idea to push that philosophy into a very easily digested self-help tome for the masses."

"You worked on some of this stuff with her, then?"

"Yes."

"Did you cite her?"

"No."

"Okey dokey, well, what it will come down to in the court of public opinion is a she-said, she-said, which is still damaging to you, to the brand. Best possible scenario is stopping it. Now. We've got the pitch meeting for the new show idea coming up next month. You don't want to mess all of that up or complicate it or anything. Yeah, they optioned the book, but all that falls through if the content isn't yours. And if that happens, you're as good as dead here. You can't afford to let this get out."

"Okay, I got it."

"Like, get this all sorted."

Caroline leaned her head back, but she misjudged the distance and slammed her head against the wall. "Ouch. The hits just keep on coming."

"Well, don't say stuff like that. You're putting it all out there or something—like a domino effect. Isn't that what you say all the time? Don't manifest that crap."

"Okay, okay," Caroline said. "I'm not. I'm going to deal with this. Let me go talk to Grant. I'll get this sorted."

Thérèse rolled her eyes. "Don't get me started on that one. Or actually, do—let me talk to Grant."

"Talk to you later, Thérèse," Caroline said and clicked off FaceTime.

Caroline continued on her way to find Grant. There was a nagging, a tug on her brain she was having difficulty swatting away. Why on earth was all this happening? And why right now? It was all too absurd, really. It had a slow start, but *Kiss My Abundance* had found its audience, and it had been on the bestseller list for forty-eight weeks. It was her breakthrough into the big leagues. She had been at it for years, feverishly working her way up the ladder from her modest upbringing, and, lo and behold, forty-eight weeks ago, it was the book that launched her to the top. Caroline Beckett had catapulted to the peak of self-help stardom and had crossed the bridge into mainstream.

Her platform had been one of self-love and acceptance, and her interviews revealed her personality to be spirited and funny. She was a media darling. She made people feel better about themselves, about their jobs, their relationships, their lives. Caroline soaked in it. She spent hours every day responding to her continuously growing fan base, taping interviews, promoting new projects, pitching TV shows and films she'd been trying to get off the ground for years. She even had plans to develop her own clothing line, consisting mostly of high-waisted yoga pants in different colors and patterns. Caroline loved her fans, and her fans loved her. They related to Caroline's everywoman image and reveled in her overcoming obstacles in her life, like the tragic deaths of both of her parents at a young age from drug and alcohol abuse. Her followers appreciated her deep spirituality, her faith in God. Yes, Caroline had paid her dues, and she had achieved her payday. She had mucked around in anonymity for long enough, and with the publication of the book and its detailed guide relating very on-trend spiritual universal laws to prayer and existential philosophies, she had cracked the code. It had all slammed into alignment, like a beefeater at Buckingham Palace.

Caroline really did have life figured out. She had what she had always wanted, ever since she was a little girl back in Massachusetts. She'd broken free from the shackles of nothingness. She was well known, rich, and successful. She was somebody. She was happy.

So why was Devorah calling her now? Why wouldn't she just stay tucked and buried in the past and out of Caroline's mind? What did she want? Hadn't she done enough?

Nope. It wasn't going to work. Caroline would not go back. She would not sink back down into the muck. She could control her thoughts, and she would not think about the past. She would not think about all the nonsense that had happened with Grant. She would not let some salacious lawsuit ruin her. She had worked too hard to become the woman she was today. She would not fail or hurt or succumb to the pain.

Ever.

Again.

Which was why the discovery of what Grant was up to in the study was all the more upsetting.

CHAPTER EIGHT

DEVORAH

Devorah sat on the floor of her cluttered office surrounded by coverless Bankers Boxes and with crumpled-up pages of typewritten notes strewed around her. Mary Magdalene was lying in a bed of paper at Devorah's feet. Devorah scrunched up another piece of paper and tossed it near the wastebasket. She turned to Mary and watched the rise and fall of the dog's stomach. She reached down and patted her head.

"How's my good girl?" she said. She kissed her hand and patted her head again. "What do you think, Mary? The good life! Plato knew what he was talking about, didn't he, old girl? What are you laughing at?"

Mary Magdalene did not move or acknowledge she was being spoken to.

"Did you know the Greeks had different terms for love? Love is a noun, but it's also a verb, Mary. Did you know that? Of course you did, my little darling." Devorah's eyes drifted around the room and finally landed on the book, *Kiss My Abundance*, sitting on the desk. With a ton of effort, Devorah rose up from the ground and took her seat at her desk. She reached for the book and opened it. There were note tabs, little colored stickies jutting out from the pages. She licked her fingers and turned the page. She read for some time before stopping and looking out the window. "I need something stronger than those damn drafts to hold my case. I want to zing her. There's got to be something else in here. Dammit," she said aloud. "Mary Magdalene, this is some kind of bullshit, that's for damn sure. Look at this—I found it—right here. Straight plagiarism! I've got her. You can't just take someone's work and pass it off as your own. You can't do that. No matter if they sat their fat derriere on that work for thirty years or not. It's not right. I connected the dots with all those philosophers and their writings. But seriously, to gobble it up and regurgitate it back in such a Hollywood way. It's insulting. I'm insulted. But she won't get away with it. That's for sure. Damn sure."

She placed the book down on the desk and swept her fingers across her touchpad, waking her laptop. She typed the words *Caroline Beckett* into her search engine and scrolled through one news story after another. What a mess. "Caroline, Caroline, Caroline . . . what the hell are you doing?"

Mary Magdalene raised her head up off the ground, blinked, then closed her eyes completely and drifted off to sleep again.

A short while later, Devorah's desk was littered with papers, lined and highlighted, and *Kiss My Abundance* had Post-it Notes in a rainbow of neon colors poking out from all sides.

She sat back in her chair and looked out the window at the waves tumbling in on each other. She studied them. They smashed against the shore and created chaos—sand, shells, seaweed pounding and scattering. But then, just as quickly, the water slipped away again, leaving what was left behind to lick their wounds, regroup, and get ready for the tide to rush back in again, to lean forward and strike.

Devorah picked up her cell phone and scrolled through until she found the name she was looking for—Caroline Beckett. She waited for the beep, then said, "Hello, Caroline. Me again. Give me a call."

~

Devorah parked her Mercedes in the middle of two parking spaces outside the beach club. She walked around to the passenger side of the car, opened the door, and carefully removed Mary Magdalene from the seat. The air felt heavy, the last remnant of a hot summer. Devorah marched over the seashell-laden parking lot, crunching as she went along. Overhead, the words *East Beach Club* were proudly painted in red, white, and blue over the distressed wooden archway, and the club's burgee flapped in the wind above it. Devorah stomped inside.

She was almost to her seat at the bar when a young man appeared before her.

"Excuse me," he said, trying to politely block her.

"You're excused," she said and moved around him. She placed Mary Magdalene on the stool next to her. The bar was starting to fill up.

"Excuse me, ma'am, but you can't bring a dog inside. So sorry."

Devorah turned and looked him up and down. "You're new."

"Yes, ma'am. I am," he said. "My name is—"

"Well, seeing as how you're new," she said, "I'll let it slide, this time. Bring me a Maker's Mark manhattan, up."

"No, ma'am, I don't think you understand. Your dog. Can't stay here."

"That so?"

"Yes, ma'am. I'm so sorry." He looked closer at Mary Magdalene. "And frankly, ma'am, I hope you don't mind me saying so, but the dog doesn't look well."

"Well, you don't look so hot yourself."

He stopped, gasped a little, and said, "Excuse me?"

"Look, I said I want my manhattan. Let's keep appearances out of this. For your sake."

"I . . . I . . ."

"I . . . I . . . what? Bring me my drink. And where the hell is Dennis?"

"Ma'am, I am not bringing you a drink. And you are going to have to leave the bar area with that dog."

"Listen to me, buddy, go get Dennis before I kick you right in your Nantucket Reds."

"Devorah," a voice called from behind. "I see you've met Nathan, our new manager in training."

"Hello, Dennis. Yes, we were just getting acquainted. You might talk to him about harassing board members."

"I'll take it from here, Nathan. Thank you so much," Dennis said. He gave Nathan a placating smile and a little nod.

Nathan, chastened, said, "So lovely to meet you, ma'am, and your little dog too."

"You don't have to call me ma'am, Nate. I'm not a hundred." Devorah turned to Dennis. "God, this place is going down the toilet. Fast."

"Devorah, he was just doing his job. And I've been meaning to talk to you. We've had some complaints about Mary Magdalene at the bar. It's against code to have an animal inside, not to mention we could really use the seat."

"Aah, the almighty dollar. Is that what it comes down to? I'll pay for her seat. Put a meal and a drink on my tab and give it to that little peon. My treat," she said, nodding toward Nathan.

"Nathan eats for free, Devorah, but that's not really the point. The issue is a nonservice animal indoors. People have complained."

"Who?"

"Devorah."

"What?"

"I'm sorry. I can't let you sit at the bar with your dog."

Devorah paused. She took a deep breath. She looked at Mary Magdalene, who blankly stared at the wall and panted.

"What's happening? I'm here to work. On my new book," Devorah said and held her brittle hand to her neck. "I'm not going to be pushed around."

"Devorah, I need you to keep your voice down," Dennis said, looking over his shoulder. "You have to go."

"What?"

"I can't have you in here raising your voice like this. Please."

"Please, what?"

"Please. Leave. I'm sorry, Devorah."

She straightened her shoulders, looked around the room, swallowed, and turned back to Dennis. She lowered her voice. "I have nowhere else to go. I can't work at home." She exhaled slowly. "I'd like to stay. We'd like to stay."

Dennis nodded and placed a finger on his mouth. He looked around the room. "I can seat you on the terrace, but you have to put the dog out of everyone's view. And you can't do this again. Like, ever. Okay?"

"Yeah, yeah, yeah, okay, okay. What, do you want me to write it in my own blood or something?" she said, stepping around him as he rolled his eyes.

CHAPTER NINE

CAROLINE

Caroline pushed on the heavy wooden door and stepped over the threshold of Grant's sanctuary, a place that was his and his alone. The rest of the house was sophisticated and feminine, but Grant's study was like an extra toe on a Hemingway cat, out of place and intriguing. The slate gray walls were covered with black-and-white photos of seductive female body parts, an old train, birds in flight, and a smattering of framed photographs of Grant through the years with various dignitaries, presidents, the Dalai Lama, and a who's who of Hollywood celebrities. The showy nature of the wall hangings were in contrast to the otherwise minimalist-styled office. The clean, dark wood desk had a sleek angular design, and all that lay atop it were a pencil-thin modern lamp, several envelopes, and one framed photograph of Grant and Caroline on the beach from years ago.

Grant had his back to Caroline, facing the window. He was on the phone, whispering as the door glided open. As he heard her behind him, Grant's body language immediately shifted from relaxed to shoulders back, tight and at attention.

He abruptly swung around to face Caroline and then loudly and rapidly spoke into the receiver, saying, "Yes, yes, you've got it, *Doug*. But listen, Caroline's just walked in, and I've got to go. Okay. Bye." And he hung up and dropped the phone onto his desk like it was a hot potato.

"Grant?" Caroline felt a fluttering sensation in her chest, but not like the gentle whizzing of a butterfly's wings—this was more sinister in nature, more like an angry wasp, or a *hive* of angry wasps.

"Hey, hi. Hi," Grant said, a smooth smile spreading across his handsome face.

"What's going on?"

"What do you mean? Nothing. I was just on the phone."

"Who was that?" Caroline asked, looking between the phone on the desk and Grant.

"Doug," Grant said matter of factly.

"Doug who? Doug Pastor?"

"Yes, Doug Pastor. He was just returning my call. I called him the other day to work out some of the details on the Tulum shoot. I told you about that, right? That it got moved up. I'll be heading out Thursday."

"You didn't tell me you're going to Mexico at all, and definitely not on Thursday."

"Oh, okay, well, I'm sorry about that, honey. But I'm telling you right now. I mean, I thought I had told you before that I was going, and now I'm telling you that the dates moved up. I think it's going to be a great shoot."

Caroline took a deep breath and looked past his shoulder at the books framing the wall behind his desk. Her eyes traveled around the room, drifting over the artwork, and paused on the ornate statue of Lord Ganesha atop a three-drawered table in the corner. Ganesha was the elephant-headed Hindu god of beginnings, revered for his ability to remove obstacles from one's path. Caroline loved that statue. But pretty much everything else in the room was garbage.

"There was an earthquake," she said. She was frowning, she realized. She turned to Grant.

"I know. I know that. I felt it. It was scary, huh?" Grant said. He came around the front of the desk and positioned himself in front of Caroline.

"It was scary," Caroline said.

Grant reached out his arms toward her, and Caroline flinched. She took a step back.

"Are you okay?" Grant asked.

"You didn't come look for me."

"I . . . I didn't think I had to. I . . . it wasn't the big one. Is that . . . is that what's bothering you?" Grant asked.

"You know," Caroline said, gesturing to the room. "You have one picture of me. In this whole room. You have one picture of me. One. And you're in it."

Grant looked down at the single silver-framed picture on his desk of the two of them smiling with the Pacific Ocean as a backdrop. He picked it up. "I like this picture of you. That was a really nice day."

"Who was that on the phone?" Caroline said and then chewed on her bottom lip.

"Oh, come on," Grant said, exasperated. He dropped the picture frame back down into its spot on the desk loudly and then tilted his head back and looked up at the ceiling. He exhaled all the air in his lungs.

Caroline closed her eyes. "Don't do that to me."

"Do what? I told you who it was on the phone. If you don't believe me, that's your problem."

"Don't try to make me sound like I'm crazy. Just don't do that to me," Caroline said. She felt shaky.

Grant shuffled a few envelopes on the desk and flung them to the side next to the photo. "Okay, fine. *Whatever*, Caroline."

Caroline bit hard on her lip. She tasted the rusty metal tinge of blood.

"If it was Doug, then you can show me, right? Show me your phone."

"Oh, come on, Caroline. What are you doing?"

"I'm listening to my gut," she said. She stared at him, and he glared back, shaking his head.

"What kind of relationship is this? Are you just never going to trust me again? Is that what it is? How long, huh? How long until you're going to trust me?"

Caroline felt heat building, rising up from the earth into her body and bubbling, burning like a flame behind her eyes, but she felt almost eerily calm.

"You humiliated me. You cheated. You did that. I didn't do that. You did that. So don't you dare try to turn this around. You were whispering into the phone when I came in here. Why would you be whispering to Doug?"

"I wasn't whispering." Grant rolled his eyes. He picked up his phone and held it out to Caroline. "You want to check? You want to see? You don't believe me? Fine. Go ahead and take a look and just know that if you are not going to trust me, you are the one who is destroying this relationship. You. Not me."

Caroline looked at the phone in his outstretched hand, the hand she'd known so well over the past ten years, with its long fingers and wide nail beds. She looked at that phone, stared at the phone, waiting for it to jump up and start talking all on its own, and then, finally, when she couldn't take the doubt and indecision anymore, she grabbed it from him.

Grant's shoulders slumped. "Well, that says a lot," Grant said, sadly.

She paused only a moment, and then she punched in his passcode.

It didn't work. Caroline looked at him. The look in her eye said, *Give me the passcode.*

Grant met her eye. "You sure you want to do this? This is where we're at?"

Caroline didn't flinch, even though her insides were jelly. Fiery, angry jelly, but jelly all the same.

"Zero eight zero eight," he said.

Caroline felt her resolve weaken. "Our wedding date."

"Yes," Grant said. "I love you, Caroline. I love you. I am an imperfect man, and I have hurt you, and for that I am so sorry. But I love you. Always."

Caroline looked back down at the phone in her hand. It felt like it was getting heavier, bigger. She wanted to put it down on his desk and throw her arms around Grant. She wanted to. But she didn't. Instead she punched in the code and saw the last call Grant had made, which was, of course, to Oaklyn.

"Let me explain," Grant said to Caroline's back as she turned from him and moved toward the heavy oak door.

"I'm done."

"You don't understand, Caroline, please," Grant said.

Caroline had her hand on the doorknob, twisting it, when Grant said, "I don't know how it happened. We just . . . we just fell in love."

All the wind was sucked out of the room. There was no sound. Caroline closed her eyes and took a deep breath.

"You fell in love with her? When?"

"Caroline, please," Grant said.

"Why?"

"It just happened."

"Oh my God. It just happened? It just happened that you fell in love with someone that wasn't me, your wife? Did I do something to make you not love me? Did you ever love me?"

"Did you ever love me, Caroline?"

"Is this where you cheating is my fault?"

Grant sighed and ran his fingers through his white hair.

"I want you out of here when I get back," she said over her shoulder. Like it was just a throwaway line, something from a movie.

"What? Why? Caroline—"

"Why? Did you really just ask me *why*? Okay, how about this? When you realize you no longer want to spend the rest of your life with somebody, you want the rest of your life to start as soon as possible."

"Where are you going?"

"Cape Cod," she said just as the door slammed shut behind her.

CHAPTER TEN

DEVORAH

Isolated from the row of beachfront houses, on a strip of sandy land, home to sandpipers, eelgrass, and fiddler crabs, sat a lone tree. Devorah couldn't see it from her house, but it was quite close, and it had been ages since she felt up to walking to it. Now that she was reclaiming her health, taking out a new lease on life, she decided that this walk would once again be her daily ritual.

The tree was old and withered, the bark black with salt and lack of nourishment. It sat at the very edge of the channel where the river met the sea of Nantucket Sound. Conch shells hung from its branches, placed there by dreamers who knew the tree held a little bit of magic.

Devorah and David used to do this walk together. David loved the mystical tree. He told her a sea witch lived nearby and would grant wishes to whoever left the prettiest gift.

Devorah never left the gift of a seashell, but she liked looking at the shells of the wishful thinkers who did. The tree was lovely and mysterious. How did it get there? Way out there on the point all alone? What had caused that first person to hang a shell from its branches?

She remembered the summer one desperate soul had strung a wind chime on those withered, gnarly branches. The music it created carried downwind and was hauntingly beautiful, and beach walkers swore they could see the tree dancing to the jingling in the warm sea air.

She put on a light sweater and began her walk to the tree. Her arthritis was bothering her more and more these days, and, on top of that, she just couldn't catch her breath. Walking toward the point took her longer than it used to, but she made it. As she moved along, she saw a couple at the tip of the land by the tree. The woman was middle aged, with short blonde hair. She wore a turtleneck with a lightweight fleece vest over it and loose capri jeans. The man wore a baseball cap, sunglasses, khaki shorts, and a matching vest, and both were barefoot. The woman looked upset, like she was crying. The man wrapped his arm around her. The matching vests made Devorah think they must be a married couple dressing like one another as they got older and, not even realizing they were doing it, blending each into the other.

Devorah felt like she was intruding, but she carried on anyway. *If you want privacy, stay the hell home,* she thought. But as she got closer, the woman turned to her and smiled. She had kind eyes, and Devorah thought she looked a little embarrassed. Her cheeks were still damp with tears. Devorah nodded at her and continued on around the tree and back toward home.

The whole walk back she wondered what had made that woman cry.

~

Devorah made her way up the well-trodden path from the water to the house. She slipped off her sandals and used the hose to rinse off her feet. From around the bend, Diaz appeared in full waders, wielding a large spike rake and a metal bucket of quahogs.

"Oh, hey there," he said. "I wanted to talk to you about something. Hungry?"

"Not really, no."

"You okay? You don't look well. You look tired."

"I'm fine," she said. "Long walk."

She suddenly felt so winded, she thought she might faint.

"Here, sit," Diaz said and guided Devorah into the weathered old Adirondack chair to the left of the garden hose.

She was too exhausted to argue about him fussing over her, so she just sat. Diaz pressed two fingers into her wrist, checking her pulse.

"Have you eaten anything today, Devorah?"

"I drank some damn juice," she said. "I'm waiting for the food to be delivered."

Diaz ran around to the front of the house and was back in a second wielding a bag of Doritos. "Had this in my truck," he said and ripped the bag open and handed it to her. "Just eat a couple. You look pale."

Cool Ranch. Her favorite. "Thanks, Diaz."

"Let me get out of this stuff, and I'll get you some water and something else to eat inside." He hosed off the rubber waders and stepped out of them. "Was slim pickings at first, and then I hit the mother lode. Mostly cherrystones good for some chowder, but I got a least two dozen quahogs. Over in Osterville, off Bay. The guys at the station house love it when I make stuffers. DeSouza thinks his are better than mine. Spoiler alert—they ain't."

Devorah nodded, noting he kept checking on her while he spoke. She looked out at the water. The beach was steady in its shifting faces, always changing, always the same. At least the sandy beach and ocean were always there. Devorah could depend on that. She'd always loved her house by the sea. It had been far more modest until David was able to support the remodel she'd always wanted. She had given up so much of herself, but she had that house on the beach. But that was long ago, and the upkeep at the ocean's edge was incessant. As the years rolled by, Devorah's attention waned.

The air was crisp and slightly warm. Devorah realized she loved this chair and hadn't sat out here in ages. Why? They'd bought these chairs when they bought the house. They used to sit here and drink wine at sunset in the summer—heaven. Where did the time go?

"Where'd you go?" Diaz asked.

"Walked out to the tree," Devorah said. "At the end of the point out there. The one people put all those shells on."

"We used to party out there when I was in high school. Lost my virginity under that tree."

"Please don't ruin it for me, Diaz," Devorah said.

Diaz laughed and pulled his chair over toward hers, sat down, and stretched out his legs. "The good old days," he said, sinking into his chair.

They sat quietly side by side for several minutes, admiring the varied blueness of the ocean and sky before them. The salty wind carried a flock of terns that shifted this way and that, a dazzling dance in the sky.

Devorah cleared her throat. It felt scratchy.

"You okay?" Diaz asked.

"Think you could get me a glass of water?" Devorah said. "My throat's really dry for some reason." She coughed and covered her mouth.

"I'll get you anything you want, queen," Diaz said and smiled, though his forehead was creased in worry.

Devorah cleared her throat again. She leaned her head back against the wooden slat and closed her eyes. She felt so tired. She was out of shape, she knew that. And she felt like her bones and all the flesh that surrounded them were like rings in a tree trunk, expanding yearly with age. After a few seconds, she dozed off.

A few minutes later, Diaz returned, and she snorted as she sat up. He looked a bit sheepish. "Sorry, sleepyhead."

"Some days I think I could sleep standing up," Devorah said. She laughed as he leaned over and placed Mary Magdalene on her lap.

"Somebody wanted to see you," he said, then placed crackers and a bottle of water on the side table before returning to his matching Adirondack chair. "So, I hear you're suing Caroline Beckett?"

"Yup," she said and sipped her water, eyes focused on the view.

Diaz leaned his head back into the chair. "Why?"

After a few moments, Devorah said, "Plato said an ideal society would be run by those meant to govern, defended by those meant to defend, and supplied with services by those who had something to give."

"Sounds reasonable enough."

"Yeah, I thought so too."

"So what does that have to do with her?"

"Guess we'll see, Diaz."

CHAPTER ELEVEN

CAROLINE

Caroline was exhausted from the long cross-country flight and had a headache from the two glasses of wine she'd ordered when they hit turbulence over the Great Lakes. She had thought about having a town car pick her up from Boston Logan Airport to make the hour-and-a-half drive south to the town of Barnstable. Per old-time rules and rhetoric, Barnstable was a town within which were seven villages; one of them was Hyannis, which would be Caroline's destination. But instead of the drive, she opted to hop on a Cape Air flight that took about twenty minutes once they were in the air and landed at the Hyannis airport, ten minutes from her destination. The plane was a tiny eight-seater Cessna, and Caroline white-knuckled her armrest the entire twenty minutes, which only made her more tired.

She rented a black Jeep Wrangler—the only vehicle they had left that wasn't either an economy car or a minivan—from the tiny car rental at the airport. In hindsight, she wished she had chosen the minivan. She could feel every bump in the road in the Jeep. Her brain was starting to feel like scrambled eggs from all the rattling around it was doing from the ride. She exited the small airport and pulled out onto Route 28.

It had been years since Caroline was last here, and she felt uneasy. She noticed there was a brand-new Target where the Sears used to be at the mall, and new stoplights to accommodate for more traffic that, despite it being the offseason, seemed heavy. She got an inkling, a memory of walking through that mall countless times as a child, on rainy days, holding her mother's hand.

She quickly shoved it away and gave herself a mental slap across the cheek. She would not go down that wormhole. She tucked away her feelings about her heavily flawed parents. Caroline's father, Jim, had been a veteran and a lifelong alcoholic with a temper. He was the antithesis of slick, put-together Grant. Jim was a big man, a strong, silent type, hardscrabble, a blue-collar conservative with calloused hands and a deep vulnerability that he did his best to dull with liquor. The sober hours of his days, when Jim was pleasant to be around, shrunk over the years, and Caroline had erected walls around her heart to keep him out. Her mother, Joan, an equally proficient substance abuser, was a teacher at the school, a part-time housekeeper, and an enabler.

Her parents' relationship had been, by all accounts, tumultuous. The echoes of their fighting and subsequent lovemaking reverberated in the recesses of Caroline's mind even now. The house was haunted by their memory, by the confusing deep love and affection Caroline felt for them, the punishing anguish of knowing she could not save them, and the anger at having been subliminally asked to.

But she could not help them. And in turn they could not help her. So she did what she had to do, which was to disconnect. To run away and leave them and all the disappointment and pain they created behind. While she worked to find a way out of that house, a way past their legacy, she latched on to Devorah and plotted her escape. She soldered the hole and closed herself off from the pain of loving. She devoted her time and attention to making something of herself and avoiding the missteps that could have been her birthright. At first, Devorah had been an inspiration. She was confident, independent, wealthy, and attractive, and she wasn't afraid to speak her mind. Caroline had emulated her. She was a sponge soaking up knowledge. But the rosy sheen wore off, and the disappointment she'd experienced at Devorah's hands was a crushing blow. So she stayed away. That was a long time ago now.

Caroline had been twenty-eight when she lost her mother. Joan's death was particularly blistering. Four years prior to that, Jim's health had declined as the cirrhosis ate away at his liver, and Joan had gotten sober. She racked focus and was on the way to turning her life around. She spoke a lot about forgiveness and making amends. Caroline was skeptical, but a little part of her held out hope. But when Jim died, Joan fell off the wagon. Or more accurately was enticed off the wagon by none other than her former employer and friend, Devorah van Buren, who presumably was missing her cocktail hour friend. At the end of Joan's biweekly shift, the two women would sit on the vast backyard veranda. Joan made the best manhattans, Devorah always said. It was something Caroline could never understand. How could Devorah be so selfish? How could she not see that Joan was an addict?

Caroline knew she could not stay. She could not be a part of her mother's decline. She could not watch it. But it all slipped away quickly enough—Joan slipped away—in an early-morning single-car crash.

But that was seventeen years ago. The period had been put on the end of that sentence at Joan's modest funeral—the last time Caroline had come home and spent any time at all. In those five years after she ran away from town, ran away from her parents and their dysfunction, skipped out on her commitment to assist Devorah, tore away from her impending vow to live the rest of her life with Danny, so much had been destroyed. Her father's liver, her mother's resolve, her relationship with Danny, her friendship with her mentor. At the funeral Caroline sat in the church and grieved mostly alone. A few neighbors, a distant cousin, some former coworkers from the elementary school attended the funeral. And Danny. Caroline saw him in the back row, but he slipped out before she could speak with him. It meant the world to her that he showed up, but she didn't tell him. He didn't want to hear it from her anyway, but she knew he knew. And Devorah sent an enormous floor bouquet, but she was traveling out of the country and did not attend. Caroline wouldn't have known what to say to Devorah anyway. So when the services were over again, she ran away from this town and everyone in it, and in her mind she had closed that chapter. She shoved away the hurt and vowed she would not come back here. She would make something of herself, and she would never, ever have a funeral like that. People would show up for hers. She would know so many people, do so many interesting things, touch so many people's lives, and she would be so loved. People would show up for *her*.

Besides her childhood home, which Caroline kept for a huge tax break as a rental property and, if she had to admit it, which she wouldn't, likely some sentimental reasons as well, she had no connection with the town or its inhabitants whatsoever. Her business manager dealt with the rental. Caroline left the past in the past. If she wasn't going to waste her energy thinking about the lying liar Grant, she was sure as hell not going to think about her parents and her boring nobody existence back here. She wanted nothing to do with that part of her life anymore. She couldn't afford to waste time being nostalgic or thinking about how new things looked or how green the trees were compared to the dry taupe of autumn in Los Angeles—she had a job to do. She had to set crazy Devorah straight and get herself back to LA, back to work, as soon as possible.

She needed to strategize with Thérèse and Jeff about Devorah's frivolous lawsuit before the truth about Grant and Oaklyn's relationship got out, but she wasn't going to think about that right now either. Things were getting out of hand. She needed to get control. She would not, under any circumstances, jeopardize or lose the brand. She would not lose everything she had worked her entire life for in one terrible week, because of Grant and a crazy old woman with a grudge whom she hadn't spoken to in years.

She gripped the steering wheel a little tighter as she turned left onto Main Street and drove along past the quaint cottage-style homes and the penny candy store, feeling anxious that all this crap had her back here once again on this damn Massachusetts road, a road she could have driven blindfolded.

She continued on toward Devorah's seaside home in Centerville, another of Barnstable's villages, on the peninsula of sand known as Long Beach, the lavish beachfront homes with a half football field of sand between them and the mighty Atlantic. Each gray-shingled house had its own unique mark: a mermaid weather vane, a horseshoe driveway. She would eventually have to go to her parents' former home, her childhood home, far inland, where the real estate was cheap and the smell of the ocean battled the exhaust of Route 6. But, for now, Caroline was heading straight for battle.

The Jeep's tires crunched over the white seashells of Devorah's beach house driveway. The house was impressive but looked tired, as though exhausted from its long battle with the spirited Atlantic. The front yard was dotted with several mature white oak trees strategically placed toward the side of the property line so as to provide just the right amount of privacy without obstructing views. As Caroline took a deep, calming breath, she shifted the car into park and watched as two large squirrels chased each other up, down, and around the trunk of one of those big oak trees. They were making a ruckus, charging and darting around, rustling branches, seemingly tireless. At first glance it looked like a lively game of chase, but upon closer examination, Caroline could see the reality was not play but war. It was a battle of territory, and the tree wasn't big enough for the both of them.

What was the point of all this? It all seemed so ugly. Why so much fighting? Why so much anger? Squirrels and analogies . . . *Really, Caroline, snap out of it.* She rolled her eyes and rested her head back against the seat.

She lowered her window and felt the salty breeze take over all her senses. She felt the rhythm. She tasted the salt. She inhaled the sea's warm wind. She felt for a moment the gentle pull, the tug, that at one time she'd enjoyed here. She had a moment of clarity, feeling that she was meant to be right here in this present moment, doing exactly what she was doing. There was an ebb and a flow to the goings-on in the world and, in particular, to her own life. New and old, rich and poor, tide in, tide out. And Caroline felt like she was in flow with it all. Sure, it was a long way from Los Angeles, and it was under duress that she was even here, but she locked into the moment, to something bigger than herself, and she let go.

And then the sound of the branches rustling and the tormented cry of the losing squirrel rang out as the razor-sharp teeth of his nemesis punctured his furry flesh.

Caroline felt the call to action. After all, she had decided long ago she wasn't the loser squirrel who got nipped. She gathered herself, flung open the door, and stepped from the Jeep.

She heard footsteps and looked over in the distance to see a man descending the stairs of the guesthouse above the garage. He wore jeans, a long-sleeve T-shirt, work boots, and a baseball cap, his hair poking out from underneath. He was backlit from the waning sun, but there was something familiar about him.

He was hurrying toward her, waving frantically, and clearly saying words, but Caroline couldn't hear him, as the crash of the ocean in the distance was too loud.

Caroline tugged on her ear to indicate to him that she couldn't make out what he was saying. She wanted to laugh. His arms were swinging this way and that, and he looked, well, rather silly. And then another feeling snapped her out of her mirth and brought her full throttle back into the present moment. That feeling was pain.

"Ow, what the hell?" she said, looking down and into the eyes of a big fat wild turkey. He pecked at her knee with a razor-sharp bill and a screw-you look in his eye.

"Ouch. Ow!" Caroline yelled and, with lightning speed, hopped up onto the hood of her car. She swatted at the ornery bugger with her purse and rubbed at her sore leg. "Get out of here!"

"I was trying to tell you," the man said, racing toward her with what Caroline now noticed was a giant stick. He shooed away the pissed-off turkey, who darted at him once before deciding to back off and rejoin the flock Caroline hadn't noticed prior, over on a nearby lawn. More than a dozen of them suddenly appeared from behind this little hydrangea bush and that little flowerpot. They strutted with cumbersome movements and major attitude across the lush grass, pecking here and there at the ground, noisily making their way around the neighbor's property.

The guy looked at her face, recognition dawning in his expression. He stopped, pulled his hand away. The shock on his face was palpable.

"Caroline," he said.

"Danny, oh my God."

She stopped moving. Her breath completely taken away like a seashell by a wave.

Danny Diaz. Oh my God.

They were locked in.

"Are you hurt?" he asked, taking control of the situation. He touched her leg. "Did he get you?"

The feel of his hand, even through her pant leg, was warm, electric. Caroline felt the heat rise all the way up her leg, through her torso, and into the middle of her chest. Diaz pulled his hand away, as if touching her had burned him.

Caroline climbed down from the hood of her car and planted her feet on the ground. "I forgot about the turkeys," she said, her mind like mush.

Off in the distance her turkey offender turned back to her and emitted a threatening gobble. But Caroline barely noticed. She was only aware of the fluttering butterfly wings in her rib cage, the beautiful man standing in front of her after so many years.

As the shock of seeing him settled in, everything surrounding them seemed to screech to a halt—the air stopped moving, the earth stopped spinning, the waves stopped crashing. There was only silent fluttering as she looked at his face, so familiar.

"Why are you here?" he asked.

"Um," she said. What was she doing here? Where was she? She looked awkwardly at Diaz and then at the ground and then back at him again as the memories flowed in, filling in the cracks of her heart, long ago battered, bloodied, broken. And then she remembered. "Oh, um. I'm here to see Devorah. Lawsuit. Copyright. She's suing me," Caroline rambled nervously.

"Yeah. Right. Of course. Well, she's inside," Danny said. His voice sounded somewhat cool. He paused just briefly. "I'll leave you to it," he added and then turned to go.

"Danny, wait. This is just so . . . ," Caroline said, feeling an unwelcome chill drape over her. "I'm . . . I just . . . I'm speechless. I can't believe I'm running into you here. It's been so long."

Caroline looked at Danny, who wasn't quite making eye contact with her. She knew his face so well. He'd aged over the years, but he was every bit as handsome today as he was as a young boy of thirteen, a young man at eighteen, at twenty-three, and from a distance, in passing, at thirty. And now at forty-five his hair was graying at the temples and a bit longer now, curling over his ears from under his Red Sox hat. Thin lines broke up the perfection of the smooth brown skin near his eyes, evidence of years of smiles and laughter. He was tall, over six feet. Caroline swept her eyes up and down his still thin, athletic build. She knew that body. She remembered how that body moved, how it felt, what it had done to her, what she had done to it.

Standing there with him, Caroline realized that there was a part of her, tucked away, that had known she would see him when she returned, that had wanted it so badly. Like magnets, they would be drawn together. Of course they would. And maybe they could talk. Maybe he would talk to her. It had been so long. They could bury the hatchet.

"Oh my God," Caroline whispered to herself and then realized he'd heard her. "I'm just so . . . it's just . . . I didn't expect to see you here. I didn't know you even knew Devorah, and, yeah, I mean, it's just so nice to see you. I just can't believe it."

"Right, yeah, well, you too," Danny said and started to walk away. "I gotta get going."

"Danny, wait," Caroline said to his back.

"No, Caroline, actually I don't think I will wait," he said over his shoulder. His footsteps crunched over seashells as he made his way back toward the guesthouse. "I'm done doing that."

"Danny," Caroline said again, her heart racing, thudding in her ears.

And then, a scratchy elderly female voice came crashing in from somewhere far outside Caroline's bubble.

"What in the hell are you doing here?"

"Oh, Jesus," Caroline said, spinning toward the front door of the house and Devorah's shadowy figure.

"Well, look at that, Mary," Devorah said to her little dog. "It's the 'Success at Life' lady." She started laughing. "Go home, Caroline! Before I get my turkey whistle." Devorah turned away. Her movement was clumsy, but the meaning was clear.

"Wait, Devorah, we need to talk!" Caroline said. But Devorah slammed the screen door behind her.

Caroline exhaled loudly, slowly, her shoulders rounding just a tiny bit. She'd known it might be a bit of a challenge to come back, to face Devorah, but this was turning out to be more than she'd bargained for.

She took a deep breath, strengthening her resolve. She *was* a success at life, dammit. And as corny as that moniker was, she could handle this. She could handle Devorah van Buren. She could handle anything. She just had to think, catch her bearings.

She could do it. She could control her thoughts. She could will what she wanted into reality. She could have anything she wanted. She just had to believe it was available to her. She had done it before. She would do it again.

She took one step forward, limping slightly as pain shot up her turkey-bruised leg. She pushed on toward the main house like a wayward sailor following a siren's call.

She rapped at the door. Nothing. No movement inside. Caroline knocked, then knocked again, and, finally, Devorah reappeared.

"Caroline! What brings you to Cape Cod?" Devorah said, through the screen.

"Come on, Devorah. We need to talk."

"We do?" Devorah said. "Why? Because you stole my book?"

"I didn't steal your book, Devorah. Mine is a guide." Caroline expelled a big fat sigh. "Can I just come in, and can we talk about this and get it all squared away? Please?"

Devorah smirked through the screen. "Nope," she said and then slammed the big heavy interior door in Caroline's face, causing the large metal anchor-shaped door knocker to clatter loudly.

Through the door, Caroline heard Devorah on the telephone saying, "Hi, yes, I want to report a trespasser."

As Caroline walked back to her car, she sighed. Before ducking into the Jeep, she looked up at the guesthouse. This wasn't going to be as easy as she'd hoped it would.

CHAPTER TWELVE

DEVORAH

From the living room window, Devorah watched the taillights fade on Caroline's ridiculous Jeep as she pulled out of the driveway. *A Jeep, Caroline? Really?* What did she think she was, on spring break or something? What happened to that girl? What the hell was she thinking? *She's drinking that LA Kool-Aid.*

Devorah laughed and turned from the window. Caroline was nervy, Devorah thought, showing up unannounced at her home. That kind of behavior was unacceptable. Ballsy, sure, but not acceptable. Hell, if that happened again, she really *was* going to call Sorrenti and tell him to get his ass over and arrest her for trespassing and harassing a poor sweet old lady. Devorah laughed, happy with herself. She had Caroline Beckett shaking in her boots. Good! Ha! She'd actually showed up back on Cape Cod. Wow.

Devorah moved on into her overcrowded office and, looking around, sank into her ugly but comfortable desk chair. Wow. The office was a stinking mess. There were Bankers Boxes everywhere. They were stacked six feet high, willy nilly, and with the tops ripped off and the guts spilling out like a squirrel's entrails in the street. Devorah liked to think of herself as having things under control, but here was big fat proof that she did not. And now, after all this time, all these years, the sheer volume of things had become overwhelming, and the room had become an oversize junk drawer of sorts, full of stuff she might need one day and didn't want to throw away but piled in with no rhyme or reason.

David used to call her a pack rat. Looking at all the materials just from teaching, she was thinking he might have had a point. She saved the papers she especially enjoyed from clever students that inspired her, or from students who she thought might complain about a grade. But now, aside from having recently torn things apart looking for her old work, she couldn't remember a single day since she'd left the university that she'd ever looked at any of these papers. It would take her forever to find all the materials she was looking for, and then, once she found them, she'd have to organize it all. But whatever; she was going to do it.

Amid all this chaos, somewhere, lay her own work, written over many years: lectures, guest speaker engagement addresses, and notes, as well as dozens of articles she had published over the years and dozens more she thought she might one day publish. She had file boxes, full to the top with printed copies of every single story or lesson she'd written. She knew the younger generations kept all their materials in digital form, or up in the cloud or something bananas like that, but that just didn't work for Devorah. She didn't trust the cloud not to burst or combust or blow away or whatever. She wanted backups, and she wanted a copy she could hold in her hand. She had no idea where to find the cloud even if something was stored up there.

She flipped the top off a box and commenced sifting through the pile. She was looking for the notebook, files, and folders she'd composed for a new book proposal two and a half decades earlier—and the thirty-eight (very wordy) chapters—covering the ancient Greek philosophers and their thoughts on love and their thoughts on women. Devorah had long focused her attention on females and their presence—or actually their absence—in the canon of philosophical thought throughout history. Devorah's focus on women in philosophy was largely centered on classical times, namely the Greeks. She was interested in how women were treated in the culture—as less than men—and she found the tie-ins of the Greeks' bacchanalian exploits and their thoughts on love incredibly relevant to a modern audience.

The success of *Kiss My Abundance*, the book she should have written but hadn't, was both annoying and intriguing. The pedantic nature of a modern-day mash-up of the law of attraction, thinking your way to a better future, and a focus on long-dead philosophers in existential crisis was irksome. But Devorah knew she had the makings for a sequel of sorts. A smart book, scholarly but approachable. She could do that, right? If Caroline could rip her research off and write it, then why the hell couldn't Devorah? Why didn't she? Anyway, this new book would pick up where that one left off but be written by her. She had so much to give, and she knew where she wanted to go and what she wanted to say. For the most part. She was ready again to dive in and let loose, just as she was before David, her soulmate, her truest love, had begged for her attention. Before he'd demanded all her time.

So the notes, the book, had sat on the back burner, or, more accurately, in the Bankers Box. Until now. And in some ridiculous way it was all thanks to Caroline. Now was her time.

Devorah was passionate about the Greek philosophers, and Plato, considered by many to be the greatest philosopher who ever lived and the father of Western philosophy, in particular. The thought of it, of those men—Aristotle, Socrates, Plato—sitting around, chewing the cud, intrigued her. Despite Plato's erroneous belief that men were superior to women, Plato also believed in the education of women as it benefited society. "What a guy," Devorah used to say to her students. It always got a laugh, and Devorah loved to hear it. Connecting with her students always filled her up.

And truthfully, Devorah carried within her a desire to connect with the masses in a broader and more expansive way. She knew that there was a stodginess, a loftiness to the material that could be off putting and boring. Devorah wanted to pull Plato's teachings of knowledge and society into the present, into the modern vernacular. And, most especially, his thoughts and teachings on love. What could be more modern than a book about love? Devorah could be crafty too. It had been a couple of thousand years since Plato was kicking around bathhouses in Athens, but just as sex had been a hot topic for the ancient Greeks, that part hadn't really changed in modern times. Love and money were still at the forefront of humankind. Sex sold, and cash was king. Just look what Caroline did with the whole "*I think, therefore I am*" business.

Devorah thumbed through the box of materials, and then she leaned back, resting her head on the seat back. She was just so tired, and looking at all the boxes made her more so.

A scratching alerted Devorah to Mary Magdalene, dutiful as ever, panting in the doorway.

"There's my girl," Devorah said, a wide smile covering her face.

The dog, seeing the messy room and the path to Devorah unclear, turned around and presumably went back to her dog bed.

"Coward," Devorah said, closing her eyes and resting her head once again.

She had so many pages to comb through, it would take her a year just to organize them. Where would she find the energy? She didn't know, but she would find a way, dammit. Caroline's treachery had awakened that old flame within her, and she was going to seize the moment. She was going to *carpe* the hell out of that *diem*. If anything, the success of *Kiss My Abundance* had alerted her to the knowledge that she had been right all along. People were hungry for philosophy, for connection, for something deeper.

As Plato said, "Reality is created by the mind." Oh, it was so New Agey at the time, she had to practically shove it down the faculty's throats, but now, you couldn't swing a cat without hitting a meditating, pondering self-care devotee. The market was begging for it. And Devorah knew with her whole heart that what you thought was your reality. She'd explained that theory to Caroline in the 1990s.

The *thought* itself was a thing.

So, if the thought was a thing, Devorah had decided that she was going to toss in a load of money and steamy sex, and bingo—bestseller.

"Wow, it's like a tree graveyard in here," Diaz said from the doorway, rousing Devorah from almost slumber. "What the hell is all this?"

"It's none of your damn business is what it is."

"Right." Diaz took up the whole frame. "Charming as ever, my lady."

She could tell he had something more on his mind. "Spit it out," Devorah said, then quickly cut him off. "Unless it has to do with our trespasser earlier. I don't want to talk about her. I don't want to talk about it."

"No, it doesn't. I have nothing to say about that, about her," Diaz said and cleared his throat. He shifted his weight to his right leg and continued. "I'm just heading out to pick up my daughter, and I wanted to know if you needed anything. Maybe an ice cream?"

"Nope."

"Did you want to think it over?"

"Listen, Diaz, when you get to be my age, one of the perks is you don't have to sugarcoat shit anymore. There's no time for that. So, I got work to do. I don't need you to hover all over me." Devorah sounded harsh, but there was a playfulness in her delivery. She was loath to admit that she liked that he'd asked.

"Got it," Diaz said and turned to go. "I'll leave you to it."

Devorah turned back to her crap on the floor, and as she listened to Diaz's footfalls down the hallway, she felt a little remorseful for her behavior.

CHAPTER THIRTEEN

CAROLINE

Caroline pulled into the driveway of her childhood home and felt a chill travel up her spine. She sat in the car for a good three minutes, steeling herself, mustering up the courage to enter the dusty two-bedroom ranch with overgrown shrubs. It was in terrible need of a paint job, at the very least. Yeah, sure, she had rented it out several times over the years, but seeing it now, it still looked like it had in the late nineties, filling up her tiny rearview mirror as she raced out of town. What the hell was she doing back here? Going in reverse?

But here she was, sitting in her car, in her parents' old crappy driveway, staring at the past. Why hadn't she just sold this place when her parents died? Her business manager had suggested she keep it as a furnished rental property. She needed to remember to fire her business manager when she got this mess cleared up. She had a caretaker who looked after the place. His name was Pete Doherty, and by the looks of the exterior of this place, she was going to have to fire his ass too.

But looking at the house now, she wondered why the hell she didn't just book a room somewhere else. Whatever. She just needed to get this mess figured out. Fast. She would find a way to get through to Devorah.

And, oh, Danny. Seeing Danny Diaz after all these years was *unsettling*. But no, absolutely not. Danny would need to stay back there in this town, in the past, where he belonged.

Caroline opened the Jeep door and climbed down. She stumbled a little bit. It was a longer way down to the ground in a Jeep than in a regular car.

As she made her way toward the house, stepping on the uneven path lined with slate pavers, she swore she could hear the loud drunken arguments from long ago playing like a soundtrack in a film. She entered the numbers on the lockbox, turned the doorknob, and pushed the door open.

It felt, as she stepped over the threshold, like a vortex transported her back to another life, her old life, the one she had run away from. The living room was tidy but cluttered, and Caroline was surprised to discover it was much the same as it was in her memories. The ceiling had wood beams; brown wainscoting adorned the walls to hip height, with nautical-themed blues and whites and dashes of red in a pillow or a vase filling in the space. Fat navy blue lighthouse pillows and starfish tchotchkes spread across the tiled fireplace. Above the worn striped blue-and-white couch was a large print of the Nauset Light, just thirty miles down Route 6, with its black top, cherry red middle, and stark white bottom, perched atop the steep beach cliff, alone and imposing. The intention was preppy, but the result was dated and smacked of trying too hard to be something that, in this neighborhood, the family was not—well off. That was Caroline's mother, Joan, to a tee. Joan believed all their problems stemmed from money or a lack thereof, so she did her best to camouflage their lack of status by scouring estate sales and accepting hand-me-downs from the owners of the homes she cleaned, including Devorah.

Caroline sniffed. There was a mustiness, typical on humid Cape Cod, that hung in the air. You could feel it, practically see it in the fabric of the curtains, the fiber in the wood beams. It was familiar, the scent and the feeling it evoked.

Caroline rolled her bag down the hallway and flicked the light on in her childhood bedroom. The room was small. A sailboat quilt adorned the queen-size bed that took up nearly three-quarters of the room, and an empty shabby-chic white bureau was pressed against the wall under a white wicker-framed mirror. Next to it stood a small navy blue nightstand with a fake Tiffany lamp.

Caroline placed her Louis Vuitton luggage on the bed and flicked the light off. From the hallway, she looked into the master bedroom—her parents' room and, as such, not an option for her to sleep in. It was dark in the room, just like she remembered it. A jumble of angry arguing voices, nervous childhood laughter, doors slamming, wind blowing through trees, dogs barking . . . that all flew away when Caroline flicked the light on.

Caroline's stomach rumbled. She hadn't eaten since the cross-country plane ride, and she was hungry. Delighted for an excuse to leave, she practically ran back down the hallway, grabbed her keys off the table by the front door, and headed for the Jeep.

~

God, nothing changes here, Caroline thought. And she was surprised to note how comforting that felt as she made the turn onto Main Street. She saw the sign on the rustic barn-looking building that read *Steve and Sue's Par-Tee Freeze*. Immediately Caroline's taste buds ignited. It was, in her opinion, the best ice cream spot on Cape Cod. She missed it. Nobody ate ice cream in Los Angeles. It was all frozen yogurt and fancy shaved ice. This place was about as New England Americana as you could get.

Grinning, she put her turn signal on. In the parking lot, she pulled into one of the empty spots facing the brown-shingled building, then walked toward the glass window to place her order. Buckets of chrysanthemums flanked large bales of hay, and white and orange pumpkins were stacked against the building's facade. To the left of the building was a mini golf course with a fountain waterwheel display and a capacity crowd despite the cool fall temperatures. There were three groups ahead of her for ice cream, so she had time to run her eyes over the menu. The offerings, everything from soft serve to sandwiches, made her realize how ravenous she was and how much she missed the simplicity of good food served in a cardboard boat with red checkered paper.

When it was her turn at the window, she placed an order for a hot dog and an M&M flurry with the teenage girl inside. She paid with cash and took a seat at one of the picnic tables between the building and the golfers. Caroline dressed her hot dog with ketchup, mustard, and relish and took a bite. It was spectacular, warm and salty, and the relish made it somewhat sweet. She couldn't remember the last time she had eaten—no, *savored*—a hot dog.

She unwrapped her paper straw and shoved it into her shake, taking a long pull to coax the ice cream up into her straw. The cold cream hit her tongue first. Her eyes closed in ecstasy as she unabashedly sucked. She chewed the little chocolate M&M bits.

She was in heaven, which is why it was a shock when her eyes fluttered open again and landed on Danny Diaz. He was at the golf window returning two putters to another teenage staff member. Caroline felt a jolt and nearly dropped her ice cream.

Danny leaned over to a little girl on his right, who was tugging gently on his hand. Undeniably his daughter, she had shoulder-length dark-brown hair and pretty, wide-set eyes. If Caroline remembered correctly, she had to be about seven years old. She was adorable, sure of herself.

"Daddy, come on, ice cream, ice cream."

"Okay, okay, one second," Danny said, allowing himself to be pulled away.

Caroline couldn't take her eyes off them. She was struck by the territorial attitude of the little girl to her father—the family-ness of it all. This cute little girl, Danny's little girl, possessed all of his attention.

He wrapped his hand around hers and positioned himself at the ice cream window, where there was now no wait. As he leaned in and placed his order, Caroline followed each of his movements, as though he were an Olympian on ice skates.

Her eyes narrowed in to focus on his strong hand. She remembered her hand being wrapped up in it at that very same window years before. How many times? One muggy day in July stood out, when the melting soft serve covered in crunch-coat topping dripped down her wrist, and Danny had shamelessly licked it all away.

As she lost herself in the memory, a bubble of glee rose up inside her, and she laughed. Danny turned from the window, and their eyes met. The look on his face was shocked, stunned, and, Caroline was unhappy to acknowledge, disappointed. She was so embarrassed, she felt like a Peeping Tom caught in the act.

She covered, smiling warmly and waving to him, signaling for them to join her. His return look of distaste nearly melted her flurry. He paused for a moment, and Caroline hung on, thinking maybe he would come to her. Only one of the other tables was empty, and she was the only person at hers. They were locked in, again, an onslaught of memories flashing by in an instant.

Danny nodded and waved, and Caroline moved over to let him sit.

And then he turned away from the picnic tables, away from Caroline, toward the parking lot.

"Come on, Chloe, let's eat in the truck," he said, again taking the little girl's hand with his free one.

"Yay! You never let me eat in the truck, Daddy!"

Caroline felt the rebuff from Danny's about-face like a slap. God, it had been years, but, still, she was hurt, stunned. She felt an impulse to run after him. She wanted to beg his forgiveness and tell him her side of everything, and this realization truly shocked her. It wasn't Danny's refusal to speak to her that hurt so much but that he wanted nothing to do with her, and worse, that she cared that he wanted nothing to do with her. She felt consumed with a desire to make him not hate her. It hurt too much to think he hated her.

But really, why? She couldn't understand it. Why did she care?

Because it was Danny Diaz, that was why.

But so what? She had messed up; she'd been hasty; but the past was the past. She was a different person today than she'd been all those many years ago. They were kids back then. She had climbed the highest mountains and made a name for herself in the world, risen above this place. She hadn't even thought about Danny and what had happened in—well, okay, that wasn't entirely true—she thought of him every now and then, when a song like "The Downeaster 'Alexa'" by Billy Joel or "Pictures of You" by the Cure came on the radio. Over the years, she'd wondered about him—if he was happy, if he was content. She'd heard he had a child, a daughter. But she didn't think about what happened between them, or about why they broke up or how they broke up, ever. She didn't think about needing to set the record straight. She didn't think about whether or not she felt any regret about not staying in town and getting married. She didn't think about what it might feel like to be the mother of Danny's child, a daughter. She didn't think about running to Danny and trying to make him understand. Not until that very moment.

Caroline realized she was staring when the bones in her hand began to ache from her cold ice cream. But that didn't mean she stopped. Like a creepy psycho stalker, her eyes remained glued to Danny the whole time he climbed into his truck. He started the engine, and she felt the brisk October breeze waft over her. Everything cold and stifling about this small town closed in around her. He put the truck in gear, and under her too-light California clothes, she felt her flesh rise into goose bumps, a chill invading her joints like she was freezing from the inside out.

He pulled out of his parking spot, and she immediately felt alone, singular, like her picnic table sat atop an iceberg, pushing farther and farther out into the cold open ocean. The happy customers at the tables surrounding her—families, couples, friends—chatted and laughed. The sound grew louder, sinister.

Caroline watched until Danny's taillights receded. It was at that moment that she knew she would have to do whatever she had to do quickly, to get this whole sordid mess over with fast. She would settle this nightmare with Devorah. She would sell her parents' house. And she would leave Barnstable, Massachusetts, once and for all.

Just then her phone pinged. Caroline looked down and saw a text from Thérèse with a link. TMZ picked up the story on the lawsuit. Defcon 5. Call me.

Caroline tossed the rest of her ice cream and hot dog into the trash and climbed back into her Jeep. She had lost her appetite.

CHAPTER FOURTEEN

DEVORAH

She had fallen asleep on the plush blue velvet love seat in her office last night, surrounded by junk, and awakened with a crick in her neck at nearly seven o'clock. In pain, grumpy and disheartened by the ever-growing Everest that was mounting in her office, she felt she had no other choice but to put on a pot of coffee and get on with her day already. She popped some ibuprofen to help with the pain in her neck and stepped outside to get some fresh air. She was seizing the day, dammit.

Devorah couldn't remember the last time she'd walked the beach before eight o'clock. The marine layer was thick and gray, and the air felt slightly damp. Off in the distance, she saw the dark gray of a storm cloud on its way inland. As she marched through the grassy, sandy path from her house to the shoreline, she marveled at the massive ospreys overhead, on the hunt for breakfast in the water below. The path gave way, and the sprawl of the sandy beach spread out before her. Devorah looked to her left and then to her right. There was not one soul in sight. She had the place to herself. She loved it.

She felt a little winded already, and the pain in her neck wasn't getting any better, but she carried on toward the seashell tree. She hung tight to the grassy flat area and away from the water's edge, as it was easier to get her footing on the drier sand. It was high tide, and the waterline lapped the shore, filling in every crevice between every grain of sand. Devorah's sneakered foot sunk low into the wet sand. It took effort to pull it back out and take another step forward, only to have to repeat the action again and again.

Up ahead, Devorah saw a seagull ripping the legs off a struggling crab. The bird pulled, undeterred by the crab's fervor, and simply tilted its head skyward and opened its beak to swallow. The carnage seemed in keeping with the oppressive gray sky, the whitecaps in the rollicking waves, and the jagged sand, yet it was there: the ugly fight, the struggle for survival, right there in front of her.

Devorah had only walked about a quarter of a mile when she decided she was too exhausted to continue. The wind had picked up a bit, and that dark-gray cloud was looming. She was hungry, she was tired, and what the hell was she trying to prove anyway?

She turned back and thought about making eggs for breakfast, or, better yet, maybe she'd order something in. She was too tired to cook . . . and then to have to clean it all up too? Forget it.

It seemed to take her twice as long to get back up the path than it had taken her to venture out. She was starting to feel a little light headed from the effort, and the sharp beach grass felt like glass needles scraping her exposed shins as she climbed back toward the house.

Once inside, she made her way to the kitchen to get some water. She was perspiring, and her cheeks felt flushed, like she was back in menopause or something.

At first she thought she was hearing things, but when the doorbell rang a second time, she journeyed back down the hallway to see who it was. She was only mildly surprised to discover Caroline on her doorstep. She knew it wasn't going to be that easy to get rid of her.

"You know this is harassment," Devorah said through the screen door.

Caroline peered in at her, looking svelte and LA chic in her khaki wide-leg palazzo pants, crisp white V-neck T-shirt, and oversize sunglasses. A large, expensive pocketbook hung from her bony shoulder.

"Jesus, are you okay, Devorah?" Caroline said, pulling her sunglasses off. "You look a little . . . flushed."

"Go home, Caroline," Devorah said, turning away. She wanted to sit down. She wanted to feel better. She was sure she looked like hell, but she didn't like that Caroline had the nerve to show up on her doorstep and insult her.

"We need to talk. Come on. This is just . . . a misunderstanding. Can you please just let me in so we can sort it all out?" Devorah turned back around. Caroline was squinting in the light, or at least the parts of her face that were still able to squint were squinting.

"Are you squinting, or what the hell is happening? I can't read you. How much Botox are you pumping into that face?"

"Nice, Devorah, very classy."

Ignoring Caroline, she continued, "I mean, does the patriarchy have you so goddamn brainwashed you've turned to self-mutilation? And for what? What's that gettin' ya?"

"And I'm sure you're still a natural redhead, right, Devorah?" Caroline said, a Cheshire-cat smile spreading across her smooth skin. "Now, come on and let me in, and let's figure this all out so I can go back home and leave you alone. Okay? I brought breakfast." She held up a white paper bag.

"What is it?"

"Egg sandwiches from the Barnacle."

Devorah took a deep breath. She was tired and hungry, and the food smelled good. Dammit, she loved those egg sandwiches, and she knew this problem wasn't just going to go away. She didn't really *want* to let Caroline in, back into her life, but she opened the door anyway and proceeded down the short hallway into the living room, with Caroline following closely behind her. She needed to deal with it, with her, and get it over with, and if the discussion came with the most delicious egg sandwich ever made—so be it.

Devorah could hear Caroline's breath catch as they entered the drop-down living room. That breathtaking view never got old. Out there, beyond those salty panes of glass in the big bay window and on full, dazzling display, rocked Nantucket Sound and the mighty Atlantic Ocean. Devorah loved its powerful audacity.

On the slightly worn navy blue couch beneath the window, Devorah took her seat like a queen on her throne, the sea at her back. She reached over and placed tiny Mary Magdalene on her lap and began stroking the dog like a Bond villain. Devorah watched as Caroline looked around, taking in the room with its high ceilings and dusty nautical decor. It was cluttered, evidence of Devorah's several decades in residence and pack rat sensibilities. She knew she had to clear things out, but she just hadn't gotten around to it. She had a long list of to-dos. The room was impressive, yes, but like the exterior of the house, it was feeling slightly dated and worn, like a beach rose in September. But Devorah would get to it. She always did.

"Nice room," Caroline said.

"I know."

Caroline laughed as she unwrapped the egg sandwiches and handed one to Devorah. Mary Magdalene picked her head up and sniffed. Devorah patted her gently.

"Look, we've known each other a long time. And I think there's been some kind of . . . misunderstanding about all this with the book," Caroline said.

Devorah bit into her sandwich and chewed. She savored the bite and hoped her heart would stop racing. She felt a nagging sensation in her chest, like anxiety or a sense that something bad was going to happen.

"Come on, Devorah."

The older woman smiled with a full mouth of food. "Something to drink? A manhattan perhaps?"

"No, thank you," Caroline said. "It's not even ten o'clock in the morning."

"I know what time it is," Devorah said.

"Why are you doing this?"

"Doing what?"

"Listen, Devorah, the book—"

"*Kiss My Abundance*. Ha! Kiss my ass is more like it."

Caroline exhaled loudly. "How much do you want?"

"I don't need money."

"What do you want, then? Why are you doing this?"

Devorah ignored her and continued between mouthfuls of her sandwich. "What a fun read. It's so accessible, good for you. Spirituality, knowledge for the common man. Bravo."

"So, what actually is your problem? Is it that my book, my platform, is popular now?"

"Platform? Yikes. Platform." Devorah nudged Mary Magdalene. "Did you hear that, Mary? A platform."

"You know . . . my life got large, Devorah. And yes—I have a platform. I have something to say, and people care about it, and right now, it's like a house of cards, and I need you to stop."

Devorah's eyes finally met hers. "*You* have something to say? That's rich."

"There are similarities. Yes, okay . . . but you weren't doing anything with it."

"Similarities?"

"Come on, Devorah, it was my idea to make it an easily accessible guide for modern-day women!"

"You know it was me who suggested the teachings as a manifesto for good living. It's as good as a guide. And I did all the research. That was all my work you used as examples! The entire framework—the principles, the tie-in with Descartes—all of that cross-referencing was my work."

"Actually, I think it was Descartes's work, Saint Teresa of Avila's work."

"Don't be daft, Caroline. It doesn't suit."

"Come on, Devorah. What's bothering you? I put a lot of work into it, and I'm proud of that book. I figured out how to mold it all and make the steps work for a modern audience. Humility, awareness, surrender, soul, prayer, freedom, and peace. It was my idea to make it a self-help guide. I sent you a note when the book was acquired. That was years ago. Why didn't you respond?"

"It's annoying, isn't it?"

"So, is that it? Are you teaching me a lesson, not to ignore your phone calls, by throwing gasoline on the dumpster fire that is my life right now?"

"Well, I'm hardly to blame, right? I mean, we are all responsible for positive or negative things in our lives. We are magnets. Isn't that true? Chapter . . . hmm, what chapter was that again?"

Mary Magdalene began to wheeze. It was a disconcerting sound.

Caroline looked at the dog. "Is she okay?"

Devorah put the dog on the ground. Ignoring the question, she leaned forward and said, "I'm not dropping the suit."

Caroline slumped, melted back into her chair. "I recognize I have made some missteps. I own my mistakes. I want to do what it takes to make this work out, for everyone."

Devorah noted Caroline's diminished pose. "Don't worry, dear. The pendulum swings, right? This is just your downturn. Hang on. People love a comeback story."

"I don't understand," Caroline said. "Why are you doing this now? I don't get it."

"Why am *I* doing this?" Devorah asked. She was annoyed now. Seeing Caroline despondent on her couch was disappointing, but that she was blaming Devorah for it was downright irritating. "You had everything figured out, right? You're the 'Success at Life,' so don't cry to me. You made your bed."

"Nice."

"You said it. 'I think, therefore I am,' right?" Devorah laughed. "You do realize that was not meant to be a self-help mantra for the woke. That was Descartes doubting his existence and recognizing that if he could doubt, he must be alive."

"Yes, Devorah, thank you for mansplaining."

"Not quite a slogan for a sweatshirt."

Caroline rolled her eyes as Devorah continued, "You took my work, my thoughts, and you made it sound stupid. Common. What were you thinking?" Devorah flung her hands out wide. "How could you?"

Caroline paused for a moment, then said, "Is that what it is? Is that what you think? That just because something is popular it's not meaningful anymore?" Caroline stood and walked to the window at the end of the couch. Devorah caught her breath. Glancing over at Caroline, she noticed the younger woman was tapping her index finger on the top of her hand. "I took that work and I did something with it. I created something. And you do this? A lawsuit? After everything that happened? After what you did," Caroline said, just above a whisper. "How can you give me one ounce of grief? How could you?"

Devorah dropped her head back, looking at the ceiling. "You blame me. All these years you've blamed me."

"You could have done more. You could have helped her."

"Your mother had a mind of her own. She was an addict, Caroline. I didn't hold a bottle to her mouth."

"No, but you did enjoy cocktail hour with her."

"I didn't know it was as bad as it was. I didn't know she was as bad as she was."

"Sure you didn't."

Devorah thought about Joan. She didn't like to think about her, the poor woman. Married to a flawed, harsh man, with her own monkey on her back. But Devorah did what she could for her. She gave her a job. She helped her daughter, Caroline, find work. And, well, okay, in hindsight she recognized she might have been a bit careless with Joan. At the time, enjoying a cocktail with Joan after her shift was over seemed like a generous offer, but if Devorah was being really honest, she thought that maybe, deep down, she had been a bit selfish. Devorah had wanted company. She wanted someone to have a drink with. And Joan was funny. She was sarcastic, well-read, hardscrabble New England

Irish with an accent and a lovely daughter that Devorah felt a bit envious of. Caroline was stylish and more worldly than this tiny island, and Devorah had known she would move on and make something of herself. She just didn't know it would involve deceit. Joan was honest and hardworking and the best housekeeper Devorah had ever had, bar none. She enjoyed sharing the beautiful view and a manhattan with her. The difference was Devorah knew how to stop at one—or maybe one and a glass of sauvignon blanc. And she looked the other way as Joan easily finished off the bottle, knowing full well she was going home to drink more. But still, that wasn't Devorah's fault. What could she do, really? And all of that was over and done with years ago.

Caroline turned and walked away from the window toward the hallway. Devorah saw Caroline notice the office off to the side of the large room and thought, dammit, why hadn't she shut the door?

"Wait, is that your office? What the hell happened in there?" Caroline stepped into the hallway and poked her head in the office door.

"None of your damn business, that's what," Devorah called out, furious at herself for not closing the door. She didn't want Caroline to see her mess. She didn't want anyone to. "Why don't you just go back to LA?" she said. "Why don't you just leave?"

Coming back into the room and facing Devorah, Caroline said, "That's all I want in the world. I want to. I want to leave. I want all this to be over, and I want to go back. I want to be far away from here."

"Good, go fix your marriage or something," Devorah said.

Caroline caught her breath. She looked stunned, pained.

"I'm sorry." Devorah was ashamed of her insensitivity. She didn't know why she felt so upset. She felt like Caroline was bringing out the worst in her, but that was no excuse. "That was a terrible thing to say. I'm sorry."

Caroline nodded.

"Look, I am. I'm sorry, Caroline."

"I know," Caroline said. She smiled and came back to sit on the couch. A moment passed before she said, "It's not really fixable, my marriage." Caroline looked out the window and continued. "And my work, my brand, that's all I have left. I want to leave, I do. But I don't know. Maybe I just don't know what I'm going back to."

Devorah felt tired. She wished that she *did* have a manhattan in her hand; she didn't care that it was morning. She wanted to maintain a hold on the fire in her belly. She didn't want to be distracted.

"All I ever wanted was to be somebody. To connect with other people. I thought that might make me feel important. To say things and be heard," Caroline said.

"And be rich and famous and all that stuff too."

"Yes, actually, I think you're right," Caroline said. "I did. I wanted all that. How sad. I know. I thought it would make me happy. Initially, it did. And I thought I was doing good. I was trying to help people take control of their own lives."

"The first and greatest victory is to conquer yourself; to be conquered by yourself is of all things most shameful and vile."

"Plato. Yes, I remember. I paid attention. Plato is fascinating. I remember how pervasive a figure he was in your research."

Devorah pulled her sweater a little tighter around her shoulders. "I was at times obsessive about his idea of virtue and living the good life, as they say." The sky was growing darker, and the wind carried a chill through the open window. She wanted to lie down. She wanted to watch TV.

She watched Caroline walk over to the office doorway again and stick her head inside the office again.

"Devorah," Caroline said. "I have a proposition."

"Christ on a cracker, here we go," Devorah said.

"Shush. Hear me out. I was thinking, you and I are both in a sort of unique position here. I need all of this bad publicity to go away, and you need some help with your book."

Devorah started to protest, but Caroline put up her hand. "Don't even start, Devorah. I was your assistant. I know you need help. I can see that your office looks like a bomb hit it. And the bottom line is this could be good for both of us. You need me, and I need you."

"How on earth do you think I need you?"

"I've been working on a new book. I think you know that. Right?"

"Enlighten me."

"Well, I'm building on the success of the brand. Building on classical philosophies and bringing them into the modern day, more mainstream. Another guide of sorts."

Devorah snickered. "Guide."

Ignoring her, Caroline continued. "The Greeks, Plato. Defining love, exploring the principles and aspects that lead to long-lasting love and how to position oneself better to identify it, be able to act on it, create more of it, et cetera."

"Plato?! You think you're going to rip me off again?"

"You don't own Plato, Devorah. Seriously," Caroline said. She had the nerve to roll her eyes.

"You know I've written many, many scholarly articles about Plato. Do you think I'm going to let you steal that book too?" Devorah added, but her heart wasn't in the slight. She really was tired.

"I'm not stealing anything, Devorah. I'm doing the work. You don't own the ideas I put forth in *Kiss My Abundance,* and you don't own the Greeks."

"Right, well, we'll just see about that."

"Listen, let's just stop for a second here. Take a breath. Hear me out. Okay? Now, listen, what if we helped each other out?"

Over Devorah's laughter, Caroline continued. "Think about it, Devorah. Who could be better equipped to help you? I know your process. I know how you work."

"What are you talking about? Why on earth would I want to work with you? Why would I give you my idea?"

"You're not giving me your idea. We collaborate. Same topic, kind of an examination of philosophy brought more mainstream. The format could be something like part guide, part lecture of sorts. Look, don't be naive. I know a lot of people. I mean, are you being realistic at all about the process to even get a book published? I can literally hand this to my agent."

"Okay, so if you've got all the key players standing by, why would you want to work with me?"

"Well, I guess it's a little hard to write a book about love when your marriage has imploded in the public eye. You are a scholar. You do lend a certain credence to the research. This could be a collaboration that served both of us very well."

"And I drop the lawsuit." Devorah's voice had just a slight catch in it, and she hated herself for it.

"And, yeah, you drop the lawsuit."

Despite being irritated by Caroline's arrogance, Devorah had to admit she saw the wisdom in the plan. She felt so very tired, and the thought of entering that office made her want to take a nap. She had had many assistants over the years, but she had lost touch with every one, and none had been as efficient as Caroline. She hated to admit it, but she needed the help, and there might be something in this collaboration that suited her. She felt a little jolt, her intuition, telling her to do this, telling her to let Caroline Beckett into her life and receive the help she'd been unconsciously asking for. She felt something stirring, like she was relevant, part of the conversation.

"How exactly would this work?" Devorah said.

"Well, we would have to break it down and get specific about what we want to achieve, what we'd like the book to be. Then we outline. We brainstorm. I will share what I have so far, and we will get you organized and set up here. Maybe after things die down a little bit and I go back to California, we can bring in another assistant, and you and I can continue to collaborate remotely. And then, yeah. All is forgiven."

Devorah looked out the window, let out a huge, long sigh, and then said, “Fine.”

“What? Okay?” Caroline said, shocked. “Really?”

“Okay, really,” Devorah said, right before the angry boom of a thunderclap ripped through the sky. “I’ll talk to my attorney. We will have a contract drawn up.”

Caroline chewed on a nail for a minute. “What would you think about issuing a press release too? Where you indicate that the lawsuit was just a misunderstanding and you’re excited to be working together now?”

“Ha! Keep dreaming,” Devorah said. The nerve of her! Hadn’t Devorah just agreed to drop the lawsuit? What else would this woman ask of her? She looked out the window and then back at Caroline. “Why do I feel like this is the part of the movie where the audience starts yelling, ‘Run, you idiot! Run!’”

CHAPTER FIFTEEN

CAROLINE

Twenty minutes later, Caroline pulled the door closed behind her and stepped down the three concrete steps onto the white shell driveway. The sky was dark gray and was dropping lower like a ceiling giving way. Caroline ran quickly to her car as the rain started to fall.

She needed to think. What had she just done? She was prolonging her stay here? Oh God! And working with Devorah? Holy moly, talk about making a deal with the devil. But she had to do something to get her to agree to drop the lawsuit, and she really could use Devorah's support on her new book.

She took a breath while she looked for her keys. This hadn't been the plan, but what else could she have done? It was the only way she could see to move forward quickly and get herself out of the mess she was in. She would have a huge amount of work in front of her, but that wasn't the worst thing. She enjoyed the process, although working with someone else presented challenges, especially when that someone made the Prada-wearing devil look like a kindergartner. But she knew this could be a good idea. And while she appeased Devorah and threw water on the flames of accusations, Caroline could also get her parents' house ready to sell. Then she would finally be finished with this place. She had everything to gain and not much to lose.

She was getting wet as she continued to dig through her bag. Where were her keys? She needed to get herself, her life, and, dammit, this stupid pocketbook organized. And it would be easy enough. She knew how Devorah worked, and, frankly, Caroline had learned so much from Devorah, crazy as she was; in the scheme of things, this would be a breeze. Who knew? Maybe she'd even enjoy it. Writing could be so lonely. It might be fun to work with someone else on it, even salty Devorah.

But dammit, where were her keys? The last time she remembered having them, they were in the pocket of her oversize palazzo pants. She dug around in them, getting more and more annoyed. The sky was dark and angry, and the fat gray cloud above her head dribbed and drabbed. She slammed her pocketbook down on the hood of the Jeep and rifled through each pocket methodically, but no luck. *Shoot,* she thought, *they must be inside.* They must have slipped out of the damn, annoying, purposeless pockets of her pants. Crap, now she had to go back in and deal with Devorah.

As she turned and ran back toward the house, the rain really started dropping, pelting her like spitballs.

She raced to the front door. Pulling open the aluminum screen door, she knocked on the hard wood. There was just a slim cover over the door, and Caroline was getting wetter by the second. She knocked again. No answer.

Dammit! She tried the doorknob, but it was locked. Devorah had been walking up the stairs to take a nap as Caroline left. She would never hear her. But she had to try. What else was she going to do?

She knocked harder on the door and peered into the side windows. Maybe Devorah had changed her mind about the nap? Caroline futilely covered her hair with her bag and carefully ducked in between the barren rosebushes and the house and began knocking on the windows. There was no sign of Devorah. She continued along the perimeter of the house until the wide leg of her pants caught on a particularly sharp rosebush and tore.

"Dammit!" she yelled as she freed her pants, scratching up her right hand as her bag slipped from her grip and fell. Her phone and Gucci sunglasses spilled out onto the dirt, which was quickly transforming into mud.

And then the lightning started.

Soaking wet, Caroline jumped away from the aluminum-lined windows, bumping once again into the prickly rosebushes and stepping accidentally on her sunglasses, breaking the lenses. She picked the pieces up, along with her wet, dirty phone.

The wind had picked up off the ocean, and the rain had taken on a diagonal trajectory, slashing Caroline, now utterly doused and freezing. She tried to turn her phone on, but it blinked a couple of times and then died.

Stepping out from the bushes into the front yard, she looked around, desperate and frustrated. She looked at the guesthouse, but hell no. No way she was going up there. He hated her. She couldn't blame him. She hated what she'd done to him. She hated that she'd hurt him.

"Dammit!" she shouted again, the words blowing away with the wind.

She blinked and swiped at the mascara dripping into her eyes and angrily made her way to the wooden staircase that climbed up to the guesthouse. She had no other option. She knew Danny was home because his truck was in the driveway. She sloshed her way up the stairs.

Knocking hard on the door, she shouted, "Danny! Danny!"

After a quick second, she saw him through the window, walking toward her, a confused frown spreading across his face as, on her side of the door, she pantomimed: keys, rain, locked out, sleeping. The door swung open.

"I left my keys in Devorah's house, and she's not answering the door."

He looked her up and down, said nothing, but opened the door wider, inviting her inside.

"Thank you," she continued. "My phone got wet, and now it's not turning on, and it started to rain."

"Did it?" Danny snickered. He walked away from her, back toward the small hallway.

Caroline was shocked at his rudeness. She wanted to pick something up and throw it at him.

She dripped on the floor and wasn't sure what to do. She looked around at the cozy but impressive room before her. A wide bay window, smaller than but similar to the window in Devorah's living room, consumed one side wall completely, facing the furious ocean. Adjacent to the window was a kitchen with a small retro gas range and mini Frigidaire. A countertop jutted out from the wall with two high-backed stools tucked under. The bathroom door was open on the opposite side of the room, and the dim hallway where Danny had disappeared presumably led to the bedroom. It felt unbelievable to her that she was back, once again in the same room with Danny Diaz.

"Maybe you could call down there, on your phone, for me? And ask Devorah?" Caroline said, craning her head like she could see through the wall. "Or are you able to enter, like on your own? I think I might have dropped the keys in the living room." She sighed heavily. She was annoyed. What the hell was he doing? Where was he? How rude! "Are you coming back?"

And then Danny reentered the living room with a big, fluffy beach towel, causing Caroline to close her mouth. He held it out to her. "Here, dry yourself off."

"Thank you," she said, sheepishly. "I didn't know where you went."

"Not everybody leaves without a word and doesn't come back."

"Oh, um. My God, that's really . . . thank you." She didn't know how to respond. She decided to ignore the innuendo and continued babbling. "It just caught me off guard. I forgot how quick and crazy intense these storms can be on Cape Cod."

"Yeah."

Caroline dabbed herself with the towel. Danny grabbed her hand at the exact moment a giant bolt of lightning lit up the room like a fireball.

"You're bleeding," he said, rolling her shirtsleeve up and taking a closer look at her right arm.

His hands felt warm. She was trembling, cold. His touch felt electric.

"Oh, I guess I got into it with the roses. They won," she said, laughing a bit nervously, a tad too much. God, what was she doing back here? "Ouch." Caroline jumped and pulled her hand away.

"I'll get my first aid kit and wrap that up. It's pretty deep," he said, looking away, a wry smile spreading across his face. "And, uh, I think I have some sweats that you can change into."

"Oh, I don't want to put you out, Danny. I just need my keys back, and then I'll be out of your hair."

"Well, I can't really let you leave, you know, in good conscience, or whatever," Danny said. At Caroline's confused look, he continued, "You can't really go out like that." His gaze dropped downward and then back up to her eyes.

Caroline pulled the towel away and, to her great horror, when she looked down, she saw her underwear on full display, and the fabric from her pant leg flapping open from her waist to her knee. She rewrapped the towel around herself.

"Oh my God, I didn't realize! I didn't know the rip was that bad." She wanted to scream as Danny left her in the room alone again. She thought she heard him laughing and then clearing his throat. This was excruciating.

"Here," Danny said, coming back into the room. He handed her a pair of sweatpants and a sweatshirt. "Do you want to change in the bathroom?"

"Thank you," Caroline said, taking the offered clothes and moving toward the bathroom. She sounded like she was stepping on sponges, she was so waterlogged. "You're being so nice to me. I am grateful, Danny. Really, thank you."

Danny turned away from her. "I have a key to Devorah's. I'll run down and get your keys. Do you know where they might be?"

"They must have fallen out of my pocket when I was in the living room. Maybe in the couch?"

"Okay, I'll be back in a sec," Danny said, walking to the door.

"Danny," Caroline said.

Danny turned back around to face her. Caroline wiped a wet lock of hair from her face. "Be careful, you know, with the lightning. Thank you so much. I really appreciate it."

"It's nothing I wouldn't do for anyone else." Danny pulled the hood of his sweatshirt up over his head. The door slapped hard against the frame as he left.

"Right," she said to his back. She squished and squeaked her way over to the bathroom.

A few minutes later, she was drier but still embarrassed. Danny hadn't yet returned, so she took the opportunity to wander around the living room. She tugged at the collar of the sweatshirt and sniffed it. It smelled like laundry detergent. And Danny.

Underneath the window was a long thin table covered with plants: bromeliads, spider plants, and ferns. Caroline remembered how Danny loved to garden, and he had brought the outdoors inside. It was beautiful.

Adjacent to the plant table was a rolling cabinet of see-through plastic drawers, and inside Caroline could see Barbie dolls, doll clothes, LEGOs, and an assortment of superheroes and lesser-known, at least to Caroline, cartoon Happy Meal characters and more. Seeing all those toys in that plastic compartment made Caroline feel sad for some reason. Something felt off, like they didn't belong in a guesthouse above a garage but strewed across the floor in a child's playroom.

On the side table, underneath the wall-mounted television, was a framed photograph of Danny and his daughter. It looked like the little girl was about two or three years old in the picture. Danny was beaming, proud, and she looked equally happy. They both wore Red Sox hats, and by the lighting and the lush green tree in the background, it looked like it had been taken in the summertime. She looked so much like him.

Caroline picked up the frame to examine it more closely, and when she did, she saw something behind it on the table that stopped her in her tracks. Resting on the table was a glass bottle filled with sand and sealed with a simple cork stopper. Caroline put the frame down and picked up the bottle. Tied around the neck with white cotton string was a small and somewhat weathered brown paper tag with writing on it. Caroline knew what was written on the tag. She ran her fingers over the word *Mayflower* written in ink with a small heart.

Caroline knew what the tag said because she had given Danny that glass bottle full of sand years earlier when they decided to get married out there on the sand, on their favorite beach.

Seeing it here, now, after all these years, on Danny's table . . . she felt shocked. Why did Danny still have it? It had been years since she'd seen the bottle or thought about it, even, and now the memories of that day, their last day, when she abruptly broke their engagement and shattered his heart, began to flood in.

The squeaking of the screen door startled Caroline, and she quickly returned the bottle and stepped into the center of the room.

"They were in between the couch cushions," Danny said, walking toward Caroline with her keys in hand. He was slightly wet as he pulled his hood off and shook the water from his hair.

"Thank you so much. Not my finest moment. But thank you. I really appreciate it." Caroline stumbled through words, attempting to compose herself. She felt like the lightning up in the sky was front and center in that room. She looked at Danny and quickly looked away. It was like she could feel him.

It was too much. What the hell was going on? She had to get herself together. She needed to get out of there, away from Danny, away from Devorah. She needed to get back to her real life.

"You okay?" he asked.

"I am. I'm fine. I'm just . . . I think I'm tired and a little bit frazzled from all of this." She quickly picked up her wet clothes from the floor by the couch and headed toward the door. "I'll return these." She pulled at the neck of the sweatshirt. His scent was part of the fabric of the clothing, and it now felt overpowering.

"You seem a little dazed or something. Are you sure you're okay?" He was looking at her, scrutinizing her, with a worried look on his face.

She felt dizzy, and all she wanted was for it all to stop. She wanted to be back in California, far away from this place and all its goddamn memories. She could not be there, in that room, for one second longer.

"Thank you, I'm fine," she said.

A loud clap of thunder boomed. Caroline jumped.

"You can wait a few minutes until it lets up a bit. It's moving quickly through here."

Caroline paused at the door, her hand on the knob. She closed her eyes. She didn't turn around but said, "Thank you, but I have to go. And Danny, I really am sorry . . . about everything."

She opened the door and stepped out into the rain.

~

That night, Caroline lay in bed in her childhood bedroom. It was only eleven o'clock on the East Coast, eight o'clock back home. Or where she now considered home to be, the West Coast. California.

The house felt so much smaller than she remembered. She realized it didn't smell the same, though. She inhaled now, breathing in an old wood scent mingled with a faint hint of mildew and neglect. But when she closed her eyes and relaxed her breath, her thoughts drifted back in time to mown grass, Downy fabric softener, smoky garlicky tomato sauce, the scent of the living. And that little space where Danny's hair met the crook of his neck and shoulder that smelled like soap and tasted like salt.

She rolled over, pulling her thoughts back to now, to this small, cramped bedroom in the wrong part of town. She was just a little lonely, and that's why she was thinking of him and their interaction today.

She fluffed her pillow. Her bed was thrust against a wall cut in half by a window with thin metal blinds. Caroline pulled the cord, raising the blinds, and peered outside. There were no streetlights, and the only light that shone through was from a neighboring house. It was too cold for the crickets to be out, and the birds who hadn't migrated south for the winter, who nested in the tall white oak trees that dotted the yard, had long since gone to bed themselves. All that remained was a certain stillness. It was so quiet. Just utterly still and silent.

In Los Angeles, even up on her perch in the Palisades, Caroline was used to the buzz of the city: helicopters, annoying neighbors and their loud parties, coyotes screaming into the night, planes, sirens, and noisy traffic. But it was the strangest thing. The silence here on Cape Cod seemed louder than the white city noise of LA.

Caroline looked out the window, peering into the dark. She tilted her head to the side, straining to hear something—anything.

She dropped the blinds and lay back against her pillow, trying to remember another time in her life when she was so cognizant of sound or, rather, the absence of it. She remembered thinking about it when she was younger. A noisy place meant more was going on, more opportunity, more everything. The silence of Barnstable had been almost deafening to her back then. She knew there was more out there, somewhere, someplace else. And it was loud out there. She wanted to be in the noisy fray.

But now, everything felt different. Here, back in this place, surrounded by memories cloaked in silence, it sounded different to her ears. She couldn't be sure if she liked it or not. She was too absorbed in the noticing. She closed her eyes and waited for sleep to come. And then, in the distance, she heard the whoosh of a car driving by, and then a few seconds after that, the heater kicked on, and warm air rushed through the vent in the far corner of the room.

CHAPTER SIXTEEN

DEVORAH

Devorah sat in the garish office chair at the cluttered oversize desk, while Caroline had piles of papers splayed out in front of her on the floor.

"Are you aware that you don't *have* to keep paper copies of everything?" Caroline said. "For example, here you have printed copies of emails with your responses. Unless you have actively deleted it, the email remains in your account, on your computer. And every time you respond to an email, the original email moves to the bottom, and so on. So, if you're printing it, it all gets duplicated. Do you know what I mean?"

"I understand, Caroline, and thank you for your demeaning and insulting tutorial."

"I wasn't trying to be offensive."

"Sure you were."

"Okay," Caroline said, taking a deep breath. "So this box is from 2010—keep this?"

Devorah rocked in her chair. "Yup."

"All of it?" Caroline said, and receiving no answer, continued. "Okay. It's a lot of stuff to go through, you know?"

"Uh-huh," Devorah said. She was looking down lovingly at Mary Magdalene at her feet. "I know. You're probably right, but that year I attended a convention in upstate New York, and there might be something useful in there, and I'm not sure what I'm going to use or not."

"Does your housekeeper not come into this room?"

"She does. When I have her in. I don't have the house cleaned as often as I used to, since it's just me and Mary." Devorah sighed. She looked at Caroline and cleared her throat. "I don't enjoy having a housekeeper in anymore. I don't like having a stranger in at all of my stuff. And it's not like it used to be."

"Right."

"Your mother was very good," Devorah said and paused before adding, "I did think of her as a . . . well, I enjoyed her company."

"Yeah." Caroline sighed heavily and continued organizing and filing papers.

Devorah nodded and looked past her out the window.

"I just want to make sure we're making the best use of our time together and we're getting all the pertinent stuff in one place." Caroline pulled another box from the shelf onto the floor in front of her, revealing a trove of tchotchkes behind it.

Devorah stood. Her knees cracked, and her hips were sore, but she wanted to get a closer look at the items. It was a collection from her many travels. Most of it was crap she could not have cared less about, really—a bust of Shakespeare, a mask from Venice—but one item caught her eye. A memory stirred, a flutter in her heart.

Devorah leaned over and, with effort, picked the piece up. The item was an ornate hourglass. It was about twelve inches tall. She retook her seat and ran her fingers over the olive wood that framed the sand-filled glass. It was intricately carved with flowers and fruit. Devorah flipped it over. The wooden floral design was a marvel. Depending on which side the hourglass was positioned, the flowers appeared to be either blooming or wilting. It was not the most expensive item in that room by a long shot, but it was precious to Devorah. Not just because it was so interesting but because David had given it to her.

I will love you until the end of time, David had said.

Whose end of time? Devorah wondered. *Mine or yours?*

"That's a nice piece," Caroline said, breaking up Devorah's reverie.

"Oh, yeah, it is. I just haven't seen it in a while." Devorah tipped the hourglass over, flowers abloom. She could feel Caroline's eyes on her, and it made her uncomfortable. She spoke to lighten the moment. "Ten minutes. That's how much time is measured by the sand."

"Are you okay?"

Devorah placed the hourglass on her desk. "Let's get this show on the road. Damn, you're slow." Her eye drifted back to the hourglass and the flowers, now wilted and dying. "Look, honey, I know you save stuff, and it's all up there in the cloud or in the air or the dust or whatever the hell you call it." She pointed at the ceiling. "I just don't trust it. And anyway, I like a copy. I like to look at it. I want to be able to pick the damn thing up and hold it in my hand like it's a real thing."

"Okay, fine." Caroline continued, "Did you have time to take a look at my outline that I printed per your very grumpy request?"

"Actually, yes."

"And?"

"It's not the worst thing I've ever read."

"Come on, Devorah."

"I like the examination of the different types of love as defined by the Greeks. And I think there's a great opportunity here to in some way tie in some modern ideas on the tenets of Plato's *Symposium*, along with some of his thinking surrounding what it means to truly live a good life, and then placing some of those ideas within a framework, such as you did with *Kiss My Abundance*, but I think you have some work to do convincing me how the Greeks and their definition of love can tie in with the modern space and exactly how that's going to be the basis of your guide."

"Oh, that's a walk in the park."

"Is it?"

"The world is set up for couples. Love, loving, being loved is an innate part of human nature. The looking for it, working on it, asking for it, celebrating it is like tapping into an eternal vortex of material. Essentially, this stuff writes itself."

Devorah harrumphed and looked at her nails. She had a hangnail. She bit at it, and it pulled away, ripping the skin and leaving a rectangular strip of white at the nail bed. It started to bleed. "Yeah, sure, whatever you say."

Outside the open window, the waves brutalized the sand. The sound of the punishment carried inside.

Caroline looked over. "What does that mean?"

"Moving on."

"Do you think I don't know about love? Why, because I'm getting a divorce?"

"Mary Magdalene, come give Mama a kiss," Devorah said, passive-aggressively—or maybe just aggressively—ignoring Caroline.

"I suppose you think you're the foremost authority on love?" Caroline laughed, waving her arm around the room.

Devorah didn't care for that. She didn't care for the implication that somehow, her messy office was in some way indicative of something negative, something loveless, perhaps?

"Well, I think you settled for someone who wasn't good enough for you. And then he did exactly what I think you always thought he would do, which was to cheat on you and humiliate you, but now you're free to play the broken heart card and run away like you always do, and then you don't have to risk anything. I know from experience the hardest thing to do after a man abuses a woman in any form is to open up again. So, put that in your book about love. I mean, try starting there. You don't even love yourself, and I don't care what all those crackpots in Hollywood, or wherever, think."

Devorah looked over to see that Caroline had stopped sorting and was just staring at the messy pile in front of her. Devorah felt like a door somewhere had slammed, loud and frightening in her brain. Bringing her back to herself, her thoughts, her words. In that moment, that split second of clarity, she felt shocked, and then instantly ashamed. "I'm sorry. That was harsh. I shouldn't have said that."

Caroline shrugged, barely.

"I don't know why I sometimes say the things that I say," Devorah said. Her eyes cast downward. She could see that Caroline was not really listening to her, lost in her own moment.

Her eyes still focused on the paper in front of her, Caroline said, "I don't know. I made a career of telling people to love themselves. I detailed daily activities, exercises, *showing* people how to do it. 'Love is all there is,' I said. 'Fear isn't real, and when you love . . . and when you love fully, you are never alone.'"

Devorah examined Caroline as she spoke. She hadn't really looked at her since she arrived. She looked . . . tired.

Caroline continued. "And the truth is, I don't think I have ever felt so afraid, and so alone, in my whole entire life. I don't feel love, not for me or anyone else or anything else. I'm starting to wonder if I ever did."

"Oh jeez, don't listen to me," Devorah said. She couldn't stand all the sincerity. "Let's just get the hell on with it. Do you remember Plato's allegory of the cave?" Devorah asked.

"The prisoners in the cave and stuff?" Caroline said. "The puppets and the fire behind them making shadows on the cave wall that prisoners thought were real. That's it, right?"

Devorah nodded. "Remember, one of the prisoners breaks free and turns around and sees the puppeteers behind him and the light from the world outside the cave."

"Yeah, yes. And he goes out there, and then he comes back to tell them what he's learned, and they threaten to kill him if he does."

"That's right."

"So the point is to stay where you are?"

"No, Caroline, Jesus. The point is to keep seeking out knowledge. And really to not give a thought about who believes you or not."

Caroline was quiet, reflective. It was a lot for Devorah. She felt uncomfortable.

"Well, look at us," Devorah said after a long moment. "Just a couple of sad sacks."

Caroline smiled. "Yeah, true that."

It looked to Devorah like she was returning to herself. Maybe she was remembering where she was and who she was with. They didn't do this. They didn't share their feelings. That wasn't the deal.

With some effort, Devorah rose from her ugly chair. "Time for a manhattan," she said. She shuffled down the hallway toward the kitchen. From behind, she heard the pitter-patter of a dog's feet, followed closely by Caroline's.

CHAPTER SEVENTEEN

CAROLINE

The cold, hard breeze off the ocean rolled in like a boulder as she exited Devorah's house. She felt cozy from the bourbon. She rubbed her hands together, blowing on them, as she stepped into the driveway.

Danny looked up as she approached, then quickly turned away.

"Hi," she said, hoping her voice sounded friendly. "Going somewhere?"

"Gotta drop something off at the fire station out in Harwich," Danny said with his back to her. He clicked the unlock button, opened the door of his truck, and placed an envelope on the seat inside. "Then stopping by a friend's."

"Oh, okay, sounds busy," Caroline said, and when he didn't respond, she continued. "Just finished up for the day with Devorah. She's pretty blasted." And then, when he still didn't say anything, she added, "Well, I won't hold you up, then."

"Sure, see you around," Danny said and, grabbing hold of the door, pulled himself up into the truck.

His eyes never ventured over to find her. He faced forward as he started up the engine. Caroline felt stuck in her spot, watching Danny purposely not watching her. What was going on? She thought maybe they'd had a moment the other day.

Danny idled in the truck, organizing his papers and checking something on his phone. Caroline turned to walk toward her car, but she didn't take a step. She didn't want to go home. She didn't want to be alone. She wanted to *do* something. She wanted to go for a ride with Danny like she used to.

She turned back around and knocked on the window of the truck. Danny slowly rolled down the window and said nothing.

"Hi," Caroline said. She cleared her throat. "I was just wondering if maybe I could ride with you?"

"What?"

"Look, I just, was thinking maybe . . . well, first of all, thank you so much for being so nice to me the other day. I know you must hate me."

"I don't hate you, Caroline. I don't *anything* you."

"Right. I get it. I understand that. I don't blame you. I've been thinking a lot about this all lately. And I just wanted to apologize to you for the way everything happened back then. I know you moved on and everything, but I thought I should address it. And I am so very sorry. Being back here and seeing you, I realize that I was selfish, and I have a lot of regrets about that, and I'm sorry. I was running away from so many things, from my parents and my fear I'd end up like them, I guess. I guess we just got caught up in that part."

"It was a long time ago, Caroline. It doesn't matter anymore."

"Well, okay. I just wanted to say that to you, because I never did."

"Okay, well . . . you said it." Danny smiled. "We were kids. We weren't ready for marriage and all of that. You took off. One-way ticket to California. Took me a minute, but I get it. So, anyway, thanks, I guess, if that's even what you say. Good luck, Caroline."

"Well, wait, just before you go, I just would really love to—I don't know—be helpful and hang out or something. So, I was wondering, can I come with you? Please? Just like old friends hanging out?"

Danny looked down at her from his perch inside the truck. He squinted at her.

"Please?"

And then he reached over and pressed the unlock button on the door.

Hearing the click, Caroline smiled and walked around the front of the truck. She pulled the passenger-side door open and climbed inside.

"Thanks, Danny," she said.

He nodded and put the car in gear. As they pulled away, Caroline thought she noticed a shadow in the window in Devorah's upstairs bedroom window.

~

Caroline fell in step next to Danny, crunching over the fallen leaves as they wandered along the exterior of a resplendent cranberry bog belonging to Danny's friend and just down the road from the Harwich fire station. They dropped off the paperwork (a permit request for fireworks for an upcoming cranberry festival) at the station (Caroline stayed in the truck), and Danny wanted to say a quick hello to his buddy Frank, a restaurant owner in Harwich, who had submitted the request. This was exactly the kind of thing that happened in person here rather than electronically, facelessly, like it did out in LA, and she appreciated it. Frank texted he was running late, so Caroline and Danny were given the okay to head out and explore.

The flaming orange sun dipped low in the sky, setting a uniquely New England autumnal scene. Caroline felt like she was walking into the "happy accident" of a Bob Ross painting. Millennia ago, glaciers tore through the earth here, leaving behind large kettle pools with marshy, sandy soil that provided the perfect conditions for the cultivation and harvesting of the tart little cranberry. The Native Americans grew them and taught the early settlers. It was a wet harvest. The bog was flooded with water, and the ripe, crimson fruit floated to the top while workers scurried to gather it. Being out there on the bog, strolling around in the crisp, clean air with Danny, who seemed to be starting to warm up to her a little bit as he pointed out wild asters and migrating birds, made Caroline feel like she was walking through time. This less complicated, less stress-inducing and artful living—growing, caring, harvesting, and celebrating growth—was as fulfilling an experience as she could ever imagine. Who needed more than that? Caroline had forgotten about the bogs and what it felt like to roam through them as a child, and it had been ages since she felt so weightless, so free of responsibility. It felt like Los Angeles was a million miles away instead of just three thousand. Or one email, one text.

She felt the warmth of Danny's hand as he gently grasped hers to ease her back from the watery edge. It was such a simple act, but it felt at once familiar, protective . . . promising. He didn't let go right away, and his hand felt rough and strong encircling hers. She hated that she was thinking how different it felt compared to Grant's softer, thinner hand.

She commanded her mind to remain firmly in the present moment, and she released everything else. She would not think about Grant and her wounded heart. It had been almost a week now since she'd left, and he'd called her only one time. He said he was calling to check in on her, to see how she was doing, but really, he wanted to know where the key to the BMW was, as the lease was coming up and he wanted to trade it in. In her pocketbook with her on Cape Cod, she'd answered. Because forget you, Grant. That had been three days ago.

"God, it is so beautiful out here. I'd completely forgotten this place existed," she said.

Danny was quiet, but she could tell he felt more relaxed, happy even. They were the only humans in that far patch of the bog, and their footfalls disrupted a flock of hundreds of migrating tree swallows, who had paused to fill their bellies and rest momentarily on their long, arduous trip to South America to wait out the bitter New England winter.

Caroline and Danny moved forward toward the birds, who scattered, putting on a stunning display, darting up into the air and back down to earth again, flapping their wings in glory. Caroline inhaled the magic in the air all around them, and, as she grew still, she felt a sensation she hadn't realized she'd been missing. There was an easiness here in this moment. It was all just so straightforward and pretty and natural. Caroline marveled at the birds. They were connected to one another, purposeful in their movements. They moved in unison and with confidence. Their aerial dancing looked effortless, making her smile. The birds didn't hinder their progress by doubting it. They weren't mumbling under their breath: *What the hell am I doing? Why am I doing this? What next? How do I know I'm doing the right thing?* They followed their instinct, plain and simple. They remained open for the signal and received guidance, and together they were greater. They knew there was plenty, enough for all of them. And together, united, they were astounding, better.

Standing there with the cool October breeze feathering her hair, Caroline flung her arms out wide like a blackbird's wings, arched her back, and faced the sky, laughing loudly. *There is a God, and He is good,* she thought. *And I am not alone. I never am.*

Danny laughed. "What are you doing?"

"I don't know." Caroline was still laughing. "I guess I just don't think I ever really knew what 'free as a bird' meant until right now. This is just so amazing. Thank you."

"You're welcome," he said and laughed again. "For what?"

Caroline stepped in a little closer to Danny. She tilted her head up. "Thank you for bringing me here to this beautiful place. Thank you for accepting my apology. It feels really wonderful to have a friend right now."

Danny went still, his face growing serious. He seemed to be searching for what to say.

Her heart thumped louder in her chest, battered and bruised but still there, pumping and fulfilling its purpose. She could hear it, and she realized she could actually feel it, like it was beginning to bulge, protrude from her chest. This feeling was at once familiar and like a distant memory, like she was a teenager about to be kissed for the first time. What was happening? The air around them was cold, but she felt warm. Her cheeks burned. She breathed him in.

He was facing her fully now, head on. A smile spread across his beautiful face, and he said, "It's good to see you."

"Yeah, it really is good to be here," she said, just as the wind picked up and roared on its way along the bog. It sped toward them and wrapped around them like an albatross. A dark cloud rolled in from the east.

Danny tugged at her hand again. Smiling, he said, "It's cold, and it looks like rain. We should go."

"Is it cold?" she said with a light laugh, her teeth just beginning to chatter a bit. "I hadn't noticed."

They turned toward the outer edge of the bog and headed back the way they came, matching their steps.

"Beer?" he asked.

"Oh, hell yeah," she said.

~

Danny held the glass door open for Caroline, and she stepped inside the large warehouse brewery at Cape Cod Beer on Phinney's Lane in Barnstable. The cement floor was painted deep red, and the towering ceilings in the metal-frame building were dotted with signs and posters brandishing the latest and most popular brews. Caroline felt like she was in an airport hangar, but the feeling was oddly cozy, with tables and chairs strewed about and a large polished-wood bar slicing through a third of the room. The large metal fermentation tanks towered behind the glass wall. Within those imposing tanks, the barley, hops, and malt were mashing about and doing their thing, and the smell was sour and overpowering, adding a literal flavor to the air.

Caroline selected a red ale, and Danny ordered the IPA from the bearded millennial behind the bar. Caroline couldn't remember the last time she'd had a beer, never mind ordered at the bar.

After a quick moment, the bearded man placed the pint in front of her, she and Danny toasted, and she took a sip. Caramel-and-honey-infused ale slid down her throat. She closed her eyes and licked her lips.

"How is it?" Danny asked.

"I feel like I'm standing in a field of peat in Killarney," she said with a brogue.

"Nice," he said and laughed. "I think these fine purveyors would be complimented by that."

Caroline scanned the room. It was slightly warm and a little bit noisy, with the sound of glass bottles clinking together and muffled conversations from other patrons seated nearby. In the corner, a woman laughed loudly and caught Caroline's attention. She was about Caroline's age, she guessed, with ruddy cheeks and shoulder-length white hair. She was seated with three men, all four in jeans and flannel button-downs, and they were playing cards. The woman looked content and at ease, the beer doing its thing. She was decidedly not glammed up and yet had the rapt attention of all at her table. It was such a departure from the culture in Los Angeles—or, really, from *some* of the women she'd seen back there. This woman looked real. She *was* real. And all that was great, sure, less effort and whatever, but this woman just looked so happy. Caroline thought it was just about the coolest thing she'd seen all day. She had to tell herself to stop staring.

"When did Cape Cod Beer become, like, a thing out here?" she said. "It's so great."

"They started out small and eventually moved into this space about ten or so years ago. When the weather's good, from spring into early fall, they have a beer garden outside and live music and a farmers' market and cornhole and all that," Danny said. "It's actually a lot of fun."

"I bet it is," Caroline said as pulsing from atop the table disrupted their conversation. She reached for her phone to see that Thérèse was calling. She flinched.

"You need to take that?" Danny said.

"Probably, but I can call her back in a few." She sent the call to voicemail and took a long pull on her beer. "You know, this might be the best, most delicious beer I've ever had in my entire life."

"Yeah, they know what they're doing here."

"They really do," Caroline said. "So, if you don't mind me asking, what happened with you and Michelle?"

Danny stretched his long legs out under the table. "You've shown a lot of restraint in not asking. Well done."

Caroline giggled. She tucked a stray hair behind her ear. "So does that mean you don't want to talk about it?"

He smiled and looked at her. He thought for a moment, then exhaled and said, "She said she'd had enough. I'm closed off to her, I'm distant."

"You? Oh, wow, I am so sorry. I never thought of you that way."

"She might not be wrong. I have some trust issues," he said, looking at his beer. "I might have carried some past stuff into our marriage."

"Oh," Caroline said. She couldn't think of anything else to say. She felt the words land. She knew what he was saying, what he was thinking, what she had done.

"What about you?" he asked, waving his hand like it was no big deal, like the fact that they had known each other and loved each other from the time they first saw one another as children was not everything. "What's your story?"

"Oh, well." Caroline fought to keep her voice steady. She was honest when she said, "Well, I really loved him . . . Grant. I thought we really made sense, you know? For a while anyway. But I noticed I was away a lot. And when I wasn't, he was. And I felt really alone, and then he pulled me in and he made me feel like we were a family, I guess. Then he cheated on me.

"The infidelity was, I don't know, I guess it was a result of . . . you know, your garden-variety growing-apart stuff. We couldn't have a baby, which was hard, but we got through that, and then one day I think our marriage became about something else. It was odd. I remember I got a celebrity chef to give us a home cooking lesson. It was expensive, and we were going to learn how to make pasta together. Grant kept canceling. He didn't want to put in the effort. And then, all of a sudden, he did. He wanted to make ravioli, and he read up on all of it and went to the store and got all the ingredients, and he rescheduled the whole thing, and then the day came, and he was ready to go, and *I* canceled. After that, I guess we just both stopped trying."

"Why did you cancel?" he asked.

"I think it was, like, a last-minute work thing that had come up, and, I don't know, I don't really remember."

Caroline paused a moment and then reached across the table. She placed her hand on Danny's. "I've made a lot of mistakes in my life, but I can say with sincerity that the way I treated you is one of my biggest regrets."

Danny looked at her hand as Caroline's phone buzzed again, this time with a text from Thérèse that read Did you get it all sorted yet? When are you coming back?

"It's okay if you want to take that." He pulled his hand away, then took a sip of his beer.

"I don't," she said. "Want to take it. I really don't." She silenced her phone and placed it face down. She took another long pull.

"Well, I've got a busy few days, so I should get you back to your car," he said. The mood, the energy, had changed.

"Oh, okay, of course," Caroline said. She wanted to say more. She wanted to ask him what was wrong. She thought they had been having a great day, like they had just shared a moment. She felt relaxed with him and more at ease than she could remember being in a long, long time. Had she done or said something that offended him? What changed? But she didn't ask him or say anything. Instead she downed the rest of her beer and said, "Okay, I'm ready."

CHAPTER EIGHTEEN

DEVORAH

It was a warm and windy fall day, and the sea glass and weathered shells held together by fishing line and tied to driftwood clanked together outside Devorah's open window. She loved listening to the music they made. She'd made that wind chime, back when her hands were far nimbler and she actually cared, but she was grateful she had.

In the distance, through the window, Devorah watched Caroline climb out of her silly Jeep parked in the driveway. She noticed Caroline's gaze travel toward the guesthouse and then back toward the main house. Devorah ambled over and unlocked the front door.

"He's not home," she said, holding the door open.

"Oh, yeah, that's fine," Caroline said stepping inside. "Whatever."

"Uh-huh." Devorah rolled her eyes and shuffled down the hallway to the office with Caroline on her heels.

She took her seat at the desk, Mary Magdalene asleep on the floor at her feet. Devorah had felt energized last night, so she'd done some organizing and searching of her own. Maybe it was the knowing that she didn't have to do it all on her own that inspired her. At any rate, overall, the office was looking slightly more organized. And she had something to show Caroline.

"What's this?" Caroline said, seeing the open Bankers Box on the floor.

"I remembered we had moved everything from 2008 out of here, because of some financial holdings and tax stuff, because I was claiming some things and retiring that year and had receipts and all that. And I had forgotten about it. It was in my closet with some other stuff."

"Great! Oh my God, that's great!" Caroline said. "So, is this it?" Caroline held up a three-ring binder resting at the top of the box.

"A lot of it," Devorah said. She was leaning back in her chair. Her eyes were closed.

"Are you okay?" Caroline leaned in, looking worried.

"I'm fine. I'm tired from doing all this crap. Get on with it, already." Devorah opened her eyes and noticed Caroline's eye roll. "Kidding, just kidding, don't be oversensitive. I'm fine."

"Well, okay, if you're sure you're not too tired to do all this now?" Caroline said, but Devorah gave her a look, and she quickly turned back to the binder and box in front of her and opened the cover. She read silently for a few minutes, then spoke aloud, jostling Devorah. "This is so cool. I remember reading this a million years ago."

"Reading what?"

"Wait, I think this could be good as far as the framework goes." Caroline read from the three-ring binder in her hand. "Love this." She paused before continuing.

"Okay, so as we know, the ancient Greeks classified love eight different ways. *Philia*, deep friendship; *ludus*, young, playful love; *storge*, familial love; *agape*, spiritual love or love for all things; *pragma*, long-standing love; *mania*, *obsessive* love"—Caroline stressed the word *obsessive*—"*eros*, passionate love; and *philautia*, love of self."

"Yes."

"So, I think we tie in the universality that is love, and I'm working on the language of the how-to stuff with some of the observations you have written about in your work—like in this paper or lecture or whatever it is—that you did on Plato's thoughts on living the good life. Then we can pull in some modern-day examples and of course tailor a little bit more to romantic, eros-type love, and wham-o! We're in business. I'm telling you, this will be commercially right on point."

A quiet moment passed, and then Devorah felt Caroline's eyes on her.

"I'm saying I like it. That it's interesting, Devorah," Caroline said. "And before you get on your high horse or whatever, that is definitely included in my book. You can't write a book about the Greeks and love and not include their classifications."

Devorah cleared her throat. "Plato believed that the physical part of love, the sex and desire, began to fade when something deeper and more permanent, more cerebral, took over. He called it the ladder. Started out as sexual attraction but built into something more."

"I can see that. I never thought about it like that, I guess," Caroline said.

"Greek mythology said that humans were originally created with four arms and legs, and when the gods felt threatened by their power, Zeus split them in two, condemning humans to live their lives incomplete. Unless they found their other half." Devorah remembered a quote—it was on the tip of her tongue. "'Every heart sings a song incomplete until another heart whispers back.'"

"Did Plato say that?"

"Yeah," Devorah said.

"Do you believe in soulmates?"

"Sure, why the hell not?" She looked at Caroline, who was unmoving, and frowning again. She looked contemplative. "What? What's your problem?"

"Jeez," Caroline said. "I don't know. I guess . . . I don't know what that's like, I don't think. I guess I wish I had a soulmate."

"Plato didn't really believe in soulmates. But screw him. How do you know you don't have one?"

"Well, because I am getting older, and now I'm alone, and maybe I might find love or refind love again or something, but for some reason soulmates sounds like a younger person's game."

"Oh, quit your squawking. Maybe you just haven't found him yet?" Devorah said. "Or maybe you had him and you got scared, so you messed up and ran away from him?"

"Jesus, Devorah, will you just lay off?"

It made Devorah laugh to push her buttons. They were so easy to push. "Look, I'm just saying that, you know, eventually, you will definitely run out of time. And seems like you're nosing around a second chance with Diaz."

"So what exactly are you trying to say here in this bit?" Caroline asked, deflecting. "Because we need some fire here. It's super interesting—but it ain't sexy. You've got to dirty it up a little bit. That's what's going to sell it."

"So, you're telling me to dumb it down and whore it up, right?"

"Yeah, a little bit. I mean, if you want to sell it. This isn't for academia, it's for one's reading pleasure. And come on, Devorah, this is love we're talking about, right? It's exciting and expansive, and this is a little less drop-your-panties and a little more—"

"You've got sex on the brain. Diaz got you all hot and bothered?"

"Listen, I know how to sell this stuff. And as far as Danny Diaz is concerned, seriously, Devorah, that is none of your business."

"He's a good man. And you need to remember that," Devorah said. And then, out of the corner of her eye, Devorah saw something that was odd, jarring.

Caroline noticed it at the same time, and a look of abject terror covered her face.

"Oh my God." Devorah leaped from the chair as quickly as her weak arthritic bones would allow and dropped to the floor next to Mary Magdalene, who was writhing around, white foamy spittle spilling from her mouth. The dog was whimpering, and her eyes darted back and forth, side to side in rapid fire.

Caroline ran to her side, and they hovered over the dog. "She's having a seizure."

"No shit she's having a seizure. I'm not blind," Devorah cried. "Mary? Mary? What do we do? What do I do? Help her. Goddammit, help her right now."

"Just hold on. Don't put your hands near her mouth—she might bite you. We have to wait until she stops seizing."

"Mary? Oh, my sweet girl, Mary." Devorah was on all fours. She put her forehead on the ground near the writhing animal and cried. "Is she in pain?"

"She's not. She can't feel it," Caroline said and knelt beside the dog.

"How do you know that? Are you a doctor or something? How do you know that?"

"Only child. Had lots of pets over the years. You have to take her to the vet."

"No shit, Sherlock," Devorah cried.

"Do you have to be so damn ornery? I'm trying to help." Caroline's voice was calm, whereas Devorah was panicked and breathless.

Devorah closed her eyes and prayed for strength. "Just please help her, Caroline. Please."

And then Mary Magdalene stopped twitching altogether. Her eyes were half-closed, her tongue hung out of the side of her mouth, and she lay very still on the ground. Her bladder freed; a pool of urine spread out and soaked the lower half of her body.

"Oh God. Is she okay?" Devorah asked, moving over and placing one hand on her still body. "Is she okay?"

"She's breathing. Is Dr. Brinkwell still practicing?"

"Yes."

"Come on, I'll take you over there. Let's go." Caroline rose up off her knees. She grabbed a throw blanket from the back of the couch and wrapped Mary Magdalene in it while Devorah struggled to get to her feet.

"Is she okay?"

"I don't know," Caroline answered. She held the limp dog in her arms, and they hurried out the front door.

~

Dr. Brinkwell hovered over Mary Magdalene, who lay on her side on the chest-high metal table, still draped with the throw blanket from home. Caroline and Devorah stood side by side across from him.

"I'm so very sorry, Devorah," Dr. Brinkwell said. "Please, don't hold back. Tell Mary all you want her to know."

Devorah sobbed into her hands. Her shoulders were slumped over, and she nodded her head up and down. She wiped away at her tears with a bundle of tissues and leaned over, pressing her face fully into the furry body of the motionless dog. She whispered, "You are a good dog. You are a really good dog."

Caroline stood to the side, a witness to suffering. The ride to the veterinarian's had been surreal. Neither woman had spoken more than a few words, stunned into silence from knowing what was coming, wishing it away.

Dr. Brinkwell said quietly, "This is a very compassionate thing you're doing, Devorah. You have so lovingly cared for Mary for so many years. She is such a loved animal and has had such a wonderful life with you. And this is truly the humane and, again, very compassionate thing to do for her. I'm so very sorry."

"Oh, just do it already," Devorah said, her voice breaking.

Dr. Brinkwell made eye contact with Caroline, and he shook his head in sad acknowledgment. He inserted the syringe into Mary Magdalene's hind leg through a small IV port. Devorah whimpered, but the dog didn't move, didn't flinch. The syringe slowly drained, and after several minutes, the body of the tiny dog seemed to deflate like a balloon. Her little jelly eyes remained open.

Dr. Brinkwell finally spoke. "She is at peace now, Devorah."

Devorah's voice was hoarse when she spoke to Caroline. "Let's go." She opened the door, facing the hallway, away from little Mary, whom she couldn't bear to look at. Behind her she heard Caroline thanking the doctor.

"I'm so sorry." Devorah heard him say.

"Yup . . . thank you," Caroline said as Devorah stepped out into the hall, with a heart aching as deep as the Grand Canyon.

Dr. Brinkwell continued speaking to Caroline. "I'm a big fan of you . . . of yours," he said.

"Oh," Caroline said. Devorah felt sick but noted with a slight bit of surprise the annoyance in Caroline's voice as she said, "Uh, thank you."

"Yes, you bet. Take care. And take care of Devorah. Sorry again about the sweet pooch."

Caroline joined Devorah in the hall, and they walked off together toward the front door. Caroline's arm circled her shoulder. It felt good.

~

The bartender, a young man in his midtwenties wearing a backward baseball cap and a T-shirt that said *Master Baiter*, slid two ice-cold manhattans across the shiny wood bar to Caroline and Devorah. Cobwebbed vintage buoys and brown fisherman's nets dangled from the ceiling, intercut by faded fiberglass fish and ornamental seashells. The dive bar was half-full with joyfully pie-eyed patrons digging their hands into the salty bar mix and washing it back with their heavy-pour cocktails.

Master Baiter squinted at Caroline. "Do I know you?"

"I don't think so," she said.

"Are you, like, a friend of my mom's or something?"

Devorah did a spit take.

Caroline exhaled heavily. "No, not likely," she said, turning her body to face Devorah and away from him.

"It'll come to me. I know it will," he said wiping the bar and turning to the new couple that sat down.

A few awkward moments passed after he walked away. The women sipped their cocktails.

"Look, I don't want to talk about it. So just don't say it. Don't say anything." Devorah took another long swig of the brown drink.

Caroline closed her eyes. She smacked her lips together. Took a drink, then another, and finally said, "But, okay, just one question?"

"Oh jeez."

"Mary Magdalene? Her name?"

"I got her from a puppy mill in Ohio. She'd had six litters, and then she was used up. She couldn't have any more, so she was no good to them. Her whoring days were over, so she was cast off."

"Right," Caroline said. "Well, apropos then, I guess." She stirred her drink before taking another sip. "Cheez-Its, this is like airplane fuel."

"Well, it's no chardonnay spritzer, or whatever the hell kind of pansy thing you drink. And, by the way, nobody asked you to order it. Or to come to the restaurant. Or to come to Cape Cod, for that matter."

"Nice," Caroline said, taking another long sip. "Mmm, yum. I stand corrected."

Overhearing the last part of their conversation, Master Baiter tossed his bar rag over his shoulder and leaned into them.

"So, how are the drinks, ladies?" he said, winking at Caroline.

"Tolerable," Devorah cut in.

He recoiled, genuinely offended.

"They're fine. Thank you," Caroline said, reaching for the bar mix as Master Baiter skulked away. She popped a cashew into her mouth and said, "She was a lucky dog."

"Am I not speaking English? I said I don't want to talk about it."

"Sorry, I get it. I understand."

"I don't think you do, actually."

"I understand loss, Devorah."

"Listen, I don't need you to feel bad because my damn dog died. I don't need your approval to grieve, nor do I need company in my grief. Your involvement, your presence here, neither increases nor decreases my feelings."

Caroline was silent, not taking the bait. "I'm hungry. Do you want to eat something?"

"I'm not hungry."

"You should eat. Especially if you're drinking this jet fuel."

"Oh, would you just stop?"

"I'm trying to help you."

"Well, who the hell asked you to?"

"Nobody asked me, Devorah. You've suffered a loss, and you're angry about it. I get it. I'm a human being, and I'm sitting here with you, and you've had a difficult time today, and I'm trying to make you feel better. Because that's what people do. Healthy, evolved humans care for other humans. It's, like, a thing."

"Don't get all snippy with me, sister. I've forgotten more than you'll ever know."

Caroline looked at the ceiling. "Well, you've certainly forgotten common decency and manners."

"Good God, moving out there really turned you into a cream puff."

"Seriously?"

Devorah took a long hard pull on her drink and gestured with her finger to Master Baiter for another round.

"Will you add a couple of house salads with some grilled fish to that order, too, please?" Caroline said.

"Grilled fish salad?" Devorah's eyes almost rolled out of her head and onto the floor. "Jesus! Gimme a burger. And cook it, for Chrissake—none of this bloody rare crap. And make sure the bun isn't stale. Last time I was in here, the bun was stale. I hate stale buns."

"She's had a hard day," Caroline said to Master Baiter.

He punched the order into his computer. "No stale buns. Got it. Man, I just love a woman who knows what she wants."

"Yeah, I doubt that," Devorah said.

He grimaced and moved away to the other side of the bar, and Devorah thought she heard a slight giggle escape Caroline's tight lips.

~

One hour and several drinks later, Caroline was red faced, glassy eyed, and midstory. "So, I reached into his pocket, and I pulled out a leopard-print thong. I mean, how utterly cliché? I mean, leopard print? Thong? What is this, 1985? And in his jacket pocket? I mean . . . I don't get it. I mean, seriously, what does one do with someone's underwear, presumably worn? It's gross. I just . . . I don't understand. It's just unhygienic, if you ask me."

"Pervert," Devorah said.

"He's a joke."

"He's a joke, but that sure doesn't sound funny," Devorah said.

"Yeah, it wasn't, actually. It wasn't funny at all. I mean, he's a photographer. He's surrounded by models and celebrities all the time. He never, ever seemed interested or wrapped up in all that crap, but I guess he was. I was just too stupid to see it. And then—voilà—dirty drawers in his pocket. Why was I surprised?"

"Well, seriously, Caroline. I don't know, why *were* you surprised?"

"I don't . . . I don't know." Caroline pushed around some of the remaining lettuce on her plate. "But I was . . . I was blindsided."

"Well, good riddance," Devorah said, and then she paused. "Right?"

Caroline looked down at her drink and ran her fingers along the rim. "Yup . . . that's the right answer, right? You going to eat those?" She pointed to Devorah's fries.

"They're all yours." Devorah pushed her plate closer to Caroline. "You need to tread carefully with Diaz."

"Oh jeez, don't start, Devorah, okay? Can I just enjoy a damn french fry, for crying out loud?"

Devorah sighed. She tilted her head back and looked up at the ceiling. "That's a lotta cobwebs up there."

Caroline looked up at the wood-beam ceiling lined with what looked like dusty woven angel hair. "This whole place is pretty nasty. And these fries are not worth it. Why are we even here?"

"I've not been asked back, so to speak, at some of the finer establishments in town."

"Yeah, I can see why."

They laughed like they were old friends. Which, of course, they were. So to speak.

The sound of a laundry-detergent commercial played in the background, covering the silence that had descended over them.

"She was a good girl," Devorah said, stroking the stem of her martini glass.

"I know she was," Caroline said.

"A really good girl."

"She definitely was."

"I mean, she only pooped indoors, but all the time, she peed outside. How could you ask for more than that?"

"You couldn't. You shouldn't. You can't. You don't."

"Yeah, yeah, yeah, I know. But she's dead."

"She is dead. Yup. Poor girl," Caroline added and put a hand on Devorah's arm. "You feel a little hot, Devorah. You hot?"

"Boiling," Devorah said and wiped at the sweat that was beading up around her hairline. "It's hot in here. I just thought I was in hell."

Master Baiter leaned over the bar. "Can I get you ladies another round?"

"What, are you trying to get us drunk or something?" Devorah asked. "You tryin' to see if she's got a leopard thong on or something?"

Caroline spit her water out on the bar, and while gasping for air between giggles, she said, "I'm not. I'm wearing boy shorts. Very comfortable, very large boy shorts."

Master Baiter scratched the back of his neck. "Well, that's good to know. I'm not really sure what boy shorts are, but I think my mom has some."

"Oh, buzz off," Caroline said as Devorah almost fell off her barstool. "Check. Just bring us the check. Or, better yet, here." Caroline reached for her bag and pulled out her card and laid it on the bar.

The two of them made difficult work of getting down off the barstools, but Master Baiter turned back around to them. "Sorry, ma'am . . ."

"Ma'am?" Devorah cried. "Ha ha, *ma'am*."

"Your card's been declined."

Devorah bent over and crossed her legs, she was laughing so hard.

Caroline, on the other hand, wasn't as amused. "Declined? That bastard must've closed my account. Can you try again?"

"I tried three times. Don't worry, though, happens all the time in here." Master Baiter shrugged. "Adulting is hard."

"Now, you listen to me, pal, don't you dare start taking perfectly good nouns and trying to make them verbs, okay? You got me? Things are not that dire yet," Caroline said, pointing a finger. "I mean, seriously."

And then Master Baiter got a funny look on his face. "Hey, wait . . . I think I know who you are. You're that lady, the one that got—"

"Here," Devorah said pulling herself back to an upright position and tossing her card onto the bar.

"You're . . ." He was snapping his fingers, trying to remember her name, while all the humor swept out of the room, and Caroline's face went completely ashen.

Devorah leaned over. "Oh, don't listen to this guy! He's a moron!"

"Hey!" Master Baiter said, rightfully insulted.

"Oh my God," Caroline said. The sides of her mouth dipped, her focus up, squarely on the television.

"What?" Devorah said, turning to look at the screen.

On a chyron, beneath a picture of smiling Grant and cleavage-baring Oaklyn, ran the word *Engaged!* And then an old smiling picture of Grant and Caroline from happier times filled the screen.

"Yes! That's it!" Master Baiter pointed at Caroline. "You're the one in all those funny memes who got jilted at that awards show."

"Look, you want a tip, kid? Run the damn card," Devorah said, and then, turning to Caroline, added, "and you—snap out of it. No crying or any of that sad-clown crap. At least wait until you get home, like every other asshole in this place."

CHAPTER NINETEEN

CAROLINE

"Oh. My. God. It's freezing," Caroline said as she dipped her hand into the frigid water. She was a little more than ankle deep, wearing rubber wader boots over her skinny jeans. Next to her, Danny, in his own waders and jeans, adjusted his floating metal bucket.

It was the following morning, and Caroline was still stunned by the news of Grant's engagement. She was also nursing a severe headache. Sitting around in her parents' house thinking about Grant engaged to someone while they were still legally married and her accounts temporarily frozen as the divorce proceedings continued was simply more than she could handle. She decided she was unavailable to sit and wallow in hurt and self-pity. She used that word—*unavailable*—a lot when she was working with clients or being interviewed, and it more than fit the bill today. "I am *unavailable* to be treated in any way other than the queen that I am."

Caroline knew full well, and was generally proud, that she possessed an ability to compartmentalize and disassociate from conflict. It was a trait that had served her well in her life and, for quite some time, in the wrestling ring that was Hollywood. She chose to call on that skill today and to file the heartache away as best she could and make herself busy.

She returned the many fervent phone calls from her team back in Los Angeles, informing them that she would be lying low and was only to be contacted if a nuclear war was underway—it never worked, but was worth a try—and then she climbed into the Jeep and made the drive over to check in on Devorah. *Misery loves company,* she thought.

On her way, she made two quick stops, one at the market, while wearing a baseball cap and dark glasses, to pick up flowers, coffee, and pastry for Devorah to brighten her mood, and the other at the real estate office that handled the renting of her parents' home.

Caroline told Wayne, the middle-aged, bespectacled, potbellied, and bald real estate agent working the desk, that she wanted to discuss putting the house on the market and beginning to show it to prospective buyers. After posing for a photo with him and accepting his condolences on her broken marriage, she was on her way.

She noticed, as she bounced along Craigville Beach Road, that her spirits were somewhat lighter. She had somewhere to go, someplace to be, something to do.

Devorah answered the door after two hard knocks and received the gifts with a grunted thank-you but told Caroline she wasn't interested in working that afternoon and quickly closed the door in her face. Caroline, of course, understood. She felt terrible for Devorah's heartache, but she knew—she hoped—a little time would help her heal.

Caroline was looking for some healing, too, but she didn't want to be alone. She was looking for some friendship, camaraderie . . . love. She was looking for someone . . .

And then Danny Diaz appeared on the steps exiting the guesthouse. How about that? He was going out to harvest oysters? Well, what do you know: she'd wanted to do that herself.

Plunk. Drawing Caroline's attention back to their present task, Danny dropped a large oyster into the bucket.

"I'm glad you were able to come out," he said.

"Me too," Caroline said. She smiled, her spirits lifted, her thoughts firmly in the present moment.

They were just off East Bay Road in Osterville, an area sanctioned by the town's shellfish regulators for oyster harvesting every Wednesday and Saturday from mid-October through April. Prime oyster-fishing time was low tide, but they were about forty-five minutes early, as most who were in the know tended to be.

"Where are the little buggers?" Caroline asked, dipping her hand into the water again. "Oh my God, it's freezing. It's like ice. The water was actually warm last week. What happened?"

"Don't be so California," Danny said, dropping two more into his bucket. "It's good for the heart. Gets the blood pumping."

"Oh jeez, is that true?"

"Shoot, I don't know. Probably?"

"Those poor bastards," Caroline said, peering into the bucket. "Look at them, out here, minding their own business, making pearls and whatnot, and then, all of a sudden, some big scary hand comes in and scoops them right up out of the water, plops them in a bucket, and that's it. Call it a day."

"Yeah, but they're delicious."

"Well, yes, they are." Caroline smirked, feeling just a little bit mischievous. "They're an aphrodisiac, you know." She looked over at Danny, met his eye.

"Why you think I'm out here?" he said and laughed. And then he made a little show of quickly finding and then dropping another three into the floating bucket.

Caroline laughed. "Yeah, you are pretty good at this."

"Practice," he said. "Lots of practice."

"So, does it work? The aphrodisiac part?"

"We'll see." He smiled and dropped another one into the bucket. "Look, they're literally everywhere. This is only the second week back for harvesting, and you can only take a certain amount. So, they've just been sitting here getting fat all summer. You're actually standing on one."

Caroline jumped. "Oh God, I was. I hate that. I don't like standing on my food." Caroline reached into the water and pulled it out. "Wow, he's a whopper!"

"He is a whopper. You know what that means?" Danny said, laughing. "Big oyster . . ."

"No, what? Big oyster, big what?"

"Big oyster, big mollusk?" He was laughing harder now as he turned away from her.

"That was terrible. Really, awful." She splashed a little water at him. "Hey, don't turn your back on me!"

"I'm not. I'm fishing. And hush, or you'll scare them all away."

"Not sure that's how it works with oysters."

"Shh." Danny turned back toward her and brought his index finger to his lips, shushing her.

"You say *oyster* and I say *erster*," Caroline sang, then asked, "Who says *erster*? I've never heard anyone say *erster* in my life."

Danny shook his head, smiling.

"Have you?" she said.

Danny took one step closer to Caroline. They were now just inches apart. He had a wicked glint in his eye as he slowly placed his cold, wet finger on Caroline's lips and said, "Shh."

Danny's finger, his touch, sent a shock through her body. He let his finger linger there for a second. She was spellbound as his eye dropped to his hand, to that finger, to her mouth. She held still, her breath becoming more ragged. A moment or a millennium later, he pulled his finger away, the absence abrupt, terrible. Their eyes met. He tilted his head just a little to the side, taking her in. The sun rose in front of them as the calm water lapped gently around their ankles.

Her body still, and with his eyes still on her, she gently ran her tongue along her lower lip where his finger had been just a second before. Her lip tasted salty and slightly sweet. He watched her tongue slide. She wondered if he still tasted the same.

"Diaz, is that you?" a male voice called out from behind them, breaking the spell and sending them crashing back into the water in Osterville.

Abruptly, they turned to see a uniformed man with crystal-blue eyes, light-brown hair poking out from under his Barnstable Division of Natural Resources baseball cap. A badge on his army green jacket read *Warden*.

"Oh, hey, man, yeah. How are you?" Danny extended his hand, the same one he'd been tantalizing Caroline with just a moment before.

"Thought that was you."

Danny turned to Caroline. "Caroline, do you remember Jason Baxter? From high school."

"Oh my God, Caroline Murphy," Jason said. "What the hell are you doing here? This guy bothering you?"

"He is actually *not* bothering me," Caroline said, giggling a bit. She wanted to kick herself. Why did she feel like such a schoolgirl? "But thank you. Good to see you, Jason."

Jason took the hint. He smiled at Danny and, pointing a bony finger, said, "No more than a bushel. I'm watching you."

"Of course," Danny said.

Jason walked away to check the other buckets.

"Wait a minute, that's not . . . or isn't he the guy who used to eat his boogers in chemistry class?" Caroline asked.

"A-yup," Danny said. "Hopefully, he's outgrown the habit." Danny dipped his hand, the hand he'd shaken Jason's with, into the water and wiped it on his pant leg. Caroline giggled.

"You hungry?" Danny asked.

"I thought you'd never ask."

~

From the guesthouse, Caroline could see the light on in Devorah's house. They hadn't wanted to interrupt her. She'd been very clear earlier when she said she would see Caroline the next day. She needed time.

"I hope she's doing okay," Caroline said.

"She's fierce, but I know. I worry about her, too, and Jesus, she loved that sweet, ugly little dog. But anyway, she just wants a little bit of time to herself right now. I think it's okay."

"I know . . . I know you're right," Caroline said, turning away from the window. "Frankly, it feels odd to be in this place of worrying about Devorah. She's not someone you think you have to worry about, right? She's always been such a force of nature. And a pain in the ass."

"I think she's wicked lonely." Danny was standing over the sink, an oven mitt on one hand and an oyster knife in the other, shucking away.

"Yeah, I think that's probably true," Caroline said. "Devorah used to have a drink with my mom after she'd finished cleaning the house."

"I think I remember you saying that," Danny said. "Back in the day."

"Yeah. It wasn't awesome."

"I never met Devorah, but I remembered you spent some time working with her." He cracked another oyster open and placed it on a cold plate. "Sorrenti knew her. His mother was friends with her. He mentioned she was here alone, so I stopped by one day and asked her if I could rent the guesthouse for a while."

"Funny how things turn out." Caroline turned from the window to Danny. He held the knife in his right hand and the shell in the mitt on his left. He worked the blade into the base of the hinge and twisted it, putting pressure on it. The muscles in his forearms popped.

"Can I help?" she asked.

"You can open the wine."

She found the corkscrew in the drawer and grabbed a bottle of chardonnay. "This is so nice, being here with you." She pierced the bottle top and pulled the cork out, then filled their glasses as her phone buzzed on the counter.

Danny noticed. "Go ahead and get that."

"Oh, it's okay. It's my business manager. I had to move some money around," Caroline said, reaching for it. "It's okay. I can deal with it another time."

She turned it off.

"You sure?" Danny said. "I know you have a lot of stuff going on right now, Caroline. I mean, I do too. It's okay. It's okay if you want to deal with it."

"Thank you, but I don't think I want to spoil this moment."

"I'm not going anywhere," Danny said.

Caroline held his glass out for him. They clinked their glasses, and each took a sip.

"I am willing to let it all go for a moment if you are," she said.

He picked up an oyster from the plate. "You want it?"

Caroline nodded. He stepped closer, and she gently opened her mouth. He placed the half shell of the oyster on her lower lip and tilted it upward. The briny liquid spilled into her mouth, followed by the creamy flesh of the oyster. Caroline chewed gently and swallowed as Danny watched her. A tiny trickle of saltwater seeped from the side of her mouth. He wiped it away, never breaking eye contact. He was so close to her she could feel the heat of his body through her clothes.

"Good?" he asked.

"Yes," she said. "Excellent."

A slow smile spread across his mouth, lifting his top lip slightly. Caroline felt a tingling in her chest. His eyes never left hers, but they did crinkle up at the corners when he smiled. She loved his crooked smile.

She reached over to the cold plate and picked up another oyster. She brought it up to his mouth and repeated the same action he'd taken with her, but Danny brought his hand to touch hers, tilting the shell up a little more and sliding the oyster into his mouth.

"Good?" Caroline asked.

"I don't think I've ever tasted anything so sweet," Danny said.

He leaned into Caroline, pressing her back up against the counter. He pressed his hips into hers. He grabbed his wineglass and took a sip, looking down at her. He brought the glass to her lips. She parted them, and he tilted the glass. She swallowed and licked her lips.

He took her glass of wine out of her hand and placed it on the counter next to his. "Well, maybe I have," he said, and he leaned his head down and brushed her lips with his.

Caroline's eyes fluttered closed, and she arched her back, thrusting her breasts into his chest and pulling his hips into hers. She opened her mouth and welcomed his tongue with her own. Like a flame, they erupted into one another, pulling and grabbing and tearing at clothes and hair until they were both naked and Danny held Caroline's leg over his hip.

He dragged a finger, then two, across her, and, feeling her slippery need, he thrust into her. She cried out, and he paused until he saw she was not in pain but in ecstasy. He pushed again into her, deeper, and Caroline clawed at his back and hips, begging him, pleading with him, not to stop. Never to stop. She wanted only to be there, in this way, with him.

Danny pulled out of her. She ached with the agony of her emptiness, but it was temporary. He pulled her to him, lifting her up and placing her down on the countertop, spreading her legs and entering her ever deeper, ever harder. The years had built up within them, and like the night sky on the Fourth of July, they ignited quickly and exploded in unison.

A moment passed. They returned to themselves. Danny gently pushed himself back and just a little away from her. He caressed her face.

"Yeah," he said. "I knew I'd tasted something sweeter."

~

They were curled into one another on the couch. Legs intertwined, toes toasty from the fire, plates and glasses empty.

"You used to say to me, 'We fit together like a puzzle.' Do you remember that?" Caroline said, leaning her head against his chest and playing with the button on his shirt. The shirt that she was now wearing.

"Oh my God, I was so cheesy." He laughed.

"No, stop. I loved it when you said that. We were adorable. And we did—we do—fit together like a puzzle." Caroline nuzzled into his chest. She felt happy, brilliantly, blissfully alive, and she was old enough to know she should soak in the moment. Float around in the happy for as long as she possibly could, which was why she kept her phone on silent.

"I think about you," she continued. "After all these years, if I'm really being honest with myself, I still do. Do you ever think about me?"

Danny didn't say anything. Caroline sat up and looked at him. "It's okay, I mean, if you don't. I get it. I mean, it's been a long time and—"

"You asked me before what the problem was with Michelle and me, or one of them anyway. Do you really want to know?"

Caroline nodded. "Yes, I mean, if you want to share that. Of course I do."

"She used to bring you up in couples therapy. She'd had all kinds of other relationships, but for me, it was different. For me, there was only you, only ever really you, that I ever cared about."

Danny looked at the fire, and then he smiled and shrugged, saying, "Michelle said I'd never really gotten over you." The fire cast a warm light on him. He adjusted his position on the couch. "More wine?"

"Yeah, I think so," Caroline said. "Danny."

He smiled at her, leaned in, and kissed her head. "It's okay. I know."

CHAPTER TWENTY

DEVORAH

Devorah had fallen asleep on her couch. She stirred, awakening to the sound of water splashing around in a half-full glass. *Thunk.* Said glass met the wood of the side table, placed there by an outstretched hand.

"Oh," she mumbled, confused and wiping at the spittle on the side of her mouth.

The hand belonged to Caroline, who was peering down at Devorah, smiling with an annoying concerned look on her otherwise unmoving face.

"What in the hell are you doing here? What the hell time is it?"

"It's eight thirty," Caroline said.

"In the morning? Well, Jesus, why?" Devorah swatted at the cobwebs in her brain. "Why are you here?" *And why is it so damn cold in the room?* she wondered. It felt gray and lonely, like the overcast sky had drifted inside. Devorah was waking up, pulling herself together. She looked down at the floor, around her feet, on the couch next to her. What was going on? What was she forgetting?

"Sorry, we didn't want to scare you," Caroline continued.

Devorah blinked again, rubbing her eyes. Her head throbbed. Resting on the table next to her, next to the fresh glass of water, was a cocktail glass, a sticky, wet cherry resting at the bottom, mashed and bloodied. *We?*

"I'm here with Danny," Caroline continued.

Danny? Devorah thought, at first confused and then remembering. She could make out Diaz standing behind Caroline. *Danny Diaz.*

"We came to check on you and see how you're doing. Help you with your work if you wanted to focus on something else, or make you something to eat or something."

Oh, right. Devorah remembered now. Sleep was dropping away, and it was all coming back to her.

Her sweet, gentle Mary Magdalene was gone. Her little friend was no more.

Devorah felt a wave of heartache crash over her, pulling her under and knocking her about in the quiet of the current. She clutched at her chest, at the big hole in it, as though she could cover it up or fill it in. And then she clutched at her head: another headache from the crying, from the drinking. Her eyes were puffy and crusty from tears.

She really was all alone now.

Devorah loathed self-pity, and as much as her heart ached, she would not drown. She closed her eyes, focused, and became aware of her present moment once again. Floating back to the surface, treading water, gasping for air, she turned her attention to a search. She'd find a way to numb herself, to make the hurt subside or at least replace it with something else that would take away the pain.

Her thoughts raged war. Why had this happened? *Did Mary know how I loved her so? Did she feel pain? Did she suffer?*

From somewhere deep in the neural pathways of her brain, a thought presented itself. It was a quote, heard long ago, almost as long ago forgotten, yet she remembered it now: "The worst suffering is a meaningless existence."

Someone had told her that once, or had she read it somewhere? And here it was. Yes, that sweet little dog had purpose. She'd meant something in this world. And aah, a sense of relief, and an area of space opened up within Devorah.

But there was more. She was forgetting something. What was it?

"Devorah? Are you okay?" Caroline asked.

Diaz stepped closer to look at Devorah, sizing her up with his fireman's eye. She looked at his left hand, resting on Caroline's lower back.

"Just give her a second," Diaz said.

They were twins standing in front of her, wearing matching looks of concern and blatantly scrutinizing her. It was annoying. Why? They meant well, right? Why should that bother her? Was it the way they looked at one another, telling a story with their eyes? The fact that they were now a pair that outnumbered her? Was it perhaps that, under their obvious concern, just this little bit of contentment lurked? Was that it? Were they . . . *happy*? They'd been in strife and struggle and were finding their way in the current to contentment.

And so what? Who cared? What the hell if they were? Mary Magdalene wasn't their goddamn dog. She wasn't their goddamn loss.

Devorah rubbed at her face again, pumping blood and building anger. And again, she felt some relief. The anger moved her up the scale from lost and despondent. Rage felt better.

"Give me a goddamn second to catch my damn breath," Devorah said.

Caroline rolled her eyes and sighed.

But there was something else, something nagging at Devorah. It wasn't just their underlying seething, spiteful happiness. She was slowly waking up, coming to, gathering information from the recesses of her furious brain.

As she picked up pieces and assembled them, she wondered at the meaning of any of it. Why was pain like this a facet of life? Were we really magnets? Was she courting this? Attracting this? Was she horribly flawed? And who the hell cared anyway? Was it even worth caring?

She was sad, sure. Her beloved furry friend was gone, so why the hell wouldn't she be sad? She was goddamn tired. Tired from grief. Tired *of* grief. But why was she sleeping on the couch? She hated falling asleep there. She rarely did it, after too many times awakening having slept fitfully and with a crick in her neck. She rubbed her neck now, struggling to remember the events of last night. What was nagging at her?

Larry had called. That's right. Her attorney. Yes, Larry called. He wanted to talk about the contract. That was it. Right? He needed her signature. He was waiting to get it back from her. He was talking about e-signing or some crap that made no sense to her. What the hell was wrong with a pen and a goddamn piece of paper, anyway? *Keep your email and pay for the messengers and send me the damn papers, for Chrissake,* she'd told him.

So they could proceed with the work. Right? The book. Caroline. That was it. Now Devorah remembered.

"We're here to help you, Devorah," Caroline said, breaking Devorah out of her momentary freeze.

"Diaz, what's your sign? Horoscope?" Devorah asked.

"I'm a Capricorn," he answered.

"Oh, that's too bad. Caroline's a Gemini." She turned to Caroline. "You should be with a Leo."

"A Leo?"

Danny chuckled, and Caroline sighed heavily.

"Don't laugh, it only encourages her," Caroline said to him.

"Yeah, a Leo, Caroline. That's what I said—a Leo. L-E-O. Jesus."

"Okay, Devorah, I'll take that into account," Caroline said in a very appeasing tone. "In the meantime, do you need anything? Want any help with anything?"

But Devorah didn't want help. Goddammit, she was sick and tired of the fight, of the helping, of the need for assistance. And Devorah had found what she needed to rid herself of heartache and grief. And it was right there in front of her, looking down on her. The sanctimonious high priestess of self-helpery was here to help—like Devorah was just some feeble old lady. "Really?" Devorah said. "Well, that's generous. Considering your own shit show."

It was clear to Devorah that Caroline and Diaz weren't sure what she meant by that. Mr. and Mrs. Fixit shared a look, then turned their focus back to her, broken and alone. Doing what they could to piece back together the old lady.

Devorah grabbed the glass of water.

"Good, you should definitely have some water," Caroline said. "And can I make you some tea or, I don't know, something else that's not coffee?"

"Why the hell do you look so—*happy*?" Devorah adjusted her body in the couch cushion, twisting so she could replace the water and grab the *New York Post* from where it had been on the side table.

"We were just talking about maybe getting out today. Doing something outside. Danny told me about the rail trail. The bike trail in Harwich? I'd like to go rent some bikes and do it," Caroline said. "It's very easy, level ground. And it sounds so great, so uplifting, to ride along past beaches and cranberry bogs, and there's even a general store we can stop in and buy an ice cream or something. It sounds so nice. Don't you think? I think you could do it too. It will really lift your spirits to be outdoors." Caroline smiled over at Danny, who nodded encouragingly.

Devorah made a *pfft* sound. Young love. *Ludus*, the Greeks called it. It was a playful, flirtatious love, full of passion. She rolled her eyes.

"I'm just feeling a little happy. What's wrong with that?" Caroline said.

"Oh, Jesus," Devorah said and shook her head.

"Don't. Come on," Caroline said. "Let's have a good day. I want to be here for you. We both do. I know this is hard."

"Here for *me*? What about you?"

Caroline looked confused.

"I think you better tend to your own garden there, missy," Devorah said, and when Caroline didn't stir, she added, "How do you not—wait—Jesus, you don't know?"

And then Devorah saw dread slide across Caroline's now frowning face. As it did so, Caroline's neck appeared to lock into a stiff, tight position, and she brought her hand up, massaging it.

Her knees buckling, she dropped down onto the couch.

Devorah opened the paper in front of her. Why the hell didn't she know? She thought Caroline was glued to her phone like everyone else on the planet. How could she be so disconnected? Didn't she know it was just a matter of time?

"What are you talking about?" Danny asked. "What is it?"

Devorah blurted out, "She's been canceled. That's what they call it, right?" Devorah directed her attention back to the paper, rummaging through it. "Susan Blunan-Flunan something or other is making some claims."

"What?" Caroline said, looking genuinely surprised. "Oh my God."

Devorah read from the paper in her hand, "Susan Noonan-Bunin." Devorah paused and looked up at Caroline. "Seriously?"

Caroline just nodded, looking simultaneously puzzled and annoyed.

"Okay, whatever. Anyway, moving on. Ms. Beckett's former assistant claims she was the victim of extraordinarily tortuous demands at the hands of her former boss."

"Like what?"

Devorah continued reading. "Beckett went off the rails when she discovered her husband's infidelity and she was notified of a pending lawsuit from her former mentor alleging copyright infringement, and she began making numerous repeated demands that her assistant adhere to strange behavior such as only looking at her left eye when speaking, never her right. She required Noonan-Bunin to walk only on the hardwood floors and never on the carpet, and she was never allowed to wear the color yellow under any circumstances. Noonan-Bunin said the work environment was hostile and that Beckett accused her of flaunting her sexuality. 'I can't help being a buxom, brawny woman,' Noonan-Bunin said. 'It's my curse. But I shouldn't have to be penalized in the workplace, or anywhere, for it.'"

"Oh, for God's sake." Caroline brought her hand to her forehead.

"That's ridiculous," Danny said.

"And it's not true."

Devorah paused reading and looked between Danny and Caroline. "There's a picture of her, too. Brawny. Huh."

"Why would she say that?" Danny asked. "You can sue her for libel or slander or whatever."

Caroline was motionless, like a deer in the headlights.

"It was on the news last night," Devorah said, thwarting the awkward tension in the room. "I thought you would have seen it or heard about it by now."

Caroline looked nauseated.

"Look, it begs the question," Devorah said. "What the hell's up with you and your assistants?"

"Right," Caroline said, avoiding Devorah's look, her voice sounding faraway. "I turned my phone off and left it in the guesthouse. I just . . . wanted an escape for a night. That was stupid of me. Really, really stupid."

"But it's not true," Danny said, looking slightly wounded. "Why would she say any of this stuff?"

"Looking to capitalize on my current misfortune and gain her fifteen minutes of fame, I guess?" Caroline shot an accusing glance at Devorah, who threw her hands up in the air. "Don't look at me, Caroline. I'm just the messenger."

"Well, you certainly seem happy to deliver the news. Jesus, I've got to call Thérèse." Caroline headed for the door. "I'm going to go get my phone."

The sound of the front door closing with a click, with Caroline on the other side of it, punctuated Devorah's perusal of the article. She looked up from the paper at Diaz. "Damn, not the most flattering picture of Caroline, but there you have it."

Diaz sighed, ran his hand through his dark hair, and positioned himself in front of the window looking out. He looked so uncomfortable, upset, and lost. What a shame. He looked like he did when he first moved into the guesthouse, but over the past few months, Devorah had seen that less and less in him. She realized over the past few days, since Caroline had arrived, he was different. He seemed pretty damn happy. He had been lost in ludus, the playful passion of a young love.

Well, not anymore.

"I'm sorry, Diaz," Devorah said. "That's a tough break."

"What do you mean? I don't know what that means. 'That's a tough break' . . . ?"

Ignoring his question, she shrugged and continued reading the article aloud. "It actually goes on to say, *It takes some nerve to proclaim perfection, sling a declaration of true love, and call yourself a 'Success at Life!' and then, after sales peak and the curtain is pulled back, the truth comes out, and the revelation is that a phony is at the controls, saying what we want to hear. Making promises that fall short, as they always do, as is always the case. Who knows, maybe next week Beckett will really be on trend and proclaim herself a lesbian? Let's see where sales go from there, shall we?* Oof." Devorah glanced up from the paper. "The gloves are really off now."

The front door swung open, and Caroline reentered the living room, a deep crease burning between her eyebrows. "She's calling me right back," she said.

"Well, I was just saying, you sure can pick 'em," Devorah said. "But then, I guess I can too. Isn't that right, Caroline?"

"What does that mean?"

"Nothing, Caroline. It means nothing. God. Relax," Devorah said, dancing around the conversation and having fun at Caroline's expense.

Danny looked uncomfortable. Caroline looked chafed, and Devorah's eyes were darting back and forth between the two of them like she was watching the US Open. Anyway, she thought, she'd made her point, and this Susan Looney-Bird one was clearly a nutjob and would be found out. The truth always came out.

"Thérèse . . . my manager . . ." Caroline looked deeply uncomfortable. "Look, I'm sorry to have to ask this again, but she said it would really help my brand, Devorah, if you'd be willing to put out a statement? You know, something announcing our collaboration and saying that you dropped the suit?"

"We'll see. Maybe. I'm just not sure."

"Right. Okay. Well, I have some calls to return and apparently a mess to clean up." Caroline turned to leave the room.

"Wait, wait, Caroline, one more thing," Devorah said as Caroline walked away. She winced and then said, "That Oaklyn one—God, what a stupid name! I mean, that is really dumb. Anyway, well, darling, she's preggers."

Caroline turned back around, shock blanketing her face. "What?"

Devorah saw the pain and the hurt, and suddenly she felt bad. This had grown out of control. She hadn't meant it to. Devorah paused for a brief moment, feeling just the slightest flicker of remorse for her callous delivery. She wasn't good at smoothing this stuff over, but Caroline needed to know this. Right? She shrugged. "It was on the news."

"Oh. Okay," Caroline said, still stunned. "I'll just . . . be outside for a little bit." She left out the front door.

Danny waited until they heard the click of the front door closing before saying, "Can I take a look at that, please?" He pointed and reached his hand out to receive the newspaper.

"I mean, it's pretty ridiculous that this stuff makes headlines in the *New York Post*," Devorah said, handing it over. "What the hell? I mean, I don't know, maybe politics in the Middle East got a little too redundant? Too bad those rich Armenian girls with body dysmorphia don't have any new sex tapes out, huh?"

Caroline's voice carried through the window as she paced in the driveway and talked on the phone. Danny put his attention on the paper in his hand, glancing only occasionally at the window and Caroline just beyond.

"Don't worry, Diaz," Devorah said. "As far as I can tell, Caroline is most likely not going to come out next week as a lesbian. Not that there's anything wrong with that, of course."

"Just stop," Danny said, turning to her, pain in his eyes. "Stop it right now."

"Jeez, take a joke," she said. "I was just trying to lighten the moment."

"It's just not funny," Danny said. "I know you're hurting, too, but sometimes it's just too much."

"Diaz," she said, chastened somewhat. "I'm sorry. It was a bad joke. You don't need teasing from me right now. And . . . Caroline's a good person. And so are you."

"Right," he said before walking out of the room and out the back door down to the beach.

Devorah found herself—as she always knew she would be—all alone.

CHAPTER TWENTY-ONE

CAROLINE

Caroline remembered reading an article about how listening to a particular song when you were doing something enjoyable would release serotonin and dopamine into your body and doing this repetitively would cause the same physical reaction within the body whenever you heard the song again. Well, this was true in Caroline's case, but in the inverse. Every time Caroline heard or felt the buzzing of her cell phone, she felt dread and despair that started in her brain and spread down to the tip of her (badly in need of a pedicure) toes.

She shook off the bad-juju vibes, picked the phone up from the desk where she sat zombielike, and, seeing it was Thérèse calling, took a breath and said, "Please just have something good to tell me."

Crackling down the other end, Thérèse said, "Well, I was kind of hoping you were going to say that to *me*."

"Oh God," Caroline said, her shoulders slumping, her head dropping to the side. She put the phone on speaker and picked a paper clip up from the pile on the desk in front of her. She pulled it apart, making it one long straight wire, and then folded it back in again on itself. The desk was brown and polished, with gold buckles and handles on the four drawers, and it was tucked into a nook in the sunny window. It had been the communal work desk in the middle of the house, mostly a coatrack or a place to rest a book to be read or a bill to be paid. Caroline remembered sitting there as a little girl and doing homework.

On one particular afternoon, her mother had leaned over her shoulder to check her work. Caroline couldn't remember the assignment now, but she did remember her mother saying, "Wow, you are so clever, Caroline."

It was a nice memory, and she smiled thinking about it. It wasn't often that she allowed herself to look back, and far less often did it make her smile when she did or when she thought of her mother. It had been a little less than two decades after that when Caroline was organizing Devorah's office on campus and the older woman leaned in, over her shoulder, and paid her the same compliment. "Wow, you are so clever, Caroline." And she never forgot that either.

Caroline thought she should stay in that mindset. She didn't want to tumble back down into the bucket of dread. There had to be a way out of this. There just had to be. And she knew it wasn't down the path of despair.

"Isn't there a cease and desist you can file again Susan? I mean, she's in breach of her NDA at the very least, right?"

"Well, yeah, about that nondisclosure agreement."

"Yeah?"

"She didn't sign one."

"What? Wait . . . *what?* Wait . . . what the actual hell are you talking about, Thérèse? How could that have happened? Did you ask Jeff about it? And where the hell is he? Why is he not returning my calls?"

"Yeah, about that . . . well, there's more."

Caroline felt dizzy. What more could there possibly be? The dread bucket was morphing into a big, fat barrel.

"What? What is it?"

"Well, it seems like Jeff might be a little conflicted right now."

"About what? For flying fig's sake, spit it out, Thérèse, or I swear to God I'm firing your ass."

"Jeff and Susan."

"What about them?"

"Well, apparently, Susan Noonan-Bunin is about to become Susan Noonan-Bunin-Truman."

"Shut the hell up. Shut up. Right now. Shut up."

"Susan Noonan-Bunin-Truman. I'm serious. She's engaged to Jeff. And she never signed an NDA or anything. At least we can't find any record of one."

"Jeff? And Susan? What? I thought Jeff was gay! Oh my God. What is happening?"

"Well, Caroline, you're sinking. The ship is still sinking. The brand is tanking. You know how fast this slide goes in this town, and you're already hemorrhaging money, plus Grant is taking half of whatever is left. Get a handle on this."

"Oh my God, I just can't believe this is all happening."

"Well, believe it. And get to work. I'm not a magician, Caroline. I need you to give me something better to work with. You've got to get Devorah to issue a statement. Okay?"

Caroline nodded.

"Okay?" Thérèse asked again.

"Uh, yeah," Caroline said. "I nodded. You couldn't see me. Whatever. Okay, yes, I'm on it. I'll do what I can, and I'll figure something out."

"That would help. And obv you're going to need another attorney."

"Right, of course."

"Good, I'll send you some names. Do it fast, okay?" Thérèse said. "I gotta run, I'm having a tapeworm implanted, you know, preholidays, so I can binge! Keep me in the loop! Kiss kiss."

Caroline hung up. She dragged the paper clip across the desktop, carving a deep worm-shaped gash into the old wood.

~

Caroline drove down Old Stage Road on her way back to Devorah's. She intended to focus on the beauty of New England rather than Susan's betrayal, her anger at Grant, and the impending dread she felt at having to beg Devorah for help. *You are more than this.* She heard the voice slap around in her head and thought, dammit, she just frigging had to be more than this.

She turned her focus on the present moment and not the scary future, and she got on the road. She'd always loved these winding country roads, and now was no different, even if she felt slightly nauseated from the less than smooth ride in the Jeep. From Old Stage, she made the turn onto Main Street. It was narrow and dotted with old stately homes built for sea captains, the long-ago celebrities on Cape Cod.

She drove along past the Centerville Historical Museum, which housed paintings, artifacts from the old shipping and whaling days, and temporary exhibits on things like Prohibition practices and ball gowns from a bygone era. A few doors down was the Captain David Kelley House, now a cozy bed-and-breakfast painted white with black shutters, sporting a rainbow flag and with a property line dotted with hydrangeas now well past their prime.

Just past that was the 1856 Country Store. Originally built in the 1840s to house harvested cranberries, it was turned into a general store in 1856 and had been a Centerville landmark from then on. The sign out front fictitiously proclaimed *Penny Candy*, but the mix of unusual, artsy souvenirs, locally made tchotchkes, and inflation-priced candy was a draw with locals and visitors alike.

Caroline slowed the Jeep and parked along the sidewalk out front. Devorah had a sweet tooth, and Caroline thought some fudge would earn her a few points. As much as she tried to consciously put one hopeful foot in front of the other, she was having difficulty shaking that antsy feeling. If Caroline was being really honest with herself, she knew this mess had been building for months, oxygen empowering a fire. And now she felt like she could have reached out and touched the tension, like a finger toward a hot stove.

Caroline shook the feeling away. She had her hand on the Jeep door and was about to swing it open when in her rearview mirror, she saw a familiar figure walking toward the store, coming from the opposite direction, closer to the town library in the distance.

She watched Danny growing bigger with each step forward, and her heartbeat quickened. He squeezed Chloe's small hand in his. The little girl looked so excited, and Caroline could hear her muffled laughter through her open window. And then Chloe's other hand stretched out behind her, tugging at the arm of a woman, her mom.

Michelle was laughing as she kept pace, single file behind Chloe and her dad.

Caroline felt her stomach rumble, hot lava bubbling. As she watched them grow larger, she ventured to bet there might be a postcard in that store with a happy family on it that looked just like the one she was peering at in the mirror. Or maybe inside a picture frame? A happy family, dressed in crisp white, with a beach setting as a backdrop, laughing, living, loving. Danny wore a light-blue button-down, a little polo-playing man above his heart. Michelle had on a bright-green-and-navy-blue paisley dress with brown riding boots, and a navy cardigan wrapped around her small waist. Chloe, in leggings and a turtleneck, was a mixture of her parents, with Danny's dark coloring and Michelle's wide-set hazel eyes. They must have been coming from Mass, Caroline thought. Our Lady of Victory church was just around the corner. There were several other families heading into the store, and now that Caroline thought about it, she could hear church bells over the chatter.

Danny threw back his head and laughed at something Chloe had said, and Michelle feigned fake horror that only delighted Chloe even more.

Caroline felt a prickle on her neck, and she sank down into the driver's seat, blocking herself from view. She prayed Danny wouldn't notice the Jeep.

She breathed a sigh of relief as they disappeared inside the store. She quickly restarted the engine and pulled into the street, checking the rearview mirror as she sped away.

When she put the Jeep in park in Devorah's driveway a few minutes—which felt like hours—later, she sat in the car a full five minutes before she stopped shaking, trying to make sense of why she felt so rattled.

~

Devorah wasn't answering the door, and, after a few minutes of ringing the doorbell, knocking, and waiting, Caroline walked around the side of the house toward the beach in the back. She thought maybe she could peer in the bay window or try knocking on the back door.

She didn't need to, though, as she found Devorah lounging in her Adirondack chair in the same clothes she'd worn yesterday. It was slightly windy. Caroline buttoned her sweater.

"Hi, Devorah," Caroline said. "I was knocking."

"Were you?"

"Yes, I thought I'd come and see how you're doing today."

"Fantastic. How are you doing?"

"Well, I'm not fantastic, really, but I'm glad you're doing better."

"Anyway, I had to get on the computer earlier and look up what a meme was, because they referenced them so much in the *Post* article about you."

"Yup, pretty humiliating," Caroline said, chafing slightly. "I used to think the worst thing that could happen on camera was maybe tripping and falling on my way up to get an award. Oh, how wrong I was."

"Indeed," Devorah said, sounding a bit like Vincent Price in Michael Jackson's "Thriller."

Caroline knew there was some test Devorah wanted her to pass or that she had something up her sleeve, but for the time being, she would just take in the beach and the salty air.

She sat in the hardwood-backed chair next to Devorah's and marveled at the view. The damn strange truth was, the past few days, working alongside Devorah and remembering—despite Devorah's cantankerous attitude and many criticisms—how truly accomplished her former mentor was, with her papers and her thoughts on philosophy, physics, and the spiritual and the metaphysical world, was all very refreshing. Back in the day, Caroline had enjoyed her time as Devorah's assistant. It was a refuge of sorts from the tumult in her life. She also knew, messed up as it was, that being with Devorah felt like the closest thing to home that she could remember. If, at times, Devorah was a bit salty and her words seemed wrapped in little packages of scorn and disdain, Caroline enjoyed a good verbal sparring session, and no one was better at it than Devorah. For so long, Caroline had been surrounded by yes-men and people who only told her what she wanted to hear. Well, what the hell had that gotten her?

And anyway, if Caroline had learned nothing else, it was that she hadn't outrun the chaos by running back home to Massachusetts. It had caught up to her. She'd been running away from this place for so long, she'd made a loop and found herself right back where she'd started.

No, that wasn't quite right. She wasn't right back where she'd started. In all the time away, she had actually accomplished quite a lot. She was proud, but her achievements meant there was so much more at stake, so much for Caroline to lose. She had to be careful. Caroline knew, deep down, that she always got what she asked for. It may have come wrapped up in different packaging or in a way that she didn't expect, but she had to believe that this mess would settle down. Her brand, her livelihood, her work, would be saved. Her broken heart would mend, and she would be happy. She believed it.

She knew that step one to getting her life back on course was Devorah van Buren.

Before Caroline could find the words or even know what it was she wanted to say, Devorah blurted out, "Plato said that our lives go wrong in large part because we almost never give ourselves time to think carefully and logically enough about our plans. And so we end up with the wrong values, careers, and relationships. Do you think that's true?"

"Oh, huh, I don't know, but yes, I guess so. I think that's probably true."

"Well, from where I sit, Caroline, you don't take the time to think. You got jaded. You wanted out of here, you wanted to be rich and famous, and you got that. Your motivation was pure, and your heart was in the right place. But then you drank the Kool-Aid, and you forgot to think. And now you're finding yourself in a little bit of a pickle, aren't you?"

Just like that, the wind changed direction and blew right at Caroline. She felt the hurt, the sting of it all: her husband's infidelity; her aching heart; her humiliation; her deep-rooted insecurity in her own abilities as a wife, a daughter, a friend, a writer. She could clearly see everything she'd worked so damn hard for was teetering on a precipice, and she felt completely ill equipped to control any of it. She had run away from the memory of her angry father and her disappointing mother. She had run away from Danny. She ran away from Grant, from Los Angeles. But now, she just couldn't run away anymore.

And suddenly, she felt pissed.

She cleared her throat, readied herself for battle. "Jesus, do you ever let up? You know, it's easy for you to say, here in your ivory tower on the beach, with your silver spoon childhood and your respectable career. I came from nothing. Everything I got, I worked for," Caroline said, and then immediately asked herself, What the hell was she doing? Why was she arguing with Devorah? She needed Devorah to stand up for her, to clear her name.

"So, you chased wealth and fame, and you got both, and tell me, did you find the happiness you were searching for? The happiness you preach to all your adoring fans?"

"Do I look happy, Devorah? No. Does that please you?"

"What are you really doing here?" Devorah asked.

Caroline took a deep breath. "I don't know if I know."

"What are you afraid of? Huh? David used to say, 'Stay out of fear; it closes you off to other people.' And you've always been fearless. What the hell is stopping you now?"

Caroline was going to respond, but Devorah continued, cutting her off. "My first husband was a bastard even worse than your dad. I got married a second time, but it didn't last because I didn't love him. But David, I took a chance with him, and I let myself love again. But his was an almost selfish love. David wanted all of me, all the time. He said he wanted me to work, to write my book, but when he retired and his world got smaller, he wanted all of my attention. And I loved him and I *wanted* to give him what he wanted. If I didn't, he always let me know how it bothered him. He was my family, all I had. So, for him, for us, I pushed my work to the side . . . my work always came second. I had some resentment, but I did it because I couldn't live without him. Or that's what I thought. And in the end I didn't really regret it; I didn't know how little time we would have together. And then he was gone, and I guess I just didn't care anymore. I lost the fire in my belly. But that was then, Caroline. It took me a while, but now, here I am. And I'm not done yet. I have more to say."

Caroline was confused, not really sure what had just happened. Devorah had never been so open with her before. She had never divulged such personal truths to her. It felt a little off kilter and not in keeping with their conversation, but more than that, it was strange to witness Devorah's vulnerability.

Devorah looked off into the distance for just a second, and then a switch was flipped, and she snapped back into the moment. "But then, you know," she said, "like the Greeks said, call no man happy until he is dead."

"Are you okay, Devorah?"

"I'm tired. I'm going to go lie down," Devorah answered, rising with great difficulty from the chair.

Devorah turned to go, but before she ducked inside, she turned back to Caroline and said, "Thank you for stopping by. Go home. We'll talk tomorrow."

~

Danny's truck pulled into the driveway as Caroline was halfway to her Jeep. There was no escape. And again, the fiery volcano bubbled in her belly. Caroline was going to have to get some damn Tums.

With a friendly wave, he pulled into his spot and joined her by her car. A flashback of the happy Diaz family ran through her overactive brain.

"Where you headed?"

"I think . . . I think I'm just going to head back to my parents' place," Caroline said without looking at him.

"Oh, okay. You doing better?"

"Yeah, yeah. Fine. I'll be fine. I'm fine."

"I called you. I wanted to find you and see how you're doing and tell you, you know, not to worry." He paused a moment, waiting for her response. "This stuff always blows over."

"Yeah. I saw that you called. Thank you."

"Are you . . . is there something else wrong? Are you upset with me for some reason?"

"No, no, of course not. I'm not upset, just . . . I have a lot going on in my life right now," Caroline said. She felt like a big eruption was building in her stomach.

"It seems like something else is bothering you. Are you okay? What's going on? Is there something else?"

"No, I don't know. I just . . . I mean . . . What are we doing here?"

"I thought we were spending time together. Enjoying each other's company," Danny said. He looked stunned.

"I know. Yes. We are. We were. I feel like there's just a lot going on. I'm sorry."

"You're sorry? What does that mean? What are you sorry for? You said that you've got a lot of stuff going on. Okay. Me too."

"I know. I know you do."

"Caroline, I want to help, or just be here for you. This time. All of this is going to go away, and you're going to be fine."

"But it's not just going to go away. And there are other people involved."

Caroline turned away from him. She felt overcome.

"What do you mean by that? Where are you going?"

She felt like a train wreck. Her marriage was a sham; her career was in flames. Every friend she had in Los Angeles had disappeared. She was a loser. And now she was bringing Danny, and in some way his family, into all this? She needed to clear her head and think about what she was doing to him. Her keys felt heavy in her hand. "I'm just trying to not be selfish."

Danny looked flustered. "I don't know. I mean . . . I don't know how, but you just need to keep putting one foot in front of the other. Isn't that what you say? Isn't that one of the main things you talk about in your book? Caroline, just don't close me out. I'm here to listen, if you want me to."

"I'm sorry. I think—I think I should just maybe work some of this stuff out on my own."

"Seriously?"

Her palms were sweaty, and she felt like running. She was so very good at running, dodging, deflecting. She wanted—she needed—to be anywhere but here. "I'm sorry, I have to go."

"You don't have to go, Caroline."

"I do, Danny. I really do," she said, climbing into the Jeep and starting the engine.

CHAPTER TWENTY-TWO

DEVORAH

Devorah slept fitfully. She dreamed an angry pack of coyotes cornered her, tormenting her with their menacing growls. Slimy drool mixed with blood dripped from her arms and legs as their sharp teeth cut into her, leaving her feeling more exhausted when she woke up than when she'd gotten into bed the night before.

A good manicure would be relaxing and make her feel better. She was feeling rebellious, so she chose a bloodred OPI color, handed it to the manicurist, and settled into the salon chair. She had been going to the same salon for years, but it had been close to a year since her last visit. She liked the manicurists here because they were fast, efficient, cheap, and they didn't ask her any annoying questions. She hated the awkwardness of sitting across from a complete stranger rubbing and massaging her hands and feet and making small talk. Devorah wanted to go in, relax, close her eyes, and then, half an hour or so later, be on her way.

Unfortunately, that afternoon, she got the new girl. And, unfortunately for the new girl, no one let her know that Devorah was (as she told the owner when she checked in and was alerted there would be a five-minute wait but she would just love the new girl) "just there for a manicure, not to make friends."

Devorah sat with her nails soaking in the soapy water, eyes closed. The strong scent of acetone and sanded plastic made her feel nauseated, but she ignored it. This was self-care at its finest. *Philautia,* as the Greeks called the love of self. She was taking the reins and doing things to make herself feel and look better. For whom?

Well, she didn't know, and she didn't want to give it too much thought either.

"Oh, wait, I think I know you," New Girl said. "I used to work at Bamboo Forest. I used to see you in there, right? You're the one with the little dog?"

Devorah's eyes fluttered open. In her most annoyed tone, she said, "I don't have a dog." She closed her eyes.

"Really? You don't have that little Chihuahua? He was . . . well, kind of cute? That wasn't you?"

Devorah didn't say anything; she just sighed a bit more heavily and looked to her left. She was so tired. She wished she had stayed home and taken a nap instead of going to the salon. She didn't feel quite right, and this wasn't helping.

"Yeah, he used to sit with you at the table. We all talked about it," New Girl said, filing Devorah's nails. "He was so cute, or you know, it was cute that you brought him all the time. Where is he?"

"I told you I don't have a dog," Devorah said, starting to feel rather unwell, like everything she was trying to file away and paint over was folding back in on her like a scratchy weighted blanket.

New Girl finally picked up on Devorah's aggravated tone and grew quiet. Then, suddenly, Devorah pulled her arm away.

"Ouch." Devorah rubbed her arm. "What are you doing, you stupid girl?"

"What? I didn't do anything. I was just filing your nails. What's wrong?"

"That really hurts," Devorah said, still rubbing her arm.

"I don't know what happened. I didn't do anything."

The owner of the nail salon, a middle-aged man called Ahntuan, came over and asked, "What's wrong here?"

"She hurt my hand. She's an idiot," Devorah said, rising from her seat.

Ahntuan said something in Vietnamese to New Girl, who pleaded her innocence, but Devorah stood up. She'd had enough, and she was taking her tingling fingers the hell out of there.

"This place is a nightmare. That really hurt. You're going to go out of business with this kind of garbage," she said over her shoulder as she made her way painfully to the front door and pulled it open. She felt breathless and pissed off and continued her tirade all the way out into the parking lot and in the car on the way home.

When Devorah entered the house, she was disappointed to discover Caroline was there. Why had she given her that key, anyway? "Hey, how are you doing?" Caroline said. "I thought I'd get a head start. It's going pretty well."

"Oh, Jesus, whatever," Devorah said as she pushed past her and into the house.

"What's up?" Caroline asked. "You okay?"

"I'm tired," Devorah said. "Can't an old lady be tired, for Chrissake? I earned it, didn't I?"

"Okay, clearly a touchy subject, but I thought you wanted to chat. You told me to come over tomorrow. Today is tomorrow."

Devorah had forgotten she'd said that.

"Well, maybe I changed my mind?"

"Jesus, Devorah, what is the deal? I'm trying to be here for you."

"Don't give me that. You're trying to cover your ass," she said. She felt winded and warm. She fanned herself with a piece of mail. "Haven't you learned anything? Haven't you been listening?"

Caroline rolled her eyes. "What are you talking about? You know, Devorah, this 'I'm old and salty' bit is getting kind of tired. Don't you think?"

Tired? Devorah thought. She was, indeed, so very tired. Is that what it was? She was getting confused, and it hurt her head to think about it. "Just shut up, will you? Why don't you just leave?"

"God, I was trying to help you."

"You were trying to help yourself."

"Why are you such a monster? You have held my feet to the flames over all of this crap with the book, and I'm tired of it! Okay? I worked for you years ago, and you did nothing with it. I took the material, and I took Saint Teresa's *mansions* and Descartes's questioning, and I found a way to make it more accessible and used it to mold a clear path to virtue. To happiness. I did that. I made something of all that work. You would have just let it sit there in a snobby, wordy, banal text that no one would read. It would sit on a shelf and rot away, like you've been doing here for the past however long since David died. And you can't stand that I did it. Me, little loser Caroline with the messed-up family, doesn't need the bread crumbs you threw at us for all those years. I achieved something. And you know what, Devorah? You want to drop all the rest of this, our new book? Fine. You want to sue me? Fine. Go ahead. Sue me!"

Devorah felt dizzy. She grabbed the side of the couch as she watched Caroline angrily picking up her things.

Caroline turned back around. She was frowning and looking at Devorah with concern. "Are you okay?"

"I don't know. I think I must have eaten some bad fish." Devorah shifted more fully onto the couch. She brought her hand to her forehead. She was feeling a little antsy, anxious, but couldn't figure out why.

"When did you eat last?"

"Will you just bring me some damn water?"

"Please?"

"Please," Devorah said.

Caroline looked at her a little closer and said, "Wait, look at me, Devorah."

Devorah looked at Caroline.

"Stick your tongue out," Caroline said.

"What? Why?"

"Just do it."

Devorah stuck her tongue out.

"Smile."

"What the hell are you doing?" Devorah said, annoyed.

"I'm trying to determine if you've had a stroke. So, *smile.*"

Devorah did as she was told.

"Okay, it's not a stroke. I don't think." Caroline looked worried. "Do you want me to call someone or call 911?"

"Look, I'm fine. I'm tired. Just please, stop with all the hysterical stuff," Devorah said. She didn't feel okay, but she wasn't sure what was going on. "I'm okay, I think. Okay? Yes, I am. I'm just thirsty, I think."

"Let me get you the water," Caroline said, moving toward the door.

"Yes, okay," Devorah said. "Water sounds good. And my Top-Siders."

Devorah waited patiently. She felt antsy. What was that sound? What was that annoying sound? And what the hell was taking Caroline so damn long? Devorah let the thought slip away as Caroline returned to the room, handed her the glass of water, and held up Devorah's navy blue leather Sperry Top-Siders.

"Yes," Devorah said. "Thank you. Will you put them on for me?"

"Sure," Caroline said and knelt on the floor in front of Devorah.

"Hurry," Devorah said.

"What is going on?"

"I just feel a little light headed, I think. I want to walk. Help me stand up."

Caroline felt her forehead. "You're not warm, but you look a little flushed," she said. "I think I should call 911."

"Don't you dare," Devorah said. "I'm fine. I just didn't sleep well last night, and I haven't been eating well. That's all. I will be fine with this water. And then I think I just want to watch television for a minute."

"I'm going to get a wet facecloth."

"Why?"

"You're sweating."

"No. Stop. Will you please just stop?" Devorah said. "I'm fine. I'm fine. Just . . . just sit with me. Don't go anywhere. Just stay with me, Caroline. Okay?" She was almost pleading with Caroline, who looked concerned.

"Okay," Caroline said. "Of course." She sat down next to Devorah and, picking up the remote, asked, "What do you want to watch?"

"I think . . . I think I'm going to throw up," Devorah said. She leaned forward.

"Oh my God, okay. Okay. It's okay." Caroline grabbed the big white vase on the side table. She pulled the flowers out and thrust the vase under Devorah's mouth. With her other hand, Caroline pulled out her phone. "That's it, I'm calling 911. You need to see someone."

Devorah retched into the vase. Not very much came out. She was very quiet and calm, which was in direct contrast to Caroline, whose energy was becoming more frenetic by the second.

"Hi. Yes. I'm with a friend, and she is not feeling well. Seventy-seven Long Beach Road, Centerville. Yes. This is my cell phone. She is seventy-three years old. She is throwing up and feels light headed. Yes. No, she's breathing. Yes, she's totally responsive. Yes," Caroline said, smiling assuredly and squeezing Devorah's hand.

"I think I feel . . . ," Devorah said but didn't finish her thought. She was not listening to Caroline. She thought she wanted to finish her sentence and say "a little better now." She thought about it, and she could feel the breath in her chest pushing inward and then out again. But she was also feeling a little more dizzy. She was starting to feel like the room and everything in it was far away from her. There was a distance forming, but then she looked over at Caroline, smiling at her, and she felt so happy. She was so happy, relieved even, that Caroline was there with her. More than just happy not to be alone, and she didn't know what was going on, but having Caroline in the room was reassuring. For once, Devorah didn't have to make the decisions about what to do.

Someone else could be in control for a bit. No one liked to be sick all by themselves, even when they were vomiting. And Caroline was so smart and so capable. Had Devorah mentioned that before? That she thought Caroline was smart? She'd have to remember to do that just as soon as she caught her breath.

Caroline was still on the phone, answering questions from the 911 operator. Every now and then she'd direct a few questions at Devorah, who wasn't really listening anymore. She heard that annoying sound again, and it was coming from the old grandfather clock directly across the room from where she was sitting. It had belonged to David's parents. She'd always hated that clock. The chimes were not pretty but rather clunky and ugly. And the dark wood that encased the gears and mechanics was depressing. Why did she keep that stupid clock? And why was it in the room she spent most of her waking hours in? And why had she never heard it before now, and why hadn't she acknowledged how much she hated the look of it?

"I hate that clock," she said to Caroline, who paused her phone call.

"I'm sorry, one second," Caroline said as she held the phone away from her mouth. "What did you say, Devorah?"

"I hate that clock. It's ugly," Devorah said. Her voice was monotone, and to her ear it felt faraway.

But Caroline laughed. She said into the phone, "No, she's just complaining. Which is a good sign. Maybe she's getting back to normal. But she doesn't look right."

Devorah heard Caroline laugh, the sound muffled. The sun was shining through the window behind them, and Devorah loved how it backlit them and cast them in a golden glow. Devorah felt sleepy, and the nausea was still there, but it was such a large, beautiful room, and she let her eyes travel around the space as if for the first time. It was a happy room where Devorah had so many cherished memories over the years. It was comfortable for her and a wonderful representation of her likes, her personality—hers and David's. All the blues and whites came together and gave one the impression of uniformity and control, that all was being taken care of. All was under control, but the lines were starting to cross over each other and fold in on themselves. Or were they? Maybe it just seemed that way.

A roar came from outside the window. The dark Atlantic was putting on her show. It was so simple in that room, but it encompassed everything: the order and beauty, the chaos and ugliness. Devorah loved every detail. Except for the stupid clock that seemed to be getting louder. Back and forth went the ugly gold pendulum. As soon as this was over she was going to get rid of that garbage.

She could hear Caroline. "Devorah? Devorah?" Caroline sounded faraway, but Devorah looked over and saw her seated right next to her. They were holding hands. It felt good to have someone holding her hand. It felt good to have that someone be Caroline.

Caroline. Caroline is here with me. I am not alone. I am never really alone.

Devorah smiled at Caroline; at least she thought she did. When she looked into Caroline's eyes, she saw the opposite emotion, Caroline's forehead crease pressing deep into her head. *Don't frown,* Devorah thought. *You've got such a pretty face. Don't frown, Caroline.* Had Devorah ever told Caroline how beautiful she was? Ever since she was a little girl. She was always such a beautiful, talented young girl, despite everything.

And then a burning from somewhere deep inside Devorah bubbled, and the pain began to spread and radiate through her with a desperation, down both arms, through her torso and legs, and back up into her shoulders and neck, until it consumed her fully.

Devorah gasped for breath, searching for some kind of escape from the horrible, terrible pain.

From many miles away, she could hear Caroline yelling into the phone. Who was she talking to? Why was she telling them to hurry? Where were they going? Devorah looked down at her hand entwined in Caroline's. The burning overwhelmed her. The heat was agony, and everything hurt, but their entwined hands kept her grounded, tethered in the room.

Devorah looked into Caroline's eyes, begging her to deliver some relief from the pain, but the eruption that had been threatening could wait no longer. The volcano burst forth with all the vengeance of an angry demon, and searing pain unlike anything Devorah had ever experienced tore through every single part of her like flames across a dry Southern California hillside.

At that very instant, their eyes locked, and Devorah squeezed Caroline's hand so tightly that Caroline screamed, "Devorah! Stay with me!"

But the pain swallowed Devorah up, and the explosion tore through her. There was nothing left. She let go, falling backward into the couch. Her eyes rolled skyward, her mouth dropped all the way open, and the last of her breath rattled out from her body.

She deflated and sank into the couch like a popped balloon as the sound of sirens and Caroline's screaming began to fade into blissful nothingness, and then . . .

David?

CHAPTER TWENTY-THREE

CAROLINE

The moment she heard the siren in the driveway, Caroline ran to and flung open the front door.

"Hurry! Oh my God, hurry! She's in there," Caroline cried frantically as the four uniformed firefighters glided past Caroline and entered the house, the EMT with the big orange case rushing in first.

"In there, down the hall. Hurry, please, please, please, oh my God."

"Ma'am?" one of them asked. "Ma'am. Can you look at me, please, ma'am? Look at me."

Caroline pulled her eyes away from the living room and looked at the young man. He had short brown hair and serious eyes but a kind face. Caroline tried to calm her brain and listen to the words he was saying to her.

"Okay. Ma'am, I need you to calm down."

"I'm sorry," Caroline said. She was hysterical. She was hot, and she couldn't catch her breath. She was on the verge of hyperventilating.

"Look at me. I need you to breathe, okay?" the man said, his eyes forcing sanity into her frantic brain. "We are doing what we can for her, but I'm going to need your help. Okay? Ma'am?"

Caroline focused on him. She willed herself to listen and do what he was asking her, but all she could see was the horrible faraway look in Devorah's eyes.

"I've got her, Tony," Diaz said from the doorway.

"Danny!" Caroline sobbed and ran to him. She crumpled into his arms. "Danny? Oh my God, Danny."

Danny wrapped his arms around her.

"We need her prescriptions," the man said.

"Okay, we'll get them," Danny said and turned back to Caroline. "Listen, I need you to go upstairs and get her prescriptions from the medicine cabinet in her bathroom. She has a daily pillbox. Can you do that? Can you find that for me?"

"Yes, yes, I can do that," Caroline said, grateful to have a task. Grateful to have Danny.

Caroline tore up those steps like it mattered. She had never been in Devorah's bedroom. She had never had any reason to be in there. It was large and white and sparsely decorated. The massive king-size bed was set against a gray wall, facing a floor-to-ceiling window. The room felt hazy. She felt like she was walking through fog, but she realized the haze was from the windows. They were coated with dried-up salt residue on the exterior of the glass.

She pushed on, into the bathroom on the other side of the room. The room was starkly white, a crisp contrast to the fuzziness in the bedroom. Subway tile with a mosaic of the moon in a dozen shades of blue took up one wall of the step-in shower. In her panic, Caroline knocked toothpaste and hairbrushes over as she dug through the mirrored cabinet in search of the pillbox and any prescription bottles. She was shocked to discover almost a dozen bottles in a drawer.

She snatched them all up and ran back through the room and down the stairway into the living room, where the men hovered over Devorah. Devorah was on the floor just in front of the couch. Her shirt was ripped open, her large pale breasts bare and splaying out on either side of her chest. They bounced around helplessly as the uniformed man pushed down on her chest, hand over hand, administering CPR. He was pushing and counting, pushing and counting.

Danny turned to see Caroline and stepped in front of her, blocking her. He reached out his hand to take the pill bottles from her.

"Thank you," he said.

"Is she going to be okay? What's happening?" Caroline choked out the words. "Danny, she just . . . she was fine, and then she said she wasn't feeling good, and then she just . . . like, fell back and made a horrible sound, like a gurgling sound."

"You did a good job."

"I can't believe it. I can't believe this is happening."

"I know. I know."

"I tried to help her. I didn't know what was happening."

"I know, it's okay. You did the right thing."

"What is it, Danny? What happened? What's wrong with her?"

"It looks like she's had a heart attack."

"Oh my God!"

"Right now, we just need to let them do what they can do, okay?" he said, looking at Caroline with sadness in his eyes.

Behind him, Caroline saw the others lift Devorah onto the stretcher they'd laid out beside her on the floor. "Why don't you wait outside? I'll come get you."

"Is she going to be okay?"

"They're doing what they can."

Caroline saw them rolling the stretcher toward the front door. "It was bad. It was really bad, right?"

There was a blue tube attached to her arm and a mask over her face, but all Caroline could focus on was Devorah's navy blue Top-Sider. It dangled off the side of the stretcher, bobbing back and forth until one of the men noticed it and lifted her leg up, placing it beside the other. Caroline felt her blood turn cold.

"What's going on, Danny?" Caroline said. "Is she—"

"Let's just hold off a minute. Okay?" Danny said. His eyes were so intense, so brown. They looked like big, sad pools of dark paint.

"Oh my God, I can't believe this. She's like . . . ," Caroline cried. "She's like my family, Danny."

"I know she is."

"Oh my God, I did this. I did this. I upset her. What's happening?"

"Listen, I need you to just stay here. I'll be back in just a second."

She waited just a moment, then followed the firefighters out the front door facing the driveway. She watched them loading Devorah into the back of the ambulance. It occurred to Caroline that they were moving slowly. Why? Why hadn't they sprinted out the door?

From her perch just inside the doorway, Caroline looked back inside at the empty house. Just seconds ago, it had been loud and filled with people and sounds and energy, and now it was completely still. And quiet. It was so, so quiet.

Caroline felt cold. She didn't want to move, stuck between inside and outside. She turned back around. She could see Danny in the distance. It felt like he was miles away from her.

She turned her head back around, taking in the large, empty blue-and-white vase, the Elizabeth Mumford painting of the Centerville penny candy store, the Claire Murray mermaid rug, Devorah's keys on the hook under the light switch by the door. In the gentleness of the moment, she knew she could feel something else, something she'd never experienced before. She could not put a name to it, but it felt like a presence. It was warm.

Caroline stepped back inside the house, feeling the quiet warmth all around her, above her, in between everything. She felt like she was not alone. Wrapping her arms around her shoulders, she felt the light, the levity, and she also felt *finality*. And suddenly that scared the living hell out of her.

She didn't want to feel that. She didn't want to feel anything anymore.

Caroline heard footsteps crunching on the seashell driveway behind her, just as her phone began to buzz. She pulled the phone out and looked at it as she turned to see Danny, his expression grim, his shoulders rounded and heavy.

As he walked the many miles toward her, she hit the off button on her phone, sending Grant's call to voicemail.

"Why are they moving so slowly, Danny?"

"Listen, Caroline." Danny had tears in his eyes. He looked at the ground. "It was bad. It was a bad one, okay?"

"I have to tell her I'm sorry. It's my fault. I was so mad at her. I said things . . ." Caroline moved toward the ambulance, still idling in the driveway. The lights flashing, spinning, but there was no urgency behind them.

"Caroline, stop, don't do that," Danny said. He stepped in her way, blocking her from the ambulance. "Caroline."

"No, don't," she said, flinching and pulling away from him. "No. No. This didn't happen. That can't be it. This can't be how this ends. It just can't! Please. I need to tell her I'm sorry."

"Sorry for what?"

"I said something terrible to her," Caroline said. "I am terrible. I've done terrible things."

"Listen, we just have to take a breath here, okay? Just take a second. This is . . . this is a shock. Okay? Let's just breathe for a second. I mean. Man. Oh God." Danny dropped his head back and looked up at the sky. He exhaled through his nose.

Caroline looked at him through her tears. She couldn't believe what was happening. She couldn't believe what had happened.

"I did it," she cried, consumed with shame and guilt.

"Did what?" Danny said. He reached out to her again, and, again, Caroline pushed him away.

"I was so mad at her. I was telling her off."

"Don't do this to yourself, Caroline. This wasn't your fault. You know that, right?"

"Everything she said I did, that I stole from her, that I used her, I think that was true."

"Caroline."

"Oh my God." She retreated back up the steps into the house to find her pocketbook and keys. She couldn't stand being there for another second.

CHAPTER TWENTY-FOUR

CAROLINE

The tiny chapel by the sea smelled of Casablanca lilies. They were Devorah's favorite flower. The church was quaint, right out of a New England picture book. Caroline felt overwhelmed, still reeling from the shock of watching the life, spirit, virility of the inimitable Devorah van Buren slip away right before her eyes. She was nauseated, wallowing around in her grief.

Around her, the pews were half-full. She had put out the word of Devorah's passing on social media and in the local and Boston papers. Former colleagues, students, neighbors, friends showed up. But not many, around two dozen total. Caroline sat behind the family, a first cousin and her husband and their two adult sons.

Caroline looked around at the other mourners, knowing hardly any of them. Most looked to be in their seventies: probably Devorah's colleagues from the university who had aged beyond Caroline's recognition. She recognized Officer Sorrenti, her old high school classmate, who was there with an older woman Caroline assumed was his mother.

Caroline closed her eyes and felt a wave of sadness wash over her. She couldn't help reliving the whole incident—watching Devorah struggle to take her last breath and wondering if she could have done something more to help her. *Could* she have done more?

Caroline inhaled slowly, then exhaled, turning her focus once again to the other congregants. She was desperate to feel a connection with them, to feel tethered to something bigger than herself. But there was no security, no structure to latch on to. In this earthly place, people like Devorah were just plucked from existence, here one day, gone the next. No one made it out of here alive. *There is no sure footing. There is nothing to hold on to. We are all just like cows in a tornado, getting tossed around and going whichever way the twister twists.*

But the real issue was, as much as Caroline wanted to feel better somehow, she didn't think she deserved to, not after all she had done.

The sun shone through the stained glass window, and the reds, greens, and yellows fell on the casket in the middle aisle near the altar. How odd. How beautiful. The church held memories of a childhood long ago forgotten. Caroline hadn't been to the church in years, not since she buried her parents. As a young girl, she used to attend Mass here with her father, who rarely missed a Sunday. It was one of the only activities he ever did alone with her, but he did it on a consistent basis. Caroline had wished they could do something else instead, like go to a water park or the candy store or mini golf or some other activity where they could at least converse, but she accepted it.

The church itself was a bright and cheerful place. It was in direct contrast to the enormous, high-ceilinged building she attended only on holidays in Los Angeles. Being back inside these walls, she recalled singing "God Bless America" during summer services on July Fourth, when the pews were filled with Kennedys and their relations and the other patriotic inhabitants of Barnstable, both rich and poor. She remembered that feeling of innocence, of childhood, of being a little girl, and she longed for the connection she had then, the sense of belonging to a church, a notion religion had given her. It felt so comforting to have a label. To believe in something good that wasn't visible but was all around her and was just as easy to put out of mind when she left the building. Caroline wanted so badly to slip back in time to those sleepy moments, listening to Bible verses in the warm, cozy church and thinking only of which donut she would choose after Mass. But she wasn't a little girl anymore. That time was over.

Her attention was pulled to Danny, who stepped out into the aisle and headed up to the lectern. Stunned and grieving, they had spoken only of Devorah and the logistics involved in planning the wake, funeral, and reception that would follow after the burial, and nothing of Caroline's admission. Everything felt different now.

"Good afternoon, my name is Daniel Diaz. I know many of you, but for those I don't—hello. We are here today to celebrate, to commemorate, the life of the inimitable Devorah van Buren."

Danny seemed nervous. She was grateful he'd offered to eulogize Devorah. There were no other candidates, really. Well, other than herself. She was a public person, a public speaker, but she worried about drawing attention away from Devorah. And anyway, it would have been too much. She couldn't do it. She couldn't do Devorah justice. Danny was a good, brave man. He would always do the right thing, unlike her.

He continued. "I first met Devorah a few years ago. I was at the Par-Tee Freeze—the local ice cream slash mini golf place here in town. Devorah was ahead of my daughter and me in line. She was holding her little dog, Mary Magdalene. Oh, she loved that dog. Anyway, it was just a regular day, and my daughter was deciding what she wanted, and as we waited, I could hear Devorah ordering. The young lady at the counter must have remembered Devorah as a regular customer, but it didn't sound like they were having a friendly exchange."

At this, the mourners laughed a bit, and Danny paused. He was looking at someone in the far corner of the church pews. He nodded and continued. Caroline glanced behind her and saw Michelle Diaz looking on from a pew midway back, her eyes glued to Danny. It was her he had been looking at. She must have heard him tell this story before. They had so much history. Chloe sat beside her on the pew. Caroline felt a pang of something . . . jealousy, probably, but maybe something closer to heartache. Michelle looked over, and they locked eyes. Michelle looked away first, which made Caroline feel worse, embarrassed. Michelle was pretty, with soft shoulder-length brown hair and sad eyes. It was too much, Caroline thought. There was so much pain in her eyes, pain in the room.

"What I could make out from their conversation was that Devorah had been a regular daily customer, but she hadn't been there in a few weeks, and she didn't want her regular order this time. No, this time she only wanted one cone. No, I heard her say again, she didn't need the other cone. She didn't want the other cone. The young girl didn't seem to connect the dots that she didn't need the extra cone because the person that cone belonged to wasn't here anymore. It filled me with such a sadness when I told the story later that evening."

As he spoke, he looked in Michelle's direction many times. It seemed to Caroline as if he were speaking to Michelle alone. They had years of stories, not all of them bad, clearly. Caroline and Danny had history, sure, but Michelle had been married to Danny Diaz for years. Pragma love, committed, long-term love. She had taken his name. She was his family. Storge love, familial love. They had a daughter together. A child! They were a unit. And, well, if you couldn't turn to your family when death reared its ugly face, well then, when the hell could you?

Caroline was torn up. But she deserved to feel twisted and unhappy. She didn't want that for him. She wanted Danny to feel comforted. If she was being really honest, when she looked at Danny and Michelle, she missed the familiarity of Grant, of their marriage, or, at least, of what their marriage used to be. She missed being wholly connected to another. Or maybe she missed something that never was. Maybe she missed the vision of what she wanted their marriage to be.

Everything felt overwhelming and slightly blurry, and she was starting to feel a rage building inside. She didn't think she could trust her thoughts. Or her heart. Devorah would find this whole mess confounding, humorous, and super annoying.

Devorah . . . where did you go?

"As she turned away from the window," Danny continued, bringing Caroline back to the present moment, "I smiled at Devorah, and she looked up at me and said, 'What the hell are you looking at?'"

Laughter filled the church. Caroline joined in until the thought of never hearing Devorah's nasty, salty mouth ever again hit her like a ton of bricks. Caroline felt the hot bubble of tears rise up and spill out of her. The shock of bearing witness to, and the comprehension of the finality of, death washed over her. She felt the loss of a unique woman, her friend. She wanted to scream and pull her hair out for all the time she'd wasted. She wept for Devorah and felt sorry for herself for wanting to be more like Devorah and not knowing how and not being able to ask her. And she acknowledged the fear, her very real fear, of not knowing how to move forward with the mess that was her life. She was terrified, knowing that even if she were provided an exact road map of how to get herself together and back on track, she wouldn't be strong enough to do it.

Danny again pulled Caroline's attention. He was speaking about the next time he saw Devorah around town. She was alone except for Mary Magdalene, and he ran into her at a restaurant in town, and they were both seated at the bar. He bought her a drink, a Maker's Mark manhattan, and after she made sure he wasn't hitting on her—people laughed again—they had a chat about Chihuahuas and how if it wasn't a Chihuahua, it was just a dog. Danny told the mourners he thought of Devorah as not so much a mother figure but more like a naughty aunt. He told them of her many amazing accomplishments as a scholar, professor, and author.

"Devorah was salty. She called it like she saw it. She had seemingly little to no filter whatsoever, but to quote Plato, someone she devoted years of her life to studying and teaching, 'no one is more hated than he who speaks the truth.' She was sometimes cutting and angry, and for some reason, people didn't think it was okay for her, this older woman, to speak her mind or be angry. I'm glad she didn't care and was exactly who she was. I will miss her."

After a moment, Caroline watched him walk back down the aisle and take his seat next to Michelle and Chloe. As he passed her, he smiled, and she nodded and wiped away a tear.

When the service ended, the mourners filed out of the church and gathered around front. Caroline felt her broken heart swell just a bit when she saw Grant in the group of people as she made her way down the few stairs to the courtyard. He had come to the funeral. Now that was something. She was so emotionally drained, she didn't have it in her to be furious with him. She was tired of being a stranger. She craved the familiarity of family.

Grant stood out in a crowd. He always did. His white hair, set against the black suit and sunglasses, made him look like one of the models he was always shooting. He made his way over to Caroline and leaned down, pressing his lips into her hair. She felt his strong arms envelop her as she slid into his embrace.

"Thanks for coming," she said, meaning it. She was grateful he was there. Sometimes it just felt so good to be held.

"Sweetheart, I got here as soon as I could," Grant said, just above a whisper, his chin resting on Caroline's head. "I slipped in and sat in the back. I didn't want to be a disruption. How are you holding up?"

Until that moment, Caroline hadn't realized that all she wanted in the world was to feel safe, protected, and loved. Across the way, she saw Danny and Michelle wrapped in their own embrace. Their little girl's arms wrapped around Danny's waist. They looked like a perfect family, a fairy tale, right out of a storybook.

She released herself from Grant's embrace, brought a tissue to her nose. "I'm okay. Thank you for coming out here. You didn't have to do that."

"Of course I did. And anyway, I wanted to. I wanted to be here for you, Caroline," Grant said. "You're my . . . well, you're my wife. At least for a little while longer, right?" He smiled sadly and then, seeing her watery eyes, pulled her in close once more. Caroline buried her head against his chest. "I'm so sorry, Caroline. I'm sorry for everything.

And Devorah was . . . well, I know she was complicated, and I know, at one time, she was very important to you. I'm glad you could come back here and reconnect with her again. It's just such a shock to have lost her like that. You're so strong, but I just couldn't let you go through all of this alone."

Caroline pulled away once more, wiping her eyes.

"I'm fine. I'm not . . . I haven't felt alone," Caroline said. But didn't she? Wasn't she? And shouldn't she be? After all the hurt and pain she had caused? It was all so exhausting. She felt sad, and she didn't want to feel sad anymore. She didn't want to feel anything.

"Well, I am, Caroline. Alone. I'm a stupid, stupid man. And I'm here all alone," Grant said. He reached up and ran a hand through his gorgeous white hair. "And I know this isn't the time for this, but I wanted you to know that Oaklyn and I are done. We're over. I don't love her. I never loved her like I loved you. I need you to know that, okay? And I want to talk when this is all over. But until then, I just want you to know I'm one hundred percent here for you."

"Oh, for God's sake, Grant," Caroline said, tilting her head back and sighing.

"I know, I know." He cleared his throat and reached for Caroline's hand.

"What about the baby?" she asked.

"Not mine," he said. "Not mine."

"Oh, Jesus, what a circus. Seriously," Caroline said, pulling on her hand, but Grant wouldn't let her go.

"I was trying to do what I thought was the right thing. I was a fool. And I messed everything up. If there's anything a time like this proves," he said, gesturing to the church, "it's that we can't waste a single second being stupid or selfish, and, Caroline, you're the only family I have and the only one I ever really wanted. Truly. I love you, and I'm so, so sorry."

"Caroline?" Danny's voice broke through the moment as he walked up to stand beside them. Caroline pulled her hand away from Grant, successfully this time. Danny's eyes dropped from Caroline's face to their now disconnected hands and back up to Caroline's face. "Are you doing okay?"

"Oh, yes, I am, thanks," she said, awkwardly. "Danny, this is Grant. Grant, Danny."

"Grant." Danny extended his hand. "Good of you to come all this way."

"Yeah, well, I wanted to be here for my wife," Grant said, stressing the last word.

Caroline looked at the ground, wondering why the hell she hadn't brought a flask with her. She could really use a drink.

"But it's nice to meet you," Grant continued. "Danny, was it?"

"Yes. Danny," Caroline said.

Grant added, "Sorry it's under such sad circumstances."

"Yeah, me too," Danny said, his gaze lingering on Caroline.

"That was a very touching eulogy," Grant said.

She wondered if anyone else had a flask or how long they had to stand there. She wondered if Devorah was enjoying this.

"She had her moments," Danny said and then added to Caroline, "You ready to head over to the cemetery?"

"Can I drive you?" Grant asked, cutting in. "I'd love to help out."

It was an awkward moment, one Caroline could have defused, but she didn't want to make another decision again ever. She had begun a slow retreat within herself. It was like a switch had been flicked and she was shutting down. She was so tired and had a terrible headache from all the crying, and the tissue she was using to wipe her red, chapped nose was soggy and gross.

"Grant," Danny said, putting a protective arm on Caroline's shoulder, "we'll meet you at the Dolphin for the reception. I'm taking Caroline to the interment. It's family and close friends only."

The onslaught of emotion from a few minutes prior had receded like a wave on the shore, and Caroline felt like she was drifting back out to sea. She could hear the men talking, the people around her, but she had zoned out, staring at the ground.

"She *is* my family. She's my wife."

"Oh, I'm sorry. I thought you were engaged. To someone else."

Caroline felt the tension rising, and she didn't have the energy. She took a step away from both men, toward the car in the parking lot. "Let's go bury Devorah, Danny."

Grant nodded. "I'll meet you back at the reception."

Caroline felt Danny in step behind her on the way to the car. She thought she heard Grant saying he didn't know where he was going, but she kept moving. She might not have the energy to push on if she didn't just keep moving forward, one step at a time.

Danny held the car door open for her, and as he walked around to the driver's side, she watched Grant walk away with the other mourners, back to his own car.

Danny started the engine. "You okay?"

"She would've liked it . . . what you said . . ."

"Thank you for saying that," Danny said and turned back to look out over the steering wheel.

They rode along, and Caroline's thoughts turned from a numb sadness to something else. She felt something hard and dark building. Despite the bright rays of the October sun, she felt nothing could be so cold or devoid of light as her soul felt at that moment. She was aware only of the chasm of emptiness within. But as her thoughts began to clear and gain focus and the light began to permeate her shell of loathing, she looked with new eyes at the reds, oranges, and yellows that adorned the large oak and maple trees alongside the road. To Caroline's swollen eyes they appeared bloody, garish, and insulting. As she and Danny sat in silence, winding their way down those old country roads to the cemetery where they would lay Devorah's lifeless body to rest, Caroline thought that if she had an axe, she'd cut every last one of those goddamn trees to the ground.

CHAPTER TWENTY-FIVE

CAROLINE

The Dolphin was an old, slate gray two-story black-shingled building on Main Street in Barnstable that looked more like a grandmother's home than a quaint restaurant. Inside, the ceilings hung low above deep–navy blue carpeting dotted with patriotic white stars. The two large dining rooms were fitted with mismatched brown wooden chairs and tables draped with white linen tablecloths. Doilies, pub cheese, packaged crackers, and small glass vases of fresh carnations adorned the tables.

It was midday, nonpeak hours, so the restaurant was only a quarter full. The funeral reception was in a smaller room just off the bar. As of yet, pretty empty, with only two old couples keeping to themselves and sharing a bottle of sauvignon blanc.

The interment had been fairly standard and rather quick, as interments went. As soon as Caroline and Danny arrived at the Dolphin, he was pulled into a conversation with a local landscaper dining with his teenage son and coworker at the front of the restaurant. Caroline tucked herself into the bar, doing her best to hide from view. She thought it was exactly the kind of afternoon Devorah would have hated, except maybe for the open bar, generously—and curiously—paid for by Devorah's attorney. Caroline's plan was to do two things: the first, to avoid as many conversations as possible, especially with the attorney, and the second, to get a couple of drinks in her and get out of there as soon as she could. The bartender placed a full glass in front of her—a manhattan, Maker's Mark, of course—and after raising her glass and toasting the ceiling, she took a long, steady sip. The smooth brown liquid slid down her throat with a slow burn.

Grant entered from the back and made a beeline toward her.

She rolled her eyes and took another sip.

"Caroline," Grant said, pulling out an empty stool and sitting down next to her. "How are you doing, sweetheart?"

"Yeah," Caroline said. "There's probably a more appropriate name you can use for me these days, don't you think? Like maybe just Caroline?"

"Of course, yes, of course, I'm sorry. Habit. I just wanted to, you know, be here for you." Grant shrugged and seemed to search for something to say. "How are you holding up with all of this?"

"I'm fine. I'll be fine."

"I know this has been a difficult time for you. It's all so crazy, isn't it? Life? It's just full of surprises."

As Grant continued to talk, Caroline swirled the brown liquor silently, and her mind wandered. She always thought the air felt different where people gathered after a funeral. It didn't matter really what season it was or who had passed or whether they were gathered in a house or a function hall, a church basement or a stuffy, sad restaurant with sad doilies and model ships. People were dressed up. Conversation flowed, and maybe it had something to do with everyone wanting to get one last story in and making sure everyone knew how they were connected to the newly deceased. Caroline didn't know. To her, the air carried with it a knowing, an understanding of the tenuousness and finality of all things. She despised being so familiar with it. She turned her focus back to Grant.

"Wait, what?" Caroline said. Grant had been blathering on, and Caroline was paying him no attention at all. But he'd said something that pulled her attention back in his direction.

"I said it's back on. They're ready. You did it, Caroline. I'm so happy for you."

"What? Who's ready? Ready for what?"

Grant laughed a little bit. "Thérèse said she's been trying to reach you for thirty-six hours, and you haven't picked up, and your mailbox is full. I know you've been tied up with all of this. Are you just not getting the messages, or are you not interested, or what?"

"I have no idea what you are talking about," Caroline said. She pulled her phone out of her pocketbook. It was dead, probably from all the buzzing.

"The show, your show, it's been green-lit. It's off the chopping block. They want you back, badly. They're ready for you to jump back into preproduction. You did it."

Caroline tried to catch up. "What? I don't understand. I thought they didn't want the show, didn't want me."

"Well, they do. Apparently, all this crap with the press release and the lawsuit getting dropped has sparked a renewed interest in you and the brand, and there are just diehards coming out of the woodwork to support you."

"Press release?"

"Yes, you're so lucky Devorah did that before she died. It really helped. There are some big names who have come out to say how much *Kiss My Abundance* helped them to really go to the next level in their lives. How it helped them find a way to be happy. And the hype about the new book is just stratospheric. The network is beside themselves. They want you back."

Caroline was confused. Thoughts swirled in her brain like the whiskey in her mouth.

"What? It doesn't make any sense."

Grant looked at her—stared at her, really. "But why wouldn't they love you? You're an amazing woman."

The booze was jumbling her thoughts. "I don't understand."

"As soon as the press release went viral, they called."

"Wait . . . what? What press release?" Caroline said. She needed to slow down her drinking. Things weren't making sense.

Danny's voice cut in. "Caroline, there's someone here who wants to speak with you."

Caroline jumped. Grant draped his arm protectively around her. Looking over her shoulder at Danny, she saw he had a strange look in his eye. He clearly wasn't thrilled about Grant.

"Hi," Grant said, getting in between Danny and Caroline. "She's not really in a place to meet with fans right now."

"He's not a fan," Danny said, clearly fighting his annoyance at Grant's presumptions. "Not really."

Caroline spun her chair away from the bar to fully face Danny. "Oh, Danny, hi," she said, feeling wobbly, like she was still spinning, even though the chair had stopped. Grant placed his hand on the back of Caroline's chair to steady her.

Danny's eye traveled from Grant's hand on the seat back up to Caroline's face.

"Oh, that's okay, Grant was just talking to me about some business stuff. I'm a bit confused." Caroline noticed her voice sounded different.

Caroline looked past Danny to the jolly-looking man with red cheeks and a receding hairline next to him.

The man extended his hand. "Hi, I'm Larry Silverstein, Devorah's attorney. I'm very sorry to be meeting you under these circumstances."

A few minutes later, Caroline was slurping her way through another cocktail while struggling to focus on the words coming out of Larry Silverstein's wide mouth.

"Well, she called me late, very late, one night to talk about a few things. She liked to do that. I wouldn't hear from her for months, then, all of a sudden, she'd get a wild hair, and she'd call me and insist that we talk that minute. She was . . . something else, a real character."

Caroline's head was foggy. *Get to the damn point.*

"I think she was lonely. She really didn't have very much that needed to be addressed, she wasn't really working anymore, and she'd taken care of all the other estate-type things years ago. But anyway, she called me, and we chatted about you."

"Right. We had the contract. We were working together," Caroline said.

"No, I'm sorry, I mean she called me after the legal details of a partnership with you had been worked out. She called again last Monday. About the press release."

"She did?"

"Yes, and I asked her about it. Why was she so adamant about going to bat for you, and she said, 'Love is a serious mental disease.'"

"She was quoting Plato."

"Yes, that's right, she was. And then she added, 'And Larry, if you don't want to die alone, date a woman your own age, dammit. You're too old, too bald, and not nearly rich enough for that crap.'" Larry laughed and shook his head. "She was salty, that's for sure."

"She was salty." Caroline laughed a little, but she didn't know what it all meant or why on earth Devorah would draw up a press release that had to do with her and not tell her.

"But she was also clever. And she clearly placed a high value on knowledge and the pursuit of knowledge." He was interrupted when little Chloe approached her father, standing beside Caroline.

"Hi, Dad."

"Baby girl!" Danny said, planting a big kiss on the top of her head. "Excuse me," he said to the group. "Let's go over here and give these folks some room."

Danny stepped away with Chloe, toward Michelle, who was waiting for him at the far end of the bar. Caroline watched them embrace, Michelle whispering something in his ear. Danny pulled away gently to peer down at Michelle, and she reached up to place her palm on his cheek. It was lovely. Tender. And Caroline couldn't stand to watch anymore. They looked nothing at all like a divorced couple.

She signaled for another drink and then turned back to Grant, who was casually slurring and speaking to Larry, and apparently had been speaking to him for some time, but she hadn't heard anything they were saying until now.

"Caroline and I built a life together. I'm the ass. I'm the one who doesn't say the right thing or do the right thing, and I don't know . . . I just hope we can find our way back to one another. I hope there's some way she can forgive me," Grant said, noticing that Caroline was finally hearing him.

Larry looked like he wanted to be anywhere but there in the bar, in the middle of a conversation that was much too personal to be having with a stranger, and at a funeral no less.

The bartender poured out the contents of a shaker into an icy-cold glass in front of Caroline. Before he could drop the speared cherry into the glass, Caroline swiped it and took a long pull.

"Caroline," Grant said, "I know—"

"You know? What? What do you know?"

The bartender dropped the cherry into what was left in the glass and found some other place to be.

"I know . . . I know this has been hard, Caroline. I'm sorry. I'm so sorry."

"This is too much. *You're* too much, Grant," Caroline said. She hadn't eaten anything all day, and the alcohol was loosening her up. Her self-loathing felt slightly less burdensome as her shoulders relaxed, the weight and stress of the past couple of days slipping away.

"I would like to find some time to discuss some other things with you, Ms. Beckett," Larry Silverstein said.

"Oh, sure, sure," Caroline said, slurring. "What's on your mind, Harry?"

"Larry," Grant said.

"Oh, right, Larry."

"But this is not really an appropriate time," Larry said, looking between Grant and Caroline. He was clearly a teetotaler and, beyond that, wanted to be anywhere but sandwiched in between a divorcing couple drinking a lot of alcohol.

"I know. I'm sorry," Grant continued as if they were midconversation and Larry hadn't spoken. "I'm coming on strong here, I know that. This isn't how I thought all this would go. Look, let's get out of here. Can we get out of here? We don't have to talk about any of this right now. Okay? I just want to be here for you. I care about you. I love you. I couldn't stand to think of you suffering. Lean on me. Let me take care of you. Let me take you home, Caroline."

Caroline's gaze again returned to Danny at the end of the bar with Michelle. It bothered her. She wanted to be better than this feeling of green envy that was percolating within her, which then became something else, another character flaw, that she disliked about herself. It folded in on all the other disappointments. She started to feel a little angry heat building in her stomach.

She swiveled her chair back to Grant. "How long were we married?"

"Ten years." Grant laughed a little at the question.

"Ten. Years." Caroline laughed too. She mumbled into her glass, "Ten. Ha. Ten. Dummy." She tipped her drink back and swallowed some more.

"Yes. You put up with me for ten years. I know it wasn't easy. You deserve better than me. I always told you that," Grant said. He was straining, focusing all his energy onto Caroline. "But if you give me a chance, I want to be here for you."

Caroline paused her drinking for a moment and faced him, her back now to the door, to Danny. She put her drink down and grabbed Grant's hands.

"Grant," she whispered and smiled, looking deep into his eyes. She leaned toward him, took his hands in hers. Her body was hot, scorching. She licked her lips. Grant dropped his head. Caroline brushed the side of his face with hers, her lips inches from his left ear. She whispered, "Will you get me another drink?"

Grant instantly pulled back. He sighed, and Caroline pulled away. "I mean, like, I'm thirsty, and maybe a little hungry too."

Grant smiled sadly. "You're angry. I get it. I deserve it. It's okay."

Caroline laughed and dropped his hands. She clutched at her belly, giggling hard. "Angry? Me?" Caroline's voice rose louder and louder as she continued. "What in the hell could I possibly have to be angry about?"

"Everything okay?" Danny's voice came from behind her.

Caroline swiveled around to face him. "Everything's fine. 'S everything fine with you?"

"It's been a hard day for her," Grant said, putting a protective arm around Caroline's barstool. "I'll take her home."

Caroline gestured to the uninterested bartender (who frankly looked like he saw this sort of bickering thing six times a week and twice on Sundays). "He's making apologies for me now. Can you believe that?"

"I'm heading that way. I can take her," Danny said. "Caroline, I am more than happy to drive you, if you'd like."

"You are?" Grant said, inching his stool closer to Caroline. He was nearly on top of her at this point. "Why? I mean, forgive me for asking, but why? Why are you heading to our house?"

Caroline laughed and said to no one in particular, "Our house. Ha. 'Our house,' he said. That's rich. That's a funny word. *Rich*." Caroline stretched her lips and tongue all over the word *rich*.

"I wasn't heading to *your* house," Danny interrupted, taking no heed of Grant's admission. "I meant Devorah's house . . . or guesthouse . . . where I live." He fixed Grant with an icy stare. The two men looked like they were in an old western saloon standoff.

"Barkeep?" Caroline slurred loudly. "One more for the road, kind sir!"

Caroline was fuzzy, but she could feel the annoyance radiating straight at her from the posture of the two men flanking her. "What are you guys doing? Grant? And you. Danny Diaz. I mean, what's your deal, dudes? Huh? I mean, seriously, fellas. Ever'body just have a drink. I mean, this is a funeral, for Chrissake. Somebody died here, and I think you should all just have some respec'." Caroline picked up her glass and held it high in the air, saying loudly, "To Devorah van Buren. Rest in paradise! . . . 'Only the dead have seen the end of war'!"

She took a long sip and then looked at the bartender. "Hey! Are you watering down my drinks?"

"No, I am not," the fed-up bartender replied.

"Why's my drink taste like water, then?"

"Because it is water."

"I think you've had enough, honey," Grant said.

"Honey?" Caroline said, the words sliding out of her mouth.

Danny laughed, but it was more like a sneer, really.

Caroline, smiling into her drink, repeated, "Honey, honey."

"You have had too much, Caroline. At least that part I can agree with," Danny added.

"Oh, is that right?"

"Yes, it is," Danny said.

Grant smirked. "Listen, buddy, I don't want any trouble, but, I mean, seriously, what are you thinking is going to happen here? With you two? I mean, how is that going to work? Do you not know how much Caroline loathes this town? Do you forget how badly she wanted to run away from this place?"

Caroline's thoughts were cloudy, but she could hear the tension in the voices rising.

"She lives in Los Angeles. *We* live in Los Angeles. She doesn't even want to be here."

"I think she doesn't want *you* here, and she's made that pretty clear," Danny said.

"Isn't there a fire somewhere you can put out or something?"

"Danny puts out fires." Caroline hiccuped loudly. "That's right. He's a hero."

"Listen, I appreciate all the help you've given my *wife*," Grant said, heavily stressing the word. "But I would like to—well, I think I can take care of my wife from here. Okay?"

"He sure says the word *wife* a lot," Caroline said, swinging her legs to and fro.

"I think you've actually done quite enough already. Don't you, Grant?" Danny said.

Grant reached for and grabbed Caroline's hand, tugging on it gently. "Come on, Caroline. Time to go."

"I said I've got her," Danny interjected.

In the background, Caroline could see Michelle coming in and out of focus. She was wearing a look of concern on her face, which Caroline realized was due to the fact that Chloe had left her mother at the other end of the bar and was halfway to her father, who was too wrapped up in besting Grant to be aware. Caroline's brain was much too fuzzy to form the words to warn the men to keep their cool, but she decided she would intervene and cut Chloe off before she saw something she shouldn't. Essentially, Caroline would save the day.

She pushed her stool back away from the bar and swung her legs around. The two men were locked in a verbal exchange, but her focus was on her hero's task and only that.

Caroline dropped her foot to the ground, but it wasn't there. There was no more floor, nothing solid. It felt like she was stepping into water. She plunged downward, eventually finding the floor as she sprawled in a decidedly undainty mess, parts of her ensnared in her barstool.

Danny and Grant leaped to her rescue, one pulling this arm, the other tugging the opposite arm, with Caroline, hanging like deadweight, laughing hysterically in between them.

As the men fought over who would be Caroline's savior and Caroline fought to not pee her pants and tried to stand up on her own, she noticed the men's voices rising. It occurred to her foggy brain that they were not enjoying this latest occurrence quite as much as she was.

As the first sloppy punch was thrown and then the second in retaliation, Caroline was able to register Michelle lunging toward a shocked, and then crying, Chloe.

But Caroline didn't remember anything after that, because that's when the lights went out real hard.

CHAPTER TWENTY-SIX

CAROLINE

Caroline awakened, not having any idea where the hell she was, with what felt like a hatchet dug into and splitting her forehead straight down the middle. She blinked to block the sun's hateful rays and swiftly vomited into a half-full glass of water resting on the nightstand next to what she was coming to realize was her bed in her bedroom at her parents' house.

She lay there, severely dehydrated, wondering how she'd gotten there, tears spilling from her bloodshot eyes, writhing in pain while rolling back and forth in search of a position that didn't make her feel like she was being bludgeoned to death. She begged for a second of silence from the drumming.

What was that sound? She recognized it, but she wasn't practiced in hearing it, and she didn't want to name it or think about it or really think about anything at all whatsoever, besides utter quiet stillness and a reprieve from the searing pain in her head. Yet still the sound thumped along, drowning out every other noise in the entire world and demanding its audience.

After an eternity, or twenty seconds, Caroline realized, with some confusion, that the thundering was the sound of her own heart beating. Her battered, broken heart, pumping and pushing blood throughout her body. She whimpered in defeat. By this point, hating life, hating herself, and being categorically confused about why exactly she had chosen to torturously destroy her body in such a way as that. Like Poe's bloody raven croaking "nevermore," the pounding between her temples and the nagging of that sad muscle in her chest continued their taunting. Seriously, who could hear their heart beating? That was definitely abnormal. Maybe she was dying? Yes, dramatically heartsick and dying. *Curse you, delicious Maker's Mark!*

But Caroline willed herself to move past the self-pity—and the worst hangover she had ever experienced—and end the infernal racket of that ticking clock, or at least her awareness of it, by deciding she would stand up.

She opened one eye, quickly regretted it, and slammed it shut once again. Too much light, too much light. Too much, too soon. She lay prone for another fifteen minutes, or three million days, until she could wait not one single second longer. Moving faster than she thought she was capable of, she ran to the bathroom. She grabbed onto the toilet and threw up for the next thirty minutes.

As reality and her sense of space and time returned, she remembered once again that she was back in the house of her childhood, her parents' home, and there was a mystery here, as she had no recollection of how she'd arrived. She knew this to be an important piece of trivia, but as she languished in her self-imposed hell, bits of the night came back to her like bullets piercing flesh.

The fight. Oh, dear God, *the fight*. Grant. And Danny. And Michelle and, oh no, little Chloe. Oh Jesus. What a nightmare.

And then she remembered Devorah . . . she remembered why they'd all been there.

She rolled over, and her hot tears spilled onto the cold tile of the bathroom floor, a movie-style montage going through her head:

Devorah, alive and barking out orders, and then the disgusting tragedy as Caroline watched the life leaving her body. It played over and over again, like a slasher movie on repeat, in her mind. So much anger and loss and disappointment; it was too much. And then it was just . . . *enough!*

One long, hot shower, sitting on the floor of the bathtub, and a couple Excedrin later, Caroline actually felt like a human being again, albeit more of a stupid, drooling, messy troglodyte. She glanced at her phone, plugged in on the nightstand, and was mortified to discover her notifications announced two hundred and forty-seven new text messages, twenty-five voicemails, and hundreds of emails. What the hell was happening?

She started to unlock the phone and get some answers, but her eyes crossed, the pain in her temples threatening to resurface. She couldn't go there yet. Feeling overwhelmed, she dropped the phone on the bed, deciding she would connect with the outside world—climb that Mount Everest of reality—later. There were more pressing issues at hand. She heard someone else in the house.

Caroline found her way to the hallway yet again. Was that coffee she smelled? She willed herself into the living room and then, somehow, made it to the kitchen, where she found Wayne, the helpful man from the real estate office, with his nose in her refrigerator.

He jumped a mile when he closed the fridge door, revealing her presence.

"Caroline!" He was basically screaming, she thought. "You scared me!"

"Shh. Shh. Oh, sorry," Caroline said, her voice hoarse from vomiting.

Wayne looked concerned. "Oh, wow, Caroline, you don't look like yourself. Are you okay?"

"Shh. I'm fine. I need coffee. Shh. And fresh air. And lower voices."

"I wish I'd known. I just got this from Dunkin'. I would've picked one up for you."

"I want it."

"Well, of course! Here you go," Wayne said. He had an eager look in his eye.

Caroline pulled the lid off and sipped from the cup. "Wait. What are you doing here? Why are you in my house?"

"Oh, ha! I'm showing the place to a prospective buyer in about twenty minutes. Remember? You came to the office and said you wanted it listed and that you are out all day and if I couldn't reach you and didn't see your rental in the driveway, all was good. So, I didn't know you were here. This is great. They'll be *so* excited to meet you. It will sell today!"

"Oh no," Caroline said, turning away. "Hush, hush please."

"Oh, sorry! Do you not want me to show the house?"

Caroline crossed to the sink and put some cold water on her face. "It's fine. You can show it."

"Fantastic! They will be excited to meet you! Especially with all the hoopla in the news and stuff."

"Yeah, no. I'm going out, Dwayne."

"Wayne. It's Wayne, actually," he replied, losing absolutely none of his enthusiasm at the slight.

"Right."

"Okay, but just one more thing before you go. Do you think I can get a photo?"

"No, Wayne. You sure as hell cannot."

Caroline retreated back down the hallway to her room.

"Ha, ha, okay, Caroline. You bet!" Wayne called out after her.

Caroline grabbed her phone and a sweater from her suitcase and was about to head out when an outlet against the far wall of her bedroom beneath a windowsill caught her eye. Something jolted in her memory, and she moved toward the wall. She knelt on the ground, running her fingers over the outlet, and, using her fingernails to separate the front panel from the wall, she tugged on the faceplate, pulling the faux outlet out and away to reveal a small hole in the wall.

Caroline reached in and pulled out a small box. She lifted the lid off, then emptied the contents out in front of her. There was an old Nintendo Game Boy. She pressed the buttons, but the battery had long since died. There was a small collection of Lisa Frank rainbow-colored dolphin stickers, a half-smoked joint, and a folded-up piece of lined paper. Caroline remembered what it was as she unfolded it, but her heart rate quickened all the same as she began to read.

Dear Mom, Well, it's been eight days and seven hours since you ~~left~~ died.

Caroline stopped reading. Refolded the paper. She took a breath. No. No, she wasn't ready for that. She reached into the hole in the wall one last time, pulling out an old photograph. It looked like it was from sometime in the 1970s or so, and it was slightly weathered and faded from age. In the photo, two-year-old Caroline had a bowl cut and wore a red, white, and blue bathing suit. Her long-haired mother and mustached father flanked her, squinting away the sun and smiling. Caroline stared at the photograph. She had so few photos of her family and none on display anywhere in her home. It felt jarring to see them there, staring back at her.

The phone pinged in her hand. It was a text from Grant. He wanted to talk. And yes, she would speak to him. But first she would go out for a walk by the sandy dunes and heal her body and mind with the salty Cape air. Out there she would feel better. Out there on the beach, where the punishing waves crashed relentlessly onto the shore and the viciousness of nature turned sinister to beautiful. She wondered if maybe, out there, she could find the strength to stop running. Maybe out there, blowing around in the sand, lapping water along the shore, there were answers to long-buried questions that propelled her forward into the mess she'd made of the life she'd created. She had run so far away she had finally caught up to herself.

CHAPTER TWENTY-SEVEN

CAROLINE

Caroline headed toward the end of the narrow beach road known mostly to locals and pulled into the small parking lot posted with *Resident Sticker Required* and *No Parking Dusk to Dawn* signs. Thérèse's voice, and its screeching intensity, worked in Los Angeles, but it felt jarringly out of place on Caroline's phone just then.

"Caroline! Listen, I was absolutely gobsmacked when I read Devorah's press release! That was perfect. And I know this must be hard for you, but you're the one who's always saying the pendulum swings, right? Well, hang on, baby, because you're swinging back like Miley Cyrus on a goddamn wrecking ball. I mean, what a woman—rest in peace!"

"I haven't seen anything. I know we need to talk," Caroline said. "But—"

"No, no, don't you dare hang up on me, Caroline! Caroline?"

"I will call you back. I promise. I just can't right now. I need to think for a minute." Caroline hung up the phone in defiance and flipped the switch to silent mode.

The beach parking lot maxed out at ten spaces, and only three others were occupied. Back when Caroline was a teenager, she used to park here with her friends from the other side of town. They would spill from the car and noisily file out onto the public walkway to the glistening beach below.

Devorah's home was just about seven houses back down the road in the opposite direction Caroline planned to walk. Caroline had passed it on her way, but she was not ready to go there yet today. Thoughts of Devorah, oh, Devorah . . . and Danny, Grant, home, work, family were swirling around in her head in such a confusing fury, she could barely breathe.

She was taking a moment and collecting her thoughts. No harm in that. Thérèse had sent a long email laying out an entire scenario for her triumphant return to good graces. She needed to evaluate it all. She realized, with much shock and guilt, that she was actually getting everything she'd wanted. The lawsuit was over. She'd gotten her show back. The brand was saved. Grant wanted to work on their marriage. Danny was somehow back in the picture. Her heart was reeling, wants and desires overlapping, intersecting, snapping, and breaking off.

Did she deserve any of this? The good or the bad? Both? Was it good or bad? And who determined that?

Caroline knew where to go to make sense of her thoughts and feelings. Years ago, at a national park, she'd seen a quote from John Muir: "I only went out for a walk and finally concluded to stay out till sundown, for going out, I found, was really going in." For Caroline, there was no greater place to find clarity than where the ocean met the land. She could think better with fresh air in her lungs, wrapped in the majesty of nature, where everything was brought down to its essence.

From the cup holder, she grabbed the black Sharpie marker she had taken from home and slipped her shoes off, tossing them back into the car. She walked to the timeworn pathway toward the beach.

Be here, be kind, Caroline begged herself. She whispered the words out loud and took pleasure in the warm sea breeze that carried them away. Stepping from the hard beach grass, she lost her feet immediately, swallowed up by the cool, damp sand. With a jolt, the sensation of her body meeting this magical land sent a shiver up her spine. She took another step forward, plunging her foot in the sand, and onward she went, stardust kicking up from her heels as she walked.

It was an unusually warm day for Cape Cod in late fall, and there were others outside taking advantage of it and enjoying their own beach strolls. With each step Caroline took toward the point away from the parking lot, away from Devorah's house and all that had occurred there, she felt the tension slip from her shoulders. With each footfall, she felt closer to the part of herself that John Muir was talking about. The part that felt timeless and purposeful; the part of herself that knew all the answers—or at least knew that taking a step forward to try and answer the question of how to reconcile the holes buried within her took conscious awareness and slight effort. She could no longer stay stagnant with her head buried in the sand. If anything, these past few weeks had taught Caroline that she must be an active participant in her life because her time on Cape Cod, in Los Angeles, on the physical plane, would end, and what a shame it would be to waste even a single second.

So Caroline forged ahead. One step at a time, the sun warming her body. She paused, picking up a near-perfect quahog shell and turning it over in her hand. In the water to her left, terns dove for the mummichogs swimming at the surface. On the land to her right, the last of the migratory sandpipers picked at insects below the sand and the shiny coat of shimmering biofilm. There, in that place that was both beach and ocean, Caroline felt the space that was at once her thoughts, her thinking, and her awareness observing her thinking.

Caroline leaned into the knowledge of her true self in this indefinable space, the part of her that transcended limitations. The burdens of her mind and of her material world lifted. She became swept away with the infinite joy of truly knowing that she was not just her thoughts, what she told herself about the roles she played, but something more.

She was the *thinker* of the thoughts, but she was more still. She was also the observer of the thinking! She eased into the voice in her head.

There, in the space between the thoughts you are thinking and your awareness of the thinking—the thinking and the observing of the thinking—lies your true essence. Thoughts are things.

Things. *Thoughts are things.*

Up ahead, Caroline could see the point in the far distance. It looked different. The beach was always morphing, moving, never the same from one day to the next, but there was a feeling of change she couldn't put her finger on. The footsteps of all the other beachcombers had fallen away, and Caroline was now far out, alone in the expanse of land at the tip of the isthmus, her only company a few uninterested gulls.

Her steps slowed until she stopped all together.

Wait.

It wasn't there.

Where was it?

She took another dozen steps, but no, it wasn't there. There was something shiny that was glinting, catching sunlight, but what should have been the large, weathered, salt-ridden tree was not there. Caroline jogged the last hundred yards forward, her confusion mounting, toward where the tree should have been, always had been, ever since she was a small girl and walked the beach with her mother.

She closed in, and the salty tree that once danced in the moonlight, swayed in the sunlight, was now just a shorn trunk with a few grotesque branches jutting out in terrifying directions.

The breath caught in her chest, and she slowed down. The quahog shell and black Sharpie she had brought from home burned in her hand. What was this? What was happening? That tree had been there as long as she could remember, a testament to fortitude. But the tree trunk was cut clean down to knee level. It must have been done with a chainsaw. Who would do such a thing? Why? This tree was so far out and away from the mainland, it was not in anyone's way. Its roots, long ago buried by the sand, caused no issues underground. Why, then, attack it? Why ruin it?

Caroline felt her heart begin to beat again and breath returning to her lungs. She noticed the remaining terrifying branches that jutted out from what remained of the trunk were covered almost completely with ribbons, notes, letters, beads, shells, and rocks. At the base of the ugly stump, someone had left a sign that read *The Giving Tree*. Piled up all alongside it were dozens of notes and mementos from a community of beachcombers who, like Caroline, were shocked by and grieved the blight of a most blessed landmark.

Caroline sank down into the sand and felt the letter in her pocket. She unfolded it and began reading.

Dear Mom,

Well, it's been eight days and seven hours since you ~~left~~ died. I just wanted to say, don't worry. I don't mean this in a bad way, but if you're worried about me being alone—being orphaned—or something like that, I've been okay on my own for a while now. I'm not saying that to be mean. But I'm an adult. I'm okay. I'll be okay. Well, I'm going to be okay. I know you loved me. And I know you did the best you could, which wasn't much, but that's okay. I want you to know that I'm sorry too. I wish I hadn't said all those things. I was angry. And, frankly, it was true—you weren't the best mother. But you tried. And thank you for talking to Devorah. She actually came through, and I'll be heading to college in the fall. I guess we will see where the road takes me. Hopefully far, far away from here. I know in my heart that I, alone, create my destiny. I will work hard. I know what I want, and I can have it. I know I will be a success at living this one and only life to the fullest. I won't be sad forever. So, you know, until we meet again . . .

Your daughter,
Caroline

A teardrop hit the page as Caroline read the last line. She thought of the girl she'd been when she wrote the letter, a virtual stranger to her now. Where did she go?

She closed her eyes, focusing on the feeling of the breath entering and then exiting her body, her rib cage rising and falling. She felt the sea air rush in through her nostrils, the tension in her neck subsiding. She heard the waves lapping on the shore and the wind blowing in the seagrass. A long way off, she heard the buzzing motor of a speedboat cutting through the water. The blackness behind her closed eyes began to give way to something lighter, and she began to feel more relaxed than she'd ever been. She focused her thoughts on letting go.

Devorah . . . Grant . . . Danny . . . work . . . home . . . family . . .

And then something clicked in Caroline's brain. The thoughts, her thoughts, the things she was thinking, the things she was telling herself . . . What if those thoughts were not real? What if they were untrue? What if none of it was real? What if it was all a big scam? Wait . . . was she doubting herself à la Descartes? *I think, therefore I am . . . what? What am I?* she thought. *Alive!* . . . a voice answered. *You are alive.*

Caroline decided right then she would own the truth. She would tell the world the truth about the book. She would set the record straight. She owed Devorah that.

She had been searching for something for so damn long, she actually hadn't realized she'd even been on a journey. Until that moment of discovery, she hadn't known how desperately she was searching. But she was. She was on a hunt, and she realized she had found what she was looking for all that time. Truth. What she hadn't expected was the feeling that came with it: relief.

Caroline had never asked for Devorah to reappear in her life. Caroline hadn't wanted a friend. She hadn't wanted her mentor back. She hadn't wanted to learn any more lessons. Yet Devorah had given all these things to her. She had added to the bonfire that ignited Caroline's life and had the audacity to up and die in her arms.

Watching the breath go out of Devorah's body and being helpless to save her had created a scar on Caroline's own heart that she knew would never fully heal. But it had happened. And she couldn't look away. She couldn't smile it away. Devorah was gone.

She pulled the top off the marker and flipped the quahog shell right side up, so the top was facing her. She thought for a moment, but only just, and then she pressed the tip of the marker to the shell. She wrote out the word *decide*, and then she laid it beside the others on one of the lower branches, still intact.

And now she would go to him.

Plato said, "Thinking is the talking of the soul to itself."

~

Grant answered the door at the Harbor Hotel on the first knock, like he'd known she was coming and had been waiting for her the whole time. Caroline stepped inside. The wind blew in through the open window, slamming the door shut behind her. The finality of the slam, the timing of it, just too precise to be accidental.

"Does it hurt much?" Caroline asked, looking at Grant's black eye.

"Not too bad," Grant said, wincing slightly. "Not enough, anyway."

Caroline reached up and touched his face. Smiled into his eyes, his face so familiar to hers.

"Caroline, darling. I've been so stupid."

"You have, yes."

"Caroline, like it or not, we have a life that is ours. I understand you. I get you. I know what you want, and I finally know how to give it to you. I know what to do. And I'm begging you, please, please, let me give it to you. Please forgive me."

Caroline was quiet. She'd heard this all before. Why did it sound so different now?

"I'm selfish. I know that. I was so stupid. I was reckless, and I was horrible, and I don't know how I have the audacity to stand here in front of you and ask you for another chance, but Caroline, forget it. I'm doing it. I don't know how not to. I don't know how I could live another day without telling you this. You deserve so much more. You deserve better. You do. You don't think I know that? You don't think I've always known that? You don't think I've done all of this, made a mess of our marriage, of my life, because, deep down, I've always known it? I've always known you were too good for me. I love you, Caroline. I've always loved you. It's always been you."

Caroline turned away. She couldn't breathe. She had wanted to hear this from Grant, but that was months ago—years ago, really. It was part of what made her so crazed, that deep down she really knew it was over and that it had been over for a while. Grant had stopped trying, and then she had. And she had to face it.

It was a death by a thousand cuts, but still, she'd been waiting. A part of her had been waiting and praying to hear those words this last time. But every time Grant came back to her, she was just a little bit different, and so was he. And now they just didn't fit anymore.

"Caroline, wait, listen to me—please—because I already know what you're going to say. That things are different this time. But that's true. They are. Things are different. I've been working with a therapist."

Caroline was shocked. "You said you'd never do therapy. You said you didn't believe in it."

"Just one visit so far. I know I have work to do, but I love you, Caroline. I love you so much."

Grant wiped away the tears that were now spilling down his cheeks. Caroline tilted her head back and looked up at the ceiling. She stretched the long muscles in her neck and studied the smooth surface with a dozen little sockets filled with soft light bulbs. She filled her lungs with air and then pushed the air back out and thought about how the breath leaving her lungs felt like relief. She could feel Grant's eyes on her, studying her movements, questioning if his method was working.

He continued, "Please . . . will you just think about it? We were happy once."

Caroline smiled sadly as her eyes filled with tears. "Grant."

His shoulders slumped, knowing what she had come to say. "Dammit," he said with resignation, walking over and sitting on the edge of the bed.

"I've spent so much time thinking about us," Caroline said. "How you made me feel, how we got here. I thought you were my soulmate."

"But you always said you don't . . . you didn't . . . believe in soulmates," Grant said.

"Well, I don't know. You know what Devorah told me? Greek myth stated that humans used to have four arms and legs, and Zeus was afraid of the power humans wielded, so he split them in two, dooming them to spend their lives looking for their other half, their soulmate." Caroline paused. "I think I actually said that *Plato* didn't believe in soulmates." She laughed. "God, I haven't thought so much about Plato and all this crap in years. Anyway, Plato believed the highest love was that for God. He said that until you were a fully formed person, an independent person on your own, you couldn't really find what would complete you in someone else. A happy, mature relationship is made up of two wholes, but that the love of another could bring you closer to a higher love."

"So, I'm hearing there's still a chance here," Grant said, a wide grin spreading across his sad face.

Caroline giggled and wiped away a stray tear. "You could always make me laugh."

"You know, I kinda think that enduring love is rather mundane. That was never really who we were."

"I think it has its moments, yeah, and maybe it's the getting there that isn't so mundane. I don't know, but I will miss you. I know that."

"I'll miss you too," Grant said. "So much."

"Forever."

"Now what are you going to do?" he asked.

At that very moment, Thérèse pinged her phone again.

"Well, I guess, first, I'll have to call Thérèse back," she said. "And then onward to the truth."

"Tell him I'm sorry, will you?"

"Sure, I'll do that."

CHAPTER TWENTY-EIGHT

CAROLINE

"Dammit, Caroline!" Thérèse shouted into the phone. Caroline had to pull the earpiece away and readjust the volume.

Caroline was idling at the intersection of Old Stage Road and Route 28, an old cemetery on her right. Out the window to her left, a small island in the road delineated lanes between traffic. The little island was maintained by a local with a green thumb and a sense of humor and community. A rubber seagull dangled on fishing wire to denote soaring over the petunias, rocks, and gravel below. The creation was well intentioned, but the seagull looked more like fisherman's catch, hanging lifeless on the line.

"I know, I know. I'm sorry. I guess I just needed to pause for a second. I'm dealing with some things out here," Caroline said, the light turning green. She accelerated.

"Well, I hope you're finished. We've got some deals to discuss!"

"Listen, stop, before we do all that. I want to come clean. I want to put out a statement, tell the truth, and do the right thing."

"Oh no! Seriously?" Thérèse said. "That sounds unnecessary. Also, why?"

"What do you mean, why?"

"Well, okay, let's just start with defining what the *right thing* is that you're talking about."

Caroline took a deep breath, mustering her strength, her courage. "In my time working here with Devorah, I realized she had far more of an influence on me, on my work, than I gave her credit for. I wrote every word in that book, but it was Devorah's research. It was her influence. They were her ideas that I laid claim to. Yes, I parlayed some thoughts and moved things into a bit more modern realm and put my name on it. But I didn't credit Devorah. I should have."

There was silence on the other end of the line. Caroline held her breath, and then Thérèse let out a big sigh in her ear.

"Oh Jesus. Thank God. I thought you were going to say you got a DUI or something. Oh God, what a relief!"

"I stole the book. I took Devorah's ideas, Thérèse."

"Hmm. I don't know. You sure about that? I'm not so sure about that," Thérèse said. She paused, then added, "And anyway, does it matter?"

"What? Yes, I'm sure. Yes, it matters. Of course it matters."

"I'm not sure it really does. Have you read the press release?"

"I didn't. I haven't, but you're like the third person to tell me about it. What did it say?"

"Devorah van Buren came out publicly and said she realized that indeed she had shared her ideas, her work, with you, and that you had taken it and run with it and put your own stamp on it, and she was a fan, and you had her full support. And she was happy about the book you were collaborating on currently."

"Wow. Well, that's . . . nice, but—I can't let that be the final word on this. I want to release a statement telling people I stole the book."

Again there was silence on the other end of the line.

"Hello?" Caroline said.

Laughter rang through. "Wow. Okay, if you want to put out a statement saying that you stole a book, I can't stop you. I don't think you should, but I can't stop you."

"Good, yes, I want to."

"Okay, I'm going to pause on the insanity for a second thought because we have other stuff to talk about. The show, the option—great stuff is happening!"

"Well, you say that now, but these people need to know what I've done. This is going to change things."

"Um, no it won't," Thérèse said. "Nobody cares."

"People care."

"Not really."

"What do you mean? I stole it. I took it. I took something that didn't belong to me."

"Again, she—the person you supposedly stole from—said that you didn't do it."

"She lied. She was lying."

"Well, she also said in the press release that . . . hang on, I'll read it to you. 'Wrinkled was not one of the things I wanted to be when I grew up, but I'd rather be my age with a Manhattan than a nimble bimbo that needs a guide to living life. But I recognize that I need Caroline Beckett to impart my wisdom, to find the through line to connect to a broader audience.' She then quoted Plato: 'Good people do not need laws to tell them how to act responsibly, while bad people will find a way to get around the laws.' And she said, 'Caroline Beckett has never shown herself to be anything other than a hardworking, smart woman with questionable taste in men and automobiles, but I am honored to share my work, and a (too small) part of my life, with her.'"

Caroline was stunned.

"Are you there?"

"I am."

"She sounds like she was a pretty 'real' woman."

"Um, yeah, the realest," Caroline said. "That's why I want to be clear. How can I live with myself if I'm laying claim to something I know in my heart wasn't true?"

"Think about it, Caroline. Okay? You're a smart woman. Would you just think about it for a minute. I mean, dammit, you did do the work, and Devorah has gotten credit for her part. It's time to move on from this so we can get on the phone with counsel and hash out the contract details with the network. Isn't the point of all of this to connect with as many people as you can? You did it. You delivered."

"Thérèse."

"Yeah?"

"I have to tell the truth."

Thérèse sighed heavily into the phone. "Send me a draft, and then can we find a time to talk tomorrow? I'm not letting this go. We've got the publisher to talk to, and the network really wants to get this new deal nailed down."

CHAPTER TWENTY-NINE

CAROLINE

A light flicked on in the guesthouse, pulling Caroline's attention to the shadowy figure descending the dark exterior stairway. Danny Diaz. He was mostly in shadow, but Caroline felt an uncomfortable flutter in her stomach, seeing the slump in his shoulders and the painful pierce of his stare when he noticed her at the bottom.

"Well," he said. "This is a surprise."

"Is it?" she said, holding her hand up to block the last bit of sunlight as it dipped completely out of sight.

Danny turned back around, gesturing for Caroline to follow him inside. He opened the door, and Caroline entered behind him. Her hand lingered on the doorknob as she closed the door, shutting out the sweet, salty air behind her.

She turned back to the room to face him.

"Drink?" he said.

"Oh God, no, I don't think I will ever, ever, ever drink again, actually, so no, thank you." She laughed awkwardly. He didn't. How had they returned to this place?

"It was a rough night," he said, not meeting her eye.

"Does it hurt?" she asked, looking at his swollen cheek. She reached out a hand to touch it, but he winced, pulling slightly away from her.

"Oh," Caroline said, the sting of his rejection coiling around her. "I'm . . . sorry."

"Yeah, you should see the other guy," Danny said, still averting his eyes and busying himself clearing off the couch for her to sit.

Caroline's eyes stayed glued to him, his every movement. He had a faraway expression. Everything about him felt faraway and distant, different.

"I don't remember much of it, or any of it, really. I'm ashamed to say."

"Well, lucky you," he said. "Chloe should be so lucky." He grabbed two beers from the fridge and popped the tops off both of them.

Caroline chewed the inside of her cheek. "Oh God. I'm sorry. That's just awful. Is she okay?"

"She will be." He took a long swig and offered her the other open beer. "Sure you don't want one?"

Caroline shook her head no, turned away, and took a seat on the couch. Strewed in a corner were several boxes that hadn't been there before. Caroline felt a lump in her throat as she looked at them.

Danny placed a bottle down in front of her. "I'll drink it if you don't," he said, taking a seat across from her. He smiled, but it didn't quite reach his eyes. "I apologize, but I don't have anything else to offer you."

Caroline picked up the bottle and held it up to her face. The glass felt good against her skin. She brought the bottle to her lips and took a sip. She blanched. It tasted awful, like chugging down regret.

"I'm sorry," she said.

"Let me ask you, Why did you come here today? I mean, really. What did you come here for? Like, what do you want?"

"Do you not think this is hard for me too?"

"I actually don't, no. You've had enough practice. This is kind of what you do, right?"

"Danny, I don't know if that's fair, really."

"I don't care if you think it's fair."

"Fine, you want to know what I want? I want you. I want you to come with me. Come with me to California! Come! Leave your job, your home, your wife, your *child*, and come with me. Let me be selfish. Let *me* win it all here. Right? I mean, you're asking me what I want. That's what I want. I want you. I want you to come with me. I'm begging you to come with me."

Danny was stone cold and silent. He glared at his beer.

"Because, Danny," Caroline continued, "I want the life I didn't live with you. And all I want in this whole world is for *this* to go on forever. I love you and I want you, and I will love you always. But you won't come. You can't. You shouldn't. And the truth is, I love you so much I wouldn't let you. Even if Chloe wasn't here, you wouldn't want to. This is your life, your work, your home, and you're happy here. I just never was. And that wasn't about you. It was about *me.* I had to leave. But it's not the right move for you. And so I won't do that. I won't ask you. I won't let you."

Danny exhaled. He ran his fingers through his hair.

"And I'm sorry for the train wreck that was last night," she said, "but I'll never be sorry for any of this."

"Well . . ." Danny looked at the floor. After a minute he sighed, looked up, and said, "I know that you're right. But . . . I don't have to like it." For the first time since she came in that day, he offered a smile. A sad smile, but it was still a smile.

Another long, quiet minute passed. Then he looked at the boxes in the corner. "The MSPCA is taking over the property, you know."

"Yeah, that was a very generous gift she left them. I think she liked the animals because they couldn't talk back," she said.

"Yeah, maybe," said Danny.

"Devorah used to talk about anamnesis in her class. It's a philosophical term. It is the remembering of something from a previous existence."

Danny nursed his beer.

Caroline continued. "We are born with innate knowledge, a knowing. And life, or learning, is really just us rediscovering all this information."

"I think you're a really amazing human, Caroline. You'll be fine."

She smiled, but like Danny, it never really reached her eyes. She drank more of the beer.

"It's okay to be afraid," he said.

Outside, the wind slowed down. The waves discontinued their rollicking and instead grew calm.

"Are you going inside?" He nodded at Devorah's house.

"I think I would like to. Just one last look. Say goodbye, in a weird way . . ."

"I understand. But you don't have to do it alone," he said. He reached for her hand. She gave it to him.

"Thank you. But I'll be okay."

"Oh, you'll be better than that."

"Thank you, Danny. Thank you so much. For everything."

"Always, Caroline."

Danny tugged on her hand, pulling her close to his chest. Caroline leaned into him as his arms encircled her. She closed her eyes and took a mental snapshot of this moment.

"Someone said once, 'If a writer falls in love with you, you can never die.'"

"I like that," he said.

"I love you, Danny," she said.

"I love you, too, Caroline. Always."

They walked down the stairs in silence, and Danny dropped a box into the cab of his truck and climbed inside. Caroline stared at the truck's red taillights as Danny turned onto Long Beach Road. Her eyes were tired, but she kept them glued to the glow of the red lights until they became blurry and finally faded out of sight.

She felt a tightness in her chest, and it was slightly hard to breathe. But she focused. Breath in, breath out. *You are all right, Caroline.* She knew, of course, that some relationships weren't meant to last forever, no matter how much you might want them to. But it didn't make it all suck any less. And she couldn't ignore it.

She had said goodbye to the two great loves of her life. She had no family, and now Devorah was gone too. But she could start over. She knew she could, even though she'd launched a grenade at her career. Thérèse would submit her press release in the morning. The potential fallout would be hard, but she would find a way to surmount the bad press. She would find something to write about, and she would publish another book. She would even tell the world about cranky Devorah van Buren, one of the greatest teachers she had ever had.

She would take her own advice. She would no longer doubt her existence, her power, but instead cherish it for the gift it was. She would think and therefore know truth. She would practice what she preached. She'd go back to the steps that she spoke about so often. Had she ever really lived them? Humility, awareness, surrender, soul, prayer, freedom, and then peace? Had she ever done the work? It was past time she did.

EPILOGUE

CAROLINE

The line of people at the old Pasadena bookstore was dwindling. Caroline had been signing copies of her book for almost a full hour. This was the last stop on her book tour. She was exhausted, but she was in heaven. She loved hearing, even if it was just a brief thank-you or anecdote, how her book—hers and Devorah's—had impacted people since its release a few months prior.

The store was growing quiet as the sky darkened outside and the few remaining customers paid for their books, making their way to the exits.

Caroline was tired, and her hand was cramped, but she soldiered on. It had been a year and a half since she'd returned to Southern California. In that time, she'd sold her house, bought a new one in Malibu, written and published their newly released book, *What, Do You Live in a Cave or Something?*, and left for her twelve-city book tour. She was looking forward to some downtime.

Looking up from her seated position at the folding table, she returned the signed book to the second-to-last person in line, thanking them and then shaking her hand out, trying in vain to return the blood to her sore fingers.

And then there was one. Just one person left in line. She looked up to see the stranger standing before her, smiling.

Her breath caught a little in her throat as she took him in. He was a tall, broad-shouldered man in green scrubs, handsome, with a square jaw, pronounced cheekbones, and soulful ebony eyes. He had a kind face, with a deep dimple in his smooth cheek when he smiled.

"Careful, you'll get a sprain," he said, indicating her sore hand.

"Exactly," she said, laughing. "I know, occupational hazard, I guess. Anybody know a doctor?"

"Wish I could help," he said and pointed at his chest. "Wrong body part—heart."

"Oh," she said, looking at his strong, ringless hand, at his chest, then back up to meet his eyes. "Right, well, I guess I'll just ice it, then, and call it a day." She wasn't sure why, but something about him, the way he was looking at her, made her feel like she was on shaky ground.

"I have to confess . . . I didn't read your book."

"Oh," Caroline said, heat rising in her cheeks.

"I would like to, though. I was actually shopping for something else, and I heard you speaking. I liked what you had to say. Bringing Plato into the mainstream for all of us cave dwellers," he said with a laugh. "I do love the title."

"Oh, thank you. It's an interesting topic. I enjoyed working on it."

"I minored in philosophy in college, briefly, but I wish I'd had a teacher, a mentor, like you did. You made it all sound so relatable."

"Well, I had help, as you said. Devorah and I, actually, we made a pretty good team."

"Sounds like she was an interesting character."

"The most interesting, yes, she was. Can't believe it's been nearly two years since I heard her yelling at me."

He laughed. He seemed so genuine. It had been a minute since just looking at a man had made her feel a little flip-flop in her stomach. She wondered if whatever was bopping around in there was covered in dust and cobwebs. And this man, well, he just kept smiling down at her. Caroline wanted the whole world to slip away all around them, but it actually felt like the opposite was happening. She felt like every eyeball on planet Earth was focused squarely on them. In reality, she knew it was only Thérèse, who was standing to Caroline's left.

Caroline pulled herself together, cleared her throat, and said, "Did you want me to sign a book for you?"

"Oh, I don't have a book," he said and laughed again. "I'm sorry. Can I get one? Let me go buy one."

"Wait, I'll get you one, hold on," Caroline said. She looked over her left shoulder. "Thérèse?"

Thérèse was rather aggressively looking the man up and down. She clearly enjoyed what she saw, as she indiscreetly licked her lips. "How can I be of service?"

"Thérèse, can you get me a copy of the book?" Caroline said, then repeated it, because she wasn't moving. "Thérèse, can you get me a copy? Of the book? Thérèse?"

"Oh, of course! One second. I took the rest back to the register," she said, turning away.

"I'm grateful," he said. His brown eyes actually twinkled.

Trying not to swoon, Caroline said, "I'm grateful you're interested in the book."

"I am. I very much am," he said.

She was, all of a sudden, very aware of her heart rate, her posture, the way her voice sounded . . . excited and too eager?

"So . . . Plato . . . the good life?" he asked. "What does Plato think is the good life? What's the secret?"

"Well, in the simplest terms—and I'm not going to give you everything, because then why would you buy my book?—Plato believed that the highest, happiest life one could achieve would be to be virtuous of character and not just have luxuries and riches. Which then brings in a question of morals and love and so forth."

"Morals and love and virtue. How refreshingly old fashioned."

"Well, what is old becomes new again, as they say."

"I'm intrigued."

"I'm flattered."

Thérèse was back. She placed the book down in front of Caroline, disrupting the smiling/staring contest she was having with this man.

"Here you go," Thérèse said. "Pay at the register."

"Of course, thank you very much," the man said, never taking his eyes off Caroline's.

Caroline finally broke away from his gaze. She opened the cover and returned her eyes to his. "Who should I make it out to?" She held the Sharpie over the paper.

"Leo," he said. "Make it out to Leo."

She paused, her breath caught in her chest. She blinked, a smile blanketing her face, and dipped back into the dark pools of his eyes. "Leo?"

"Yes."

"Leo, really?" she asked again, and then had the self-awareness to feel slightly embarrassed.

"Yup, L-E-O, Leo."

She felt a little bubble of laughter rise up from the center of herself. *Of course.*

"What's so funny?" he said.

"No, nothing. Leo's a really nice name. I like the name. It's just . . . that just reminded me of something an old friend said to me one time. Anyway . . ." she said, returning to planet Earth.

"So, I was wondering—and let me just say, as you talked about in your book, I'm bringing some awareness into my life, asking for what I want—so, would you like to have dinner with me sometime?"

Caroline felt a breeze as the warm Santa Ana winds blew inside the store. She felt the shift. The pages of the books rustled. She felt the electrical charge spark in the air.

She smiled. "Yes."

Acknowledgments

This book represents the culmination of a couple decades of writing, honing, crafting, and creating a body of work, and none of it, this book especially, could have happened without many colleagues, friends, family, and supporters. I am forever grateful for the people and circumstances that allowed me to get to this point with this book. What a joy to be able to express my gratitude now to all those who helped me along the way.

On a warm, sunny Cape Cod afternoon I had a Zoom call with a very smiley Tina Schwartz, who told me she wanted to be my agent, and that changed everything. Thank you, Tina, for taking me on, believing in me, and getting this book out there into the world. A few months later we chatted and laughed with an equally upbeat and inspiring editor, Erin Adair-Hodges, and through Erin I was welcomed into the formidable and comforting arms of Lake Union Publishing. It's been an absolute honor. Thank you both so much. And thank you to the wonderful group at Lake Union Publishing, Jenna Free, Angela Elson, Adrienne Krogh, Rachael Clark, and everyone else who has helped bring this book together. It has been a fabulous experience working with all of you.

Along the winding path to publication, a few key players helped immeasurably by providing thoughtful editorial critiques. Thank you, Dawn Ius, Pat Verducci, and Shannon Cave. My early readers were invaluable as well. Thank you, Gail Shapiro, for your friendship, readership, and support along the way.

Over the years, I leaned on so many for support, encouragement, favors, friendship, and so much more. I could not have stayed the course without all of you. Thank you, Ainsley Davies Morgan, Chris Morgan, Ashley Brucks, Elise Allen, Alicia Wyld, and Katrina Escudero. Thank you to the many friends, readers, editors, idea suppliers, and advocates of my work over the years. Thank you, James Grace, Claire McNabb, Joseph McNabb, Vicki Dunn, Ellen LeBlanc, Lauri Rizzo, Melissa Dorsey (forever in my heart), Jodi Gerardi, Peter and Linda Hulne, Julie Iadanza, Katie and Alex Leon, Anne Boland, Angie Edgar, Johanna Stein, Darla Delayne, Angela Kinsey, Pat and Donna Finn, Joel and Liza Murray, Mike Coleman, Betty Cahill, Jeff and Theresa Mulligan Rosenthal, Donna and Gordon Rattigan, Clay Hazelwood, Kris Cahill, Myra Goethals, Nadia Seikaly, Father Mike Wakefield, Patty Fellows, Dawn Kinsky, Caitlyn Wojkowski, Laura Rudnick, Liz Carney, Claire Wright, Nadine Guy, Olivia Guy-McCarvill, and Hannah and Olivia Donnellan.

Thank you to my talented and inspirational brother, the writer Andrew McNabb. Thank you, John McNabb. You are so missed. A very special thank-you to my mother and father, who, despite years of tumbleweeds rolling through my inbox, never failed to believe in me or in this book. Thank you to my mother especially, who read every version and provided thoughtful critiques. To be honest with you all, I'm not convinced this book didn't find its way to publication based solely on the power of my mother's belief in me. As we know, thoughts are things. Thanks for that, Ma!

And thank you, of course, from the bottom of my grateful heart, to my Liam, my Oona, and my Marigold. You three inspire me always, and being your mother is easily my proudest achievement.

And finally, thank you to David for so very much . . . the love, friendship, laughs, and the desk in front of that sunny window.

About the Author

Photo © 2023 Elizabeth Carney

Marion McNabb is an author and screenwriter for film and television whose work includes the animated series *Rainbow Rangers* on Nick Jr. and Netflix. She studied film at NYU and received a theater degree from Arizona State University. McNabb lives on Cape Cod with her family, swimming with the mermaids when not working on her next novel.